TUGGEL
A GNOKGOBLIN GROOM.

'So, another class of squires to be welcomed into the Hall of Grey Cloud. Bright-eyed, keen to learn and eager to please. I'm looking forward to the challenge of teaching them all I know . . .

Oh, my fine young squires, here you're going to learn so much of the ways of these beautiful creatures we call prowlgrins. How to care for and nurture them – oiling their great toes, rubbing their high humps; combing their beards and tickling their nostrils.

Then you'll learn to ride. How I envy you! Climbing into the saddle for the first time and taking the reins. There is nothing to compare with the thrill of soaring through the air on the back of a prowlgrin . . .

Not only will you groom, train and ride them, but like old Tuggel, you'll grow to love them.

How could you not? For a hand-reared prowlgrin is the most loyal, faithful and obedient companion any knight could wish for – which is just as well! One day, you'll need all those qualities as you journey back from the far-off Twilight Woods on prowlgrinback with your sacred shards of stormphrax.

Study hard, young squires, and learn well, and above all, when it comes to prowlgrins, listen to your heart . . .'

THE DEEP WOODS

THE TWILIGHT WOODS

THE EDGELANDS

The Edge.

The Edge Chronicles

THE QUINT TRILOGY
The Curse of the Gloamglozer
The Winter Knights
Clash of the Sky Galleons (coming soon)

THE TWIG TRILOGY
Beyond the Deepwoods
Stormchaser
Midnight Over Sanctaphrax

THE ROOK TRILOGY
The Last of the Sky Pirates
Vox
Freeglader

Also available:
Cloud Wolf
(an introductory novella featuring Quint,
published for World Book Day)
The Stone Pilot
(an introductory novella featuring Maugin,
published for World Book Day)
The Edge Chronicles Maps

Join the Edge fanclub at
www.kidsatrandomhouse.co.uk/edgechronicles!

THE EDGE CHRONICLES

THE WINTER KNIGHTS

PAUL STEWART & CHRIS RIDDELL

CORGI BOOKS

THE WINTER KNIGHTS
A CORGI BOOK 978 0 552 55126 7 (from January 2007)
0 552 55126 0

First published in Great Britain by Doubleday
an imprint of Random House Children's Books

Doubleday edition published 2005
Corgi edition published 2006

1 3 5 7 9 10 8 6 4 2

Papers used by Random House Children's Books are natural,
recyclable products made from wood grown in sustainable forests.
The manufacturing processes conform to the environmental regulations
of the country of origin.

Corgi Books are published by Random House Children's Books,
61–63 Uxbridge Road, London W5 5SA,
a division of The Random House Group Ltd,
in Australia by Random House Australia (Pty) Ltd,
20 Alfred Street, Milsons Point, Sydney, NSW 2061, Australia,
in New Zealand by Random House New Zealand Ltd,
18 Poland Road, Glenfield, Auckland 10, New Zealand,
and in South Africa by Random House (Pty) Ltd,
Isle of Houghton, Corner Boundary Road & Carse O'Gowrie,
Houghton 2198, South Africa

THE RANDOM HOUSE GROUP Limited Reg. No. 954009
www.kidsatrandomhouse.co.uk

A CIP catalogue record for this book is available from the British Library.

Printed and bound in Great Britain by
Bookmarque Ltd, Croydon, Surrey.

For William, Joseph, Anna, Katy and Jack

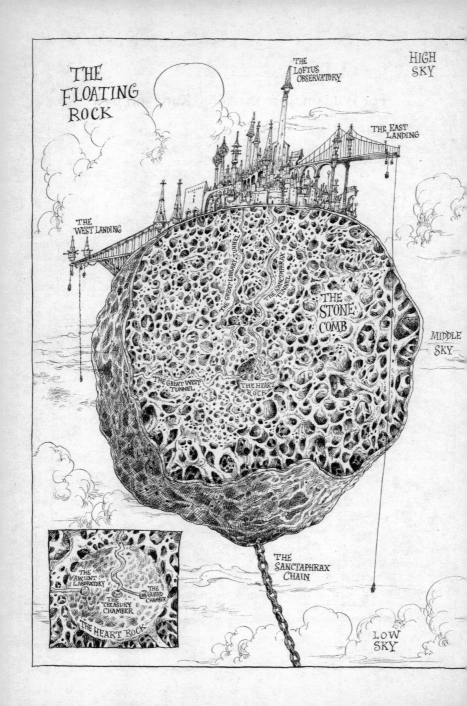

THE
FLOATING
ROCK

'THE
LOFTUS
OBSERVATORY

HIGH
SKY

THE EAST
LANDING

THE
WEST LANDING

THE GREAT LIBRARY TUNNEL

THE SANCTAPHRAX TUNNEL

THE
STONE
COMB

MIDDLE
SKY

THE GREAT WEST
TUNNEL

THE HEART
ROCK

THE
SANCTAPHRAX
CHAIN

THE
ANCIENT
LABORATORY

THE
GUARD
CHAMBER

THE
TREASURY
CHAMBER

THE HEART ROCK

LOW
SKY

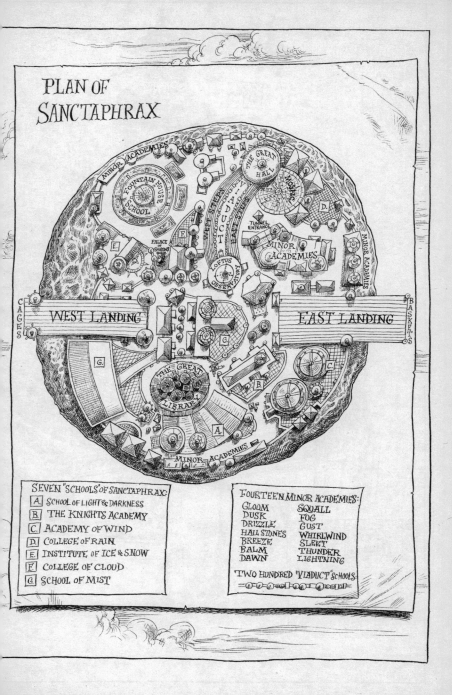

THE
GANTRY
TOWER

HALL
WHIT
CLOU

THE
UPPER
HALLS

CENTRAL
STAIRCASE

HALL OF
STORM CLOUD

HALL OF
HIGH CLOUD

ACADEMY
BARRACKS

THE THIRTEEN TOWERS

THE EIGHTWAYS

HALL OF GREY CLOUD

THE TILT TREES

THE DORMITORY CLOSETS

THE INNER COURTYARD

THE GATES OF HUMILITY

THE WEST WALL

THE KNIGHTS ACADEMY

INTRODUCTION

A cloud of uncertainty hangs over Sanctaphrax, the magnificent centre of sky-scholarship. Perched high up on top of the great floating rock, the city has been in a state of crisis ever since its Most High Academe – Linius Pallitax – fell mysteriously ill.

Since that time, the academics have talked of little else. Rumours are rife that Linius Pallitax did things he ought not to have done – that he gleaned forbidden earth-scholar knowledge from the Great Library; that he ventured down inside the rock and broke into the Ancient Laboratory, which the First Scholars had taken such care to seal up; that he used their scientific paraphernalia and, in an act of terrible folly, attempted to create life.

Of course, no-one has any proof that this is what actually happened, but the further the rumours spread, the more certain they seem until the whole city is convinced that Linius Pallitax is to blame for his own illness. And after all, what *was* the Most High Academe doing up on the rooftops the night the Palace of Shadows burned to the ground?

There are two individuals who are especially concerned about the ailing High Academe's health. One is his daughter, Maris, who loves him deeply and can't bear to think about what will happen to her if he should die. The other is Quint Verginix, son of sky pirate captain, Wind Jackal, and the Most High Academe's former apprentice.

The youth has been promised a place in the prestigious Knights Academy as Linius Pallitax's protégé. Without sponsorship Quint will have to leave Sanctaphrax once and for all, and learn instead to be a sky pirate.

Of course, there would be no shame in this. As a young lad, Quint often dreamed of standing up at the helm beside his father, the wind in his hair and sun in his eyes as they sailed high above the Edge. Indeed, the pair of them have already had many adventures together as they voyaged between the dark Deepwoods and bustling Undertown, the hold of the *Galerider* laden with all manner of illicit cargo.

Quint, though, has tasted the heady excitement of life up in the floating city in the service of the Most High Academe, and knows that this is only the beginning. He dreams of entering the Knights Academy and learning how to become a full knight academic who, Sky willing, might one day be sent off to the Twilight Woods on a stormchasing voyage – the greatest adventure of them all.

For the great floating
city depends for its
very survival on
the amazing
properties of
stormphrax –
tiny shards of
lightning
found only
in the far-off
Twilight
Woods, that in
darkness weigh
more than a thousand
ironwood pines. Used to
weigh down the Sanctaphrax rock,
stormphrax is the prize that has been sought
by the Knights Academic on their solitary stormchasing quests ever since the days of their illustrious
founder, the great Quode Quanx-Querix.

But now, with Linius Pallitax's life hanging in the
balance, all that has suddenly been thrown into doubt.
All Quint can do is hope and pray that, for Maris's sake
and his own, and for the good of Sanctaphrax itself, the
Most High Academe will recover. Yet as Linius's eyes
dim and his breathing becomes ever more laboured, the
signs are not looking promising.

The Deepwoods, the Stone Gardens, the Edgewater
River. Undertown and Sanctaphrax. Names on a map.

Yet behind each name lie a thousand tales – tales that have been recorded in ancient scrolls, tales that have been passed down the generations by word of mouth – tales which even now are being told.

What follows is but one of those tales.

PART 1

THE LOWER
HALLS

CHAPTER ONE

THE SCHOOL OF COLOUR AND LIGHT STUDIES

The academic, in his grubby, paint-spattered robes of faded 'viaduct' blue, turned the crank lever with his free hand. The cog wheels in the rotating tower high above him chattered and squealed like angry ratbirds, and a shaft of light cut through the dusty air. The academic levelled the brush in his other hand and tilted his head to one side, his pale yellow eyes fixed on the youth before him.

'A little more to the left now, I think, Master Quint,' he said, his voice soft but insinuating. 'So the light catches you. Just so . . .'

Quint did as he was told. The early morning light streaming in from the high tower window fell across his face, glinting on his cheekbones, the tips of his ears and nose and, with its rusting pipes and gauges, the battered armour he wore.

'Excellent, my young squire,' the academic muttered approvingly. He dipped the tip of the hammelhornhair brush into the white paint on his palette and dabbed lightly at the tiny painting on the easel before him. 'Now we must let the light work its magic,' he murmured. The dabbing continued. 'The highlights complete the picture, Master Quint. But I must insist that you hold still.'

Quint tried to maintain the pose – but it wasn't easy. The tower was small and airless, and the heady odours from the pigments, the pinewood oils and the thinning varnishes were combining to make his eyes water and his head ache. The rusty, ill-fitting armour chafed his neck, and his left leg had gone quite numb. Besides, he was dying to see the finished portrait. It was all he could do not to turn right round and inspect it for himself.

'The dawn light,' clucked the academic. 'There's nothing like it for illuminating the subject . . .' His pale yellow eyes darted back and forth over Quint's features. 'And what an *illustrious* subject we are, my young squire.'

He chuckled, and Quint tried not to blush.

'The protégé of none other than the Most High Academe of Sanctaphrax . . .' He turned away and began stabbing at the palette like a woodthrush after a spanglebug. 'How lucky you are, Master Quint, not to have to scrabble about with the rest of us in the minor schools, but to be given a place at the most prestigious academy of them all. I wonder . . .' The academic's voice was laden with sudden spite. 'I wonder what you actually did to deserve it?'

The academic's eyes were fixed on Quint's face once more. They were so pale that there was almost no difference between the irises and the yellowish white that surrounded them. It was a mark of his trade, Quint told himself, trying not to shudder. Just as years of working as an Undertown rope-turner resulted in spatula-shaped fingers, and just as a slaughterer tanner from the Deepwoods ended up with skin the colour of blood, so, as the years passed, the eyes of Sanctaphrax portraitists were gradually bleached by the vapours of the thinning varnishes they used – and Ferule Gleet had been a portraitist for many, many years.

'I was the Most High Academe's apprentice . . .' Quint looked down, his cheeks blazing as he remembered the monstrous gloamglozer and the night of the terrible fire.

'Keep still!' rasped Gleet, irritatedly dabbing at the portrait. 'Ah, yes,' he smiled thinly. 'There was that fire at the Palace of Shadows, wasn't there? Strange and dreadful business . . . How *is* the Most High Academe? Recovering well, I hope.'

The pale yellow eyes bored into Quint's once more.

'As well as can be expected,' the youth replied, but the words rang hollow in his ears as he thought of his mentor lying in the gloomy bedchamber at the School of Mist.

Linius Pallitax had suffered grievously at the hands of the terrible gloamglozer. He had almost been destroyed. Perhaps it would have been better if he had, for now he

never left his bed, and his haunted eyes stared into the distance, seeing neither his faithful servant, Tweezel, nor Quint, his apprentice – nor even his own daughter, Maris, who sat beside him for so many hours, praying for him to recover.

Ferule Gleet daubed at the tiny painting in silence for a moment.

'As well as can be expected, eh?' he mused at last. 'Doesn't sound too good. You wouldn't want anything to happen to him, my fine young squire. Not in your position.'

'My position?' said Quint, trying not to move.

'You're the High Academe's protégé, aren't you? Without him, you don't expect that the Knights Academy would accept you into its hallowed halls, do you? Of course not!' Ferule shook his head. 'Sanctaphrax born and bred, that's always been the rule. The rest of us have to get by at the minor academies as best we can.'

He wiped his brush on a piece of rag, and turned the easel round.

'There,' he announced.

Quint found himself staring at the miniature painting of a young knight academic in gleaming armour, with deep indigo eyes and a smile on his face. Ferule Gleet of the School of Colour and Light Studies had done a fine job all right. Quint shivered.

'Is anything wrong?' Ferule asked.

'It's nothing,' Quint said quietly.

He had no intention of telling the pale-eyed academic about the memories the miniature painting had stirred – memories of the first time he'd had his portrait done.

How young he'd been then. Four, maybe five years old; the youngest of six brothers. His father, Wind Jackal, had commissioned the mural of the whole family for the grand hall of their palace in the Western Quays. What happy days they'd been. But they hadn't lasted, he thought bitterly. Within a year of the painting being completed, Turbot Smeal – his father's treacherous quartermaster – had torched his master's house. Quint's mother and brothers had perished in the blaze, and with them, the painting itself had been destroyed.

'Of course, there's one thing you haven't captured at all accurately,' Quint said quickly.

'Indeed?' said Gleet, raising his eyebrows.

Quint tapped the pipes and gauges on the armour he was wearing, each one more corroded and tarnished than the next; then nodded towards the picture. 'The armour there sparkles like burnished brass and silver,' he said, 'newly forged and freshly polished. Whereas this . . .' He looked back down at the breast-plate.

Gleet laughed, revealing a mouthful of thin, pin-like teeth. 'You're right, Master Quint,' he said. 'The armour you are wearing has indeed seen better days. I use it as a mere prop. Once you enter the Knights Academy, you will have to work hard to win the honour of wearing a suit of armour as fine as the one I have painted; a suit of armour fit for a knight academic on a stormchasing voyage. That is why every squire has a portrait painted – to remind him always of his ultimate goal.'

Quint nodded solemnly and reached for the miniature portrait.

'Not so fast!' snapped Ferule Gleet. 'There is still the background to do. The School of Mist is your mentor's academy, I believe. I must go up to the balcony at the top of the tower to paint in the Mistsifting Towers before the sun rises too high and I lose the shadows.' He began packing up the paints and brushes into a small leadwood box. 'If you would care to join me?' he said.

'I certainly would,' Quint replied, rubbing his eyes. 'I could do with some fresh air.'

With Gleet carrying the heavy box in one hand and the tiny half-finished picture in the fingertips of the other, and Quint manoeuvring the cumbersome easel up the circular stairs, the two of them made their way to the upper balcony.

At the top, Quint leaned over the balustrade and took deep gulps of air. It was a crisp, clear morning, with broad billowing clouds sweeping majestically across the sky, and a golden light falling across the towers of Sanctaphrax.

To his left and right, lining the broad span of the mighty viaduct, were the minarets and turrets of the two hundred minor schools. At one end was the stately Great Hall, its dome and belfry gleaming in the morning light; at the other end, towering above every other building in Sanctaphrax, was the magnificent Loftus Observatory, with the unmistakable outline of the twin Mistsifting Towers just beyond.

Quint looked across at them. The huge globes, like two vast balls of twine, rotated and shimmered in the morning breeze and, as they did so, they produced a soft, haunting music of exquisitely subtle harmonies.

It was the sounds of Sanctaphrax, even more than the sight of its resplendent buildings, that always thrilled Quint. Now, on the balcony of the viaduct School of Colour and Light Studies, there was music all round, filling the air, the paraphernalia of every tower adding to the mighty symphony. It was said that the blind could never get

25

lost in Sanctaphrax. All they had to do was keep their ears open to know exactly where they were. Quint didn't doubt for a moment that it was true.

Cocking his head to one side and closing his eyes, he listened dreamily. There was the buzz of pinwheels, the clatter of hail-weights, the timpani of wind-vanes and fog-clappers. From the Academy of Wind, there came flute-like notes as the breeze blew over the calibrated air-apertures, and the mesmeric hum of the sifting-combs; while from the Raintasters' Tower there came a constant tinkling sound, as the glass collecting-bottles which hung down in great bunches from the jutting gantries overhead knocked softly together.

It wasn't only the buildings that were making a sound that morning. As Ferule Gleet began sketching in the outline of the Mistsifting Towers, Quint could hear a babble of voices bubbling up from the viaduct below.

He opened his eyes and looked down at the viaduct walkway, flanked by towers on each side, stretching into the distance. Every one of the two hundred towers was different – some were castellated, some had spires; some were shaped like pepper pots, others like colanders. One, tall and conical, was bedecked with small lanterns that hung from hooks. Another was strung with wind-chimes. And one, he noticed, had fluted columns, like a small-scale parody of the School of Light and Darkness itself. The only thing they all had in common was the number of individuals scurrying in and out of them.

Most wore robes of 'viaduct' blue, showing that they were academics from the lowly viaduct schools, housed in the towers. On one side of the School of Colour and Light Studies was the School of Refraction and Reflection, full of academics polishing and grinding lenses for the telescopes of the major academies. On the other, Quint could see the School of Sight and Smell-Filtering, where academics busily spun spider-silk and soaked woodmoth gauze in scented tinctures for the delicate weather instruments of the more important schools of Wind, Rain, Cloud and Mist.

Across the way, a group of academics in the red capes and black and white chequerboard collars of the School of Mist barged the blue-robed scholars aside. Approaching them, a dozen white- and grey-robed professors from the Institute of Ice and Snow raised their noses snootily in the air, and close behind, a gaggle of yellow-caped apprentices from the College of Cloud gossiped and laughed noisily.

'A little more ochre, I think,' Gleet was saying.

Just then, a furtive-looking individual caught Quint's eye as he emerged from the door at the bottom of a battered turret opposite. He glanced over both shoulders – clearly forgetting that someone might be looking at him from above – and pushed a gleaming phial of dark red liquid inside his gown, before scurrying off. He was thin and stooped, and from his flapping green gown with its distinctive fur trim Quint could tell he was an under-professor from the Academy of Wind.

Quint looked more closely at the turret. It seemed neglected. The windows were shuttered, the roof had missing tiles, while the walls were cracked and in need

of serious repair. He wondered what viaduct school it might be. Maybe the clue lay with the dried corpse of the vulpoon – an ungainly bird of prey with straggly plumage, a viciously serrated beak and razor-sharp talons – suspended from a jutting hook above the door.

'What do they study there?' Quint asked Gleet, nodding down at the strange tower.

The portraitist followed Quint's gaze and shook his head. 'A fine young squire of the Knights Academy doesn't need to concern himself with such schools.' He smiled thinly. 'Or the services they offer.'

He held up the disc of wood and Quint could see, in the background, the two Mistsifting Towers of the School of Mist.

'Once it is dry,' said the academic, gathering up his brushes and paints, 'you can get it fixed to the handle of your sword. You do have a sword, I take it?'

'Of course,' Quint nodded, unsheathing the long, curved sky-pirate sword his father had given him.

Gleet laughed unpleasantly as he eyed the sword with disdain. 'Yes, well,' he sniffed. 'There won't be many squires at the Knights Academy with swords like *that*, I can tell you.'

Quint's face fell.

'Just as well you're the protégé of the Most High Academe is all I can say . . .'

Just then, as Ferule was turning to go, the loud sonorous tones of a tolling bell filled the air. Quint looked up to see the huge bell of the Great Hall swinging back and forth. As if in answer, rising up from the Stone Gardens and filling the sky above Sanctaphrax like a mighty swirling snowstorm, there appeared a vast flock of white ravens. They wheeled through the sky, a great halo high above the Viaduct Towers, looping round at the Great Hall and the Loftus Observatory. And as their numbers grew, so the raucous cawing became a deafening cacophony that drowned out the sound of the ringing bell that seemed to have summoned them all in the first place.

Quint gripped the balustrade, his face ashen white. 'No!' he cried. 'It can't be! Not now, after everything . . .'

Ferule Gleet turned and shook his head, his yellow eyes glinting and a malicious smile on his thin lips.

'The tolling bell; the white ravens . . . It can mean only one thing.' He handed Quint the miniature portrait. 'Your mentor, the Most High Academe . . . is dead.'

CHAPTER TWO

THE CHORUS OF THE DEAD

The gnokgoblins and mobgnomes in charge of the hanging-baskets had been busy since daybreak, lowering load after load of academics from the East and West Landings down to Undertown below. They'd had all types coming their way and using their services that chilly morning. Old and young, venerable and callow: professors, apprentices, squires and knights-in-waiting – academics from every institute, college and school in the great floating city and representing every department and discipline of Sanctaphrax life.

There were solemn mistsifters, their chequerboard hoods pulled down over their faces so that only their metal nose-pieces were visible, poking out like vulpoon beaks. There were under-professors from the School of Light and Darkness in robes of every shade of grey, from slate-flecked white to stormcloud black; and cloudwatchers who, despite the occasion, were looking decidedly crumpled.

Then there were the academics from the College of Rain, sticking close together and carrying parasols and umbrellas of every shape and size, from huge spiky canopies to tiny delicate funnels. And apprentices from the different faculties of the Academy of Wind, who were walking in step, ten abreast. Behind them, the flimsy black kites they were pulling fluttered like a flock of excited ratbirds.

Following the representatives of the seven major schools of Sanctaphrax, there came the scholars from the fourteen minor academies. Less formal than those preceding them, they were chattering and jostling each other, their robes of bright colours merging and mingling.

In one place, the white and yellow hoods of the Academy of Squall surrounded the deep orange robes of the Academy of Dawn, creating a pattern that, from above, resembled the early morning sun itself. Some way back – behind a group of excited whirlwind apprentices – the patterned cloaks of the Academies of Breeze, Hailstones and Gust intermingled like the clouds of a gathering storm. And at the back, like a river breaking its banks, the blue robes of all those from the viaduct schools stood out in the stark, early-morning light.

With lanterns, lamps and flaming torches held high, the procession of academics wound its way through the streets of Undertown and along the narrow tracks to the furthest tip of the Edge. Those too old or infirm to manage the journey on foot were transported in barrows and hand-wagons by lugtrolls and cloddertrogs, and in golden carriages drawn by teams of prowlgrins in spangled livery and feathered head-dresses.

Ever since the break of dawn, the procession had been streaming along the road from Undertown to the Stone Gardens. Hundreds of the Sanctaphrax academics had already gathered, yet still they were coming, each one keen to be seen paying their last respects to the former Most High Academe – and even more eager to learn of his successor.

Quint himself had got up and left his small room in the School of Mist well before dawn. He'd paused outside the High Academe's chamber below and listened to Maris's anguished sobs, uncertain what to do for the best.

Then, before he had a chance to make up his mind, he'd felt a glassy claw on his shouder and, looking round, had found Tweezel standing behind him.

'We've been expecting it for some while now,' the spindlebug had trilled mournfully, 'but it has still come as a terrible shock. Give her time, Quint, to come to terms with her loss.'

Quint had nodded, but inside, he was in turmoil. He wanted to comfort his friend, to be with her at this, her hour of need. Yet he knew that, as the daughter of the late Most High Academe, Maris Pallitax also had official duties to perform. Reluctantly, he'd agreed that they should meet later, to talk and share memories and console one another.

In the meantime, Quint had duties of his own to see to. Leaving the mistsifting school behind him, he had hurried off towards the baskets on the West Landing. He'd found Sanctaphrax bustling. Word of the Most High Academe's passing had spread quickly, and even at that early hour, there were scores of academics outside in the streets, milling about, gathering in groups, and the air buzzed with rumour and supposition.

By the time the sun had risen over the horizon, Quint was standing by the entrance to the Stone Gardens, peering back anxiously in the direction of Sanctaphrax. He blew on his hands and stamped his feet, for despite the pink-tinged dawn, it was icy cold and a bitter wind was blowing in from beyond the Edge.

The place was filling rapidly. Groups of Undertowners mingled with the academics all round him, too superstitious to enter the Stone Gardens, yet eager not to miss the funeral procession. Suddenly, coming through the crowd, Quint caught sight of a tall, upright individual in the long coat and tricorn hat of a sky pirate. His heart missed a beat.

'Father!' he cried. 'Father! Over here!'

As the figure of Wind Jackal approached, Quint threw himself into his outstretched arms.

'I said sun-up, and here I am,' Wind Jackal smiled, hugging his son. 'I only wish we could have met under happier circumstances.'

'Oh, Father!' Quint cried, burying himself in Wind Jackal's coat. 'So much has happened since you left me at the Palace of Shadows.'

'I know, son,' said Wind Jackal. 'I was raiding league ships beyond the Great Shryke Slave Market when I received word from the Professors of Light and Darkness. I came immediately.'

He put an arm around Quint's shoulders. 'You have been very brave, my boy.'

Around them, the gathering of academics was growing larger by the minute. The sky pirate urged his son forward.

'Come, Quint,' he said, 'we'll have time enough to talk of the past, and the future, but first we must pay our respects to my friend and your mentor.'

Quint nodded and, wiping his eyes with the back of his hand, walked with his father through the Stone Gardens towards the great stone stacks in the distance. It wasn't long before they approached the highest of these stacks, a towering pillar of rocks, each one larger than the one beneath, and capped with a broad flattened slab. Around it, in concentric circles organized strictly by rank, the vast procession of academics was congregating.

There were murmurs and grunts of disapproval as Wind Jackal pushed through the throng, but no-one challenged him, for all of Sanctaphrax knew of the late Most High Academe's boyhood friend, the sky pirate. He and Quint stopped and took their place in the front rank, among the under-professors of the School of Light and Darkness, who moved aside with stiff nods of the head.

'Not long now,' whispered Wind Jackal, glancing back.

Quint followed his gaze back towards the Sanctaphrax rock, silhouetted against the sky. And there in the distance, just visible above the towering Loftus

Observatory, was a magnificent sky ship with billowing, black sails.

'It's a stormchaser,' breathed Quint, shivering as the icy wind picked up.

As he watched, the stormchaser – sky ship of the Knights Academy – gathered speed and headed towards them, a blizzard of circling white ravens blurring the top of its tall mast. And as it drew closer, Quint saw all those who were on board the funereal vessel.

There were thirteen knights-in-waiting from the Knights Academy making up the crew, each one dressed in shining, burnished armour. On the foredeck stood Maris, flanked by the unmistakable figures of the Professors of Light and Darkness.

And there, before them on a raised platform, the winding-cloth pale against the dark wood, lay the shrouded body of Linius Pallitax.

Quint longed to wave to Maris, or call out. He wanted so much to let her know that he was there, and felt the loss of her father almost as much as she did. But he knew he could not. He hung his head in sadness – and felt his own father's reassuring arm round his shoulders.

And at that moment, Quint realized that it had all been no more than a dream. The magnificent city upon the floating rock. The life he'd had in the Most High Academe's employ ... Now Linius Pallitax was dead, and his dream was over.

What madness it had been to imagine that he could have ever fitted in. He could see that now. How could he become a knight academic like those proud, noble figures approaching in the stormchaser? It was never going to happen. The academy would never accept *him*. A sky pirate's son, with no mentor ...

Quint returned his father's reassuring hug.

No, his future lay on board his father's sky pirate ship, where it always had. His time in Sanctaphrax had been a mirage, an illusion; a strange and beguiling dream that he would soon leave far behind.

The floating rock, the Knights Academy, the Most High Academe, and ... Maris.

Quint felt a lump in his throat.

The stormchaser was now hovering directly overhead, the swirl of white ravens circling above it like a great storm. Slowly, carefully, the shrouded body of Linius Pallitax was lowered over the side of the vessel, suspended on golden ropes.

Quint could hear Maris's sobs, louder than ever, and the mournful trilling of Tweezel, Linius's faithful spindlebug. He bit into his lips, his eyes full of tears.

The body came to rest on top of the huge boulder that topped the stone stack, and the ropes were released from above. The voices of the Professors of Light and Darkness rang out in unison.

'Linius Pallitax, Most High Academe of Sanctaphrax, we commend your spirit to Open Sky!'

At the sound of their voices, the academics below – Wind Jackal and Quint included – bowed their heads, and the raucous cries of the white ravens rose to an ear-splitting crescendo.

All around him, he could hear the academics. 'Chorus of the Dead,' and 'Spirit unbound,' and 'Sky  take him,' they whispered under their breath, before bowing and turning to leave.

Quint looked up. On the great boulder, Linius Pallitax's body was covered in a soft down of screeching ravens busily devouring his remains, while above, the black sails of the sky ship billowed afresh as it returned slowly to Sanctaphrax.

'Goodbye, and may Open Sky take you, Linius Pallitax,' whispered Quint, turning to go. 'And goodbye, Sanctaphrax,' he added, looking up at the floating city in the distance.

'Not so fast,' he heard his father's voice in his ear. 'I told you we'd have time to talk of the past and the future.'

'Yes,' said Quint, following his father through the crowd of academics shuffling back through the Stone Gardens. 'My future with you, aboard the *Galerider* . . .'

Wind Jackal turned and looked deep into Quint's eyes. 'Are you truly so keen to turn your back on this great floating city of yours?' he asked him, with a smile.

'Of course I'll be sorry to leave, Father,' Quint began. 'But I'll never get into the Knights Academy without a mentor and I don't want to end up as a gossipy old under-professor at the School of Mist or a scheming funnel-tender at the College of Rain. I'd much rather come with you.'

'Before you decide,' said his father, 'perhaps you had better see what the new Most High Academes of Sanctaphrax want with you.'

Academics all around stopped and stared.

'The new Most High Academes?' said Quint.

'Yes,' said Wind Jackal. 'They haven't announced it

yet, but Linius passed the chain of office on to them when he was being carried from the fire at the Palace of Shadows. He decreed that they should be joint Most High Academes on his death, and told them to send for me.' He smiled. 'And now, they want to see *you*.'

'But . . . but who . . . ?' Quint began.

Wind Jackal smiled. 'The Professors of Light and Darkness, of course,' he told him.

Around him, the academics burst into an excited frenzy of whispers and muttering.

'And we'd better hurry,' said Wind Jackal, turning the collar of his coat up and holding out a hand as a soft white flake fluttered down. 'I know I'm just a battered old sky pirate without all the sky learning and weather wisdom of these fancy professors of yours – but it looks like snow to me!'

·CHAPTER THREE·

THE KNIFE-GRINDER

News of the unprecedented appointments to the highest office in Sanctaphrax spread rapidly as the crowds of mourners made their way back to the great floating rock from the Stone Gardens. No-one could quite believe that it was true. And all the while, the snow grew steadily heavier, swirling round them thickly, yet doing nothing to cool the feverish atmosphere.

Quint and Wind Jackal headed towards the hanging-baskets at the centre of Undertown as quickly as the worsening weather and clumps of gossiping academics allowed. But it seemed to be taking for ever. An hour later and they were still only halfway to their destination.

All round them, the buzz and clamour of conversation filled the air. Whoever was talking – be it scholars from the seven main schools, apprentices or under-professors from any of the fourteen minor academies, scribes from the viaduct schools, or even Undertowners returning home – the subject under discussion was the same.

'Not one, but *two* Most High Academes,' a mistsifter – his face as red as his robes – was expostulating to his three companions. 'Absolutely unbelievable! The *pair* of them!'

'Who'd have thought it?' his neighbour chipped in.

'And I'll tell you this for nothing,' a third added, his chequered hood raised and metal nose glinting. 'It doesn't bode at all well for any of us at the School of Mist.'

'Aye, you're right enough there, Pentix,' the first one said, nodding vigorously. 'At least Linius was one of us. There's no knowing how these professors from the School of Light and Darkness are going to treat us.'

'There'll be changes,' the one with the nose-piece said darkly. 'And you can bet your brass beak that they won't be for the better.'

As he pushed past them, Wind Jackal shook his head. 'For all its splendid towers and magnificent academies, Sanctaphrax is just as full of spite, intrigue and petty rivalry as any Deepwoods slave market,' he said, eyeing the academics with scorn. 'And twice as dangerous.'

'That's something I know only too well, Father,' said Quint with a rueful smile. 'And yet . . .'

'And yet?' said Wind Jackal.

'And yet,' Quint continued as they approached the Anchor Chain Square, with its rows of hanging-baskets, 'there are such wonders to be found in the floating city. The bustle and colour of the Viaduct Steps, the Mosaic Square at twilight as the last rays of the sun hit the tiles, and the Great Library!'

Quint clasped his hands together and his eyes glazed

over. Lost in his thoughts, he noticed nothing around him. Neither the hooded figure with four muzzled fromps on leashes hurrying past, nor the gang of cloddertrog young'uns darting in and out of the crowds, relieving the unwary academics of their valuables. And nor did he hear the strident calls of the Undertowners hawking their wares – everything from heavy ironmongery to tawdry lace.

'The Great Library?' said Wind Jackal, prompting his son to continue.

Quint turned and smiled. 'Oh, Father! The wealth of knowledge in that place!' he said animatedly. 'You can't imagine. I tell you, a scholar could spend a thousand years in its rafters and still not read a tenth of the barkscrolls it contains!' His face fell. 'And yet it just sits there, shut up and forgotten . . .'

Wind Jackal smiled. 'I can see that Sanctaphrax has certainly got to you,' he said. 'You sound like Linius, may Sky rest his soul. Despite all its faults and failings, he loved the place, and did his best to serve both academics and Undertowners alike . . .'

'Hear, hear!' came a voice to their left.

Wind Jackal turned to see a wizened mobgnome with grizzled side-whiskers and a threadbare jacket, who was suspended just above the ground in a hanging-basket.

'Linius Pallitax was a fine Most High Academe,' he said, 'and there are many of us humble workers who have reason to be grateful to him.' He frowned. 'Going up?'

Wind Jackal nodded.

'Then climb aboard,' said the mobgnome gesturing behind them. 'Before all those academics push in front. Hanging-baskets are like gold dust today.'

Quint climbed into the hanging-basket after his father and held on as the mobgnome unhitched the crank-brake and began turning the set of hand-pedals. The basket began its long ascent.

'So you knew the Most High Academe?' said Wind Jackal to the mobgnome as the streets and alleys of Undertown fell away below them.

The mobgnome grinned. 'That I did, sir. When I was an earth-scholar.'

'You?' said Wind Jackal, surprised.

'Under-librarian, I was, sir,' he said. 'In charge of the library baskets. Until the sky-scholars drove us earth-scholars out of Sanctaphrax.'

He hawked and spat over the side of the basket.

'At the time, Linius Pallitax was a young mistsifter professor,' he went on, 'but he stood up for me when they closed the Great Library. And even though it made him unpopular, he saw to it that those of us that wanted them got jobs around the city.'

'Excellent,' said Wind Jackal.

'Yeah, thanks to him, I make a very good living as a basket-puller.' He grinned, to reveal a smile more gaps than teeth. 'And I never miss an opportunity to overcharge those pompous sky-scholar types!'

Wind Jackal chuckled.

'But for a fine sky pirate gentleman like yourself, sir,' he added, 'and a friend of the late Most High Academe, there'll be no charge.'

'That's very good of you,' said Wind Jackal, raising his hat to the basket-puller.

'And as for you,' said the mobgnome, eyeing Quint up and down when they arrived at the top. 'You spoke well of the Great Library, Earth and Sky bless you. I thank you for that.'

Night had fallen and, by the time Wind Jackal and Quint had shaken the basket-puller's hand and bade him farewell, the lamp-lighters had already lit all the streetlamps lining the broad Grand Avenue which led into the centre of Sanctaphrax. Pools of golden light spread out across the intricate patterns of red, black and white tiles beneath their feet, while to their left and right, every building – from the squattest, sturdiest hall to the tallest, slenderest tower swaying in the rising wind – was illuminated by the light streaming from their windows.

'It's this way,' said Quint, leading his father over a finely wrought curved bridge to his right.

They passed between a tall palace with elongated diamond-shaped windows and a curved wall, with honeyed light pouring out of the narrow slits along its length. The sound of muted rustling came from somewhere high up above them, and there was a hint of mildew in the air. Then, at the end of the wall, where a high-pitched squeaking noise seemed almost to be keeping time with a dull and distant throb, Quint turned sharp left, and the pair of them entered a narrow, unlit alley. Wind Jackal stumbled on the irregular cobblestones.

'Whooah! Slow down a bit,' he protested, and grabbed hold of his son's arm for support. 'Quite the Sanctaphrax academic, aren't you?' he said a moment later. 'You seem to know this place like the back of your hand. Even by night.'

Quint nodded, and felt a warm glow of pride. His father was right. What with the sights and sounds and smells of Sanctaphrax around him, he would always be able to find his way around. It was as if, without his ever having to learn it, his senses had absorbed the essence of the great floating city.

'We're nearly there,' he said.

Sure enough, a moment later, they emerged onto a large square. Before them stood the palatial School of

Light and Darkness, bathed in light – and surrounded by a vast crowd of baying academics.

Constructed on a framework of narrow pillars and flying buttresses, the great school seemed almost to be floating; an illusion enhanced by the ornamental lake which ran the length of its front wall. Soaring up gracefully, storey after storey, each one designed to combine light-filled promontories with darkness-defined alcoves which pitched and shifted with the passing of the sun and phases of the moon, the School of Light and Darkness had been designed to illuminate and reflect. There were countless blazing lanterns fixed to its outer walls, at once lightening the façade and casting dark shadows; while its windows – that great mosaic of crystal-glazed openings which lanced every wall – were divided into those through which you could see into the opulent interior, and those which reflected back what was outside.

Wind Jackal and Quint approached the front entrance, where the crowd was at its thickest and most agitated. Elbows were flying and voices were raised as the academics jostled and scuffled with one another. In front of them, a line of impassive flat-head goblins of the Sanctaphrax Guard blocked their way, their arms folded and weapons stayed.

Representatives of every school were gathered there, Quint realized. Raintasters, cloudwatchers, mistsifters; scholars of gloom, of gust, of drizzle, dawn and dusk, all jockeying for position and vying with one another for attention. They were waving their staffs of office and barkscroll petitions in the air, each one desperate to be granted an audience with the new Most High Academes as soon as possible – and, more importantly, ahead of their rivals.

'Behold the falling snow!' a gaunt under-professor from the Institute of Ice and Snow was bellowing. 'I must see them at once!'

'And I,' screeched the Professor of Balm, his rose-coloured robes flapping wildly, 'must insist that I am allowed to address the venerable Most High Academes about this unseasonable weather . . .'

As Quint and Wind Jackal approached, a huge flat-head goblin, his tattoos and rings gleaming in the lamplight, stepped forward from the ranks of the guard and raised his sword.

'Academics of Sancta-phrax,' he bellowed. 'You shall all be heard tomorrow when the announcement of who is to succeed the late Linius Pallitax as Most High Academe is formally made . . .'

'But we know who's succeeded him!' protested the under-professor from the Institute of Ice and Snow, 'and I must see them this instant, Captain Sigbord, or . . .'

'Or what, Palvius Quale?' Sigbord bared his teeth in a grim smile and grasped the under-professor's white hood in one massive fist. In the other, he raised his curved sword.

'You . . . you . . . wouldn't dare,' trembled the under-professor.

'Just you try me,' snarled the captain as, behind him, the guards took a step forward and began slowly beating their shields with their swords.

With mutters and curses, the crowd began to disperse. Pushing through them, Wind Jackal and Quint approached the entrance to the School of Light and Darkness where Sigbord was standing, still clutching the under-professor by the throat.

'Haven't lost your touch, I see, Sigbord, you old hive-hut skulker!' laughed Wind Jackal, sticking out his hand.

The goblin let go of the under-professor, who quickly scurried off after his companions, and shook Wind Jackal's hand warmly.

'Captain Wind Jackal, you old sky fox. It's good to see you. The professors . . . or should I say, Most High Academes are expecting you. Please, follow me.'

He turned, raised his fist and hammered at the heavy leadwood door. It swung open at once, and Quint and his father followed the brawny flat-head inside. The three of them strode across the echoing hallway of black and white marble flags, past a vast curved staircase and on towards the tall, pointed archway at the far end.

On many occasions, Quint had peered into the

venerable school from the doorway, but never before had he actually set foot inside. This was the grandest and most prestigious Sanctaphrax institution of them all, and there were few academics who did not wear the sombre grey robes of the School of Light and Darkness who had ever managed to get past the Treasury Guard; and fewer still who had been allowed to proceed beyond this entrance hall.

Quint gasped as he followed the others through the pointed archway and found himself in a cavernous atrium, so vast that a whole flotilla of sky ships could have comfortably moored there. Gallery after ascending gallery ringed the atrium, each one supported upon a forest of slender, fluted pillars. They rose up as far the eye could see, a broad, encircling staircase linking one with the other, and were crowned at the top by a vast dome, painted on its concave face with intricate scenes of light and darkness.

This same theme – light and darkness – was repeated throughout the great school. There were chambers so brightly lit that they were blinding, with marble walls and crystal chandeliers; there were also dark rooms, lined with black leadwood and wreathed in sombre shadows. And everywhere, like grey wraiths, the academics of the School of Light and Darkness moved about on soundless feet, absorbed in their various tasks, calculations or hushed discussions.

They went from chamber to chamber, muttering under their breath, or clustered together in twos, threes or small whispering groups. Some would hurry off in this direction, that direction, as if engaged in the most pressing work; while others sauntered – even stopped completely – their eyes staring and brows furrowed.

Apart from the grey robes they wore, they could be identified by the distinctive carved staffs they clutched, each one with a lens or spyglass attachment set into its ornate hilt. Those, and the spectacles they wore. All but a few wore several pairs at the same time – on their noses, on the tops of their heads, with more of different strengths hanging from chains and thongs around their necks, so that, with the minimum of fuss, they could easily replace those they were wearing with ones more suited to their needs in the chambers they entered.

How different they seemed, thought Quint, to the noisy, scheming academics in the other schools of Sanctaphrax. Indeed, not only was the School of Light and Darkness the grandest in the floating city, but its academics were also the most secretive, seldom involving themselves in matters beyond its walls.

Yet with the Professors of Light and Darkness becoming the new Most High Academes, Quint mused, surely that would all have to change.

They had reached the upper chambers, near the great dome, when Sigbord abruptly turned down a long corridor. At the end of it were two huge doors; one black, one white. Sigbord turned to Wind Jackal.

'The Most High Academes will see you now,' he said, opening a door and ushering Quint's father inside.

Quint was about to follow when he felt the flat-head goblin's hand on his shoulder.

'Not you, young sir,' he growled. 'Take a seat over there until you're called.'

Glancing round at where Sigbord was pointing, Quint saw a gangly youth in a faded tunic and patched breeches. He was sitting, hunched over, on a bench to the right of the door. Quint crossed the floor and sat beside him while Sigbord marched off down the stairs. When the flat-head's footsteps had faded away, Quint broke the heavy silence that descended.

'My name's Quintinius Verginix, apprentice to . . .' He paused. 'Well, former apprentice to Linius Pallitax.'

Quint held out his hand. The youth eyed it suspiciously, then looked down.

'Sanctaphrax born and bred, no doubt,' he said with an unpleasant sneer. 'Surprised you can be bothered to talk to the likes of me, a humble Undertown knife-grinder.'

'Actually,' said Quint, a little stiffly, 'my father's a sky pirate, and I was born in Undertown myself.'

The youth looked up at him, his eyes narrowed into suspicious slits.

'So what are you doing here?' he asked.

'I was sent for,' said Quint. He certainly didn't like the youth's unfriendly tone. 'But I could well ask you the same question.'

'I am the protégé of the Professor of Darkness,' said the youth, sitting up and puffing out his chest. 'Plain old Vil Spatweed, I was – 'til I found the professor's telescope half-buried in the mud of Anchor Chain Square.' He smiled, his lower jaw jutting forward with pride. 'Cleaned it up, polished the lens, made a few improvements of my own and then returned it to him. And mighty impressed he was, too. Invited me up here himself, he did. Said I had a rare talent which could be put to good use.'

The youth stood up and smoothed down his tattered tunic.

'And now,' he announced, a grin of smug satisfaction spreading across his features. 'You see before you none other than Vilnix Pompolnius, soon to be a squire of the Knights Academy – and with the Most High Academe, no less, as my mentor!'

'One of the *two* Most High Academes, Vilnix, my lad,' came a deep rumbling voice. 'And must I remind you again not to boast?'

55

Quint spun round. There, emerging from the black and white doors, was the owner of the voice, the Professor of Darkness, in a robe of deepest black, together with the white-robed Professor of Light and Quint's father, Wind Jackal.

Quint bowed his head in respectful greeting, but not before he glimpsed the scowl on the youth's face.

'Ah, making friends already?' the Professor of Light said, smiling benevolently at Quint and Vilnix. 'Excellent, excellent.'

Vilnix stepped forward and inclined his head respectfully. 'Yes, sir,' he replied.

'We have an announcement to make,' the Professor of Darkness said, looking from Vilnix to Quint, and back again. 'An important announcement.'

'This is indeed a day for the breaking of traditions,' the Professor of Light said, his voice high-pitched and reedy. 'Not only are there now two Most High Academes where before there was only one. But there will also be two Undertowners amongst the twenty-two apprentices from the Sanctaphrax schools chosen to enter the Knights Academy this year.'

'You mean . . .' Quint began.

'We would like to invite both of you,' said the Professor of Darkness, nodding. 'Vilnix, you shall be my protégé.'

'And you, Quint, shall be my protégé,' said the Professor of Light. 'It is what I had intended all along. You served our dear friend Linius well and would have made him an excellent protégé. Now you shall make *me* proud. The pair of you will carry the honour of the School of Light and Darkness into the Knights Academy.'

'*If* you choose to accept,' the Professor of Darkness added.

'Oh, I accept, all right,' said Vilnix eagerly, seizing the professor's hand and shaking it vigorously.

Quint glanced round at his father, his brow furrowed. Wind Jackal stepped forwards and embraced him warmly.

'It's up to you, Quint, what you decide to do,' he said.

'Oh, Father,' said Quint, looking up into Wind Jackal's concerned face. 'I'm part of Sanctaphrax now – and it's a part of me.'

'Yes,' said Wind Jackal, 'I can see that.'

Behind them, Vilnix gave a sneering laugh, which the Professor of Darkness silenced with a disapproving look.

'Besides,' said Quint, 'it isn't just for the Knights Academy that I want to stay in Sanctaphrax. There is another reason, too.'

'And that is?' said Wind Jackal, staring deep into his son's dark, troubled eyes.

For a moment, Quint was lost in memories of the past. Dark memories. Painful memories. He returned his father's gaze.

'Maris,' he said.

CHAPTER FOUR

THE GATES OF
HUMILITY

'Maris!' Quint called, seizing the handle of the heavy gilded door and pushing it open. 'Maris! Maris, I . . .'

He stopped, scarcely able to believe his eyes. He was standing in what had been Linius Pallitax's magnificent personal apartment in the School of Mist. But now the place was an empty, echoing hall, with open doors leading to other deserted rooms. In the middle of it all sat a great, glassy-bodied spindlebug trilling mournfully to himself.

'Tweezel?' Quint began uncertainly. 'What in Earth and Sky . . .?'

'Gone,' trilled the spindlebug, shaking his huge angular head slowly from side to side. 'All the master's things. His scrolls, his instruments, even his bed . . . and Mistress Maris with them. Gone, all gone.'

'Gone where?' Quint demanded.

'To Undertown,' Tweezel replied, turning and fixing his sad eyes on the youth. 'They had an order, signed in the master's own hand,' he added sorrowfully. 'Mistress Maris didn't want to leave, but when she saw her father's signature, she couldn't argue. So she left with them . . .'

'Left with *who*?' Quint demanded angrily. 'I don't understand, Tweezel. What's going on?'

'Heft Vespius and his wife, Dacia,' the spindlebug trilled. 'He's a prominent leaguesman in the League of Wicktwisters and Waxdippers. She's a distant cousin on Mistress Maris's mother's side.'

'Cousin,' Quint repeated.

'Yes. Always pestering the master for favours, they were, and in the name of his poor, dear wife,' said Tweezel scornfully. 'Most distasteful. Mind you, he never gave in to them . . .' He paused. 'Never until, it seems, now. Made them Mistress Maris's guardians, he did . . .'

'Her guardians?' said Quint, frowning.

'They showed me the scroll, signed in his own hand. It said that they should look after her until she came of age,' the spindlebug continued. 'They came at noon, Master Quint. Cleared the place out. By the time Maris returned from her father's funeral, they'd all but emptied her room, and then they whisked her away, too. I scarcely had time to say goodbye myself.' The spindlebug gave a sharp trill of misery. 'And then they dismissed me, just like that!' He gave a click of his claws.

'They dismissed you!' said Quint, shocked.

'And Welma too,' said the spindlebug, nodding vigorously. 'After all the years we've served the Master, and the young Mistress . . .'

'What are you going to do?' asked Quint.

'Oh, they can't get rid of old Tweezel that easily,' he said fiercely. 'Welma and I are going to follow them down to Undertown. And we'll stay close enough to keep an eye on the young Mistress. You see if we don't. Which reminds me,' he added, handing Quint a small barkscroll he'd been clutching in one of his front claws. 'She left you this.'

Quint looked down at the familiar handwriting on the outside, a painful lump forming in his throat. With a sigh, he pulled the ribbon and unfurled the scroll.

Dear Quint, he read, *it seems that Father has entrusted my care to my mother's cousin, Dacia, and her husband. He is rather fat and short-tempered, but I'm sure it must be for the best, or Father wouldn't have arranged it.*

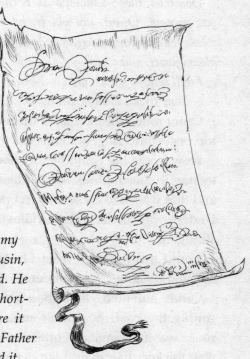

Don't forget me, Quint, now that I am to be a lowly Undertowner while you are to become a lofty squire at the Knights Academy. Yes, I heard your good news! The Professor of Light told me himself at the funeral. It'll help me, to think of you up there in beautiful Sanctaphrax if the sorrow I'm feeling now should become too much to bear . . .

As he read those last words, Quint pictured Maris's face, her green eyes full of tears but her jaw set firmly, and her eyebrows furrowed in that look of brave determination he knew so well. As he turned back to the letter, he knew just how much he was going to miss her.

Don't let those Sanctaphrax born-and-bred squires push you around, Quint, my old friend. You're better than the whole lot of them put together. I bet none of them has fought a gloamglozer, and won!

I will send word as often as I can.

Your friend always, Maris.

Quint rolled the barkscroll up and pushed it inside his top pocket, his fingers trembling.

How ironic life could be, he thought. He had wished to stay in Sanctaphrax so that he could be near Maris, and that wish had come true. Yet now she herself was in Undertown, alone and friendless, and in the care of strangers.

Could this *really* be what Linius had wished for his beloved daughter? he wondered. It didn't make sense.

Quint shivered, though whether from unease or simply the cold, he wasn't sure. Certainly the empty room was freezing, and outside the window, the snow was thicker than ever. Like a mighty swarm of white woodbees, it swirled this way and that in the shifting eddies of wind, obstructing the view and muffling every sound.

All at once, Quint was stirred from his reveries by the sound of someone clearing his throat. He turned to see his father standing beside Tweezel, his arms folded.

'Come, son,' he said gently. 'It's time to pack your things and get ready. You're to be at the Knights Academy at dawn.'

The morning broke even colder than the night it had followed, with a blistering wind slicing through the air, as sharp as slaughterers' knives. The frozen snow creaked and crunched beneath the feet of the sky pirate captain and his son as the pair of them made their way through the city. It lay thick and even, covering every step, every statue, every dome, cupola, bridge and buttress in a featureless white blanket that rendered everything the same. What was more, fresh snow was still falling from the slate-grey skies above.

'And there was me saying it was too cold to snow,' a young under-professor from the Institute of Ice and Snow commented to his older colleague as the pair of them hurried past.

'Never known anything like this in all my born days,' the older academic, his hair as white as the snow itself, replied solemnly. 'It's so cold, the quicksilver in the cloudmeters has set hard.'

As Quint and his father turned the corner of the Academy of Wind, the west wall of the Knights

Academy came into full view. Its polished surface, made of rock hewn from the cliff-face of the Edge itself, shone and shimmered, as if countless million glisters were trapped beneath its surface. At its very centre was a small entrance in front of which a line of shivering squires-to-be had formed.

Wind Jackal laid a hand on his son's shoulder. 'This is where I must leave you,' he said gravely. 'If it gets any colder, it will be impossible to keep the flight-rocks warm enough for safe flight, and I've got business to take care of at Wilderness Lair.'

Just then a shadow fell across the snow-covered square and, looking up, Quint saw the huge hull of a sky ship looming over the tops of the towers.

'The *Galerider*,' he breathed. 'Wilderness Lair . . . I almost wish I was going with you, Father.'

'No, Quint. Your future lies over there,' said Wind Jackal with a wave of his arm. 'Through that gateway.'

Quint looked across and nodded. The squires were clearly freezing, stamping their feet and hugging their arms tightly about them. There were twenty-one others in all, waiting patiently for the hefty gatekeeper in the white tunic with its red logworm badge emblazoned on the front to motion them forward to enter. Quint was the last of them. They wouldn't be going anywhere until he joined them, he knew that – and yet he was finding it so hard to leave his father.

From above his head, a rope-ladder dropped down. Wind Jackal grasped it and put a foot on the first rung.

'I must bid you farewell,' he said, 'but before I go . . .' He paused, reached inside his greatcoat and pulled out a small open-fronted box, with a lufwood perch inside and a large ring at the top. 'This is in case you need me, my son,' he said.

Quint took the cage and peered in. A small creature tethered to the perch peered back at him. 'A ratbird,' he said.

Wind Jackal nodded. 'From the *Galerider*,' he said. 'If you need me, tie a message to its foot and release it. A ratbird always finds its way back to its roost ship, wherever it may be.'

Quint smiled and nodded.

'Make me proud of you, son!' called Wind Jackal as he climbed the rope-ladder towards the hull-rigging of the mighty skycraft.

An icy blast of wind made the *Galerider* lurch upwards as its flight-rock was cooled to the core. There was a bright burst of flame from the rock cage as the stone pilot battled to keep the sky ship steady. The *Galerider*'s sails billowed, and it soared off into the slate grey sky.

'I'll do my best,' Quint shouted after it.

'"I'll do my best,"' came a mocking voice behind him, and Quint turned to see Vilnix Pompolnius at the back of the line of squires, an unpleasant sneer on his lips. 'Well, you could start by doing your best not to keep the rest of us waiting. It's freezing out here,' he added, 'or hadn't you noticed?'

The other squires had turned and were staring at him. Quint felt the blood rush to his cheeks as he joined the back of the line. The squire next to Vilnix winked at Quint.

'Sky pirate for a father,' he said, whistling through his teeth and smiling. 'I envy you. My father's a fusty old raintasting professor. Not nearly as much fun!'

He stepped aside as Vilnix pushed past him, and joined Quint at the back of the line. A shock of brown, curly hair fell over his wide forehead and across one of his smiling grey-blue eyes.

'Belphinius Mendellix,' he grinned, holding out a hand. 'But you can call me Phin. Pleased to meet you.'

'Quint,' said Quint, taking his hand and shaking it.

'You there at the back!' came the gruff voice of the keeper. 'The Gates of Humility await.'

Quint and Phin turned to find the other squires had already entered, and that they were alone at the entrance.

'Here goes!' said Phin, with a smile, and bowed almost double as he disappeared through the low opening in the West Wall.

'You next,' said the gatekeeper. 'And hurry up about it. I haven't got all day.'

Quint stooped low and entered what he discovered was a low-ceilinged tunnel. Behind him, a metal door clanged shut, while in front, Phin and the other squires shuffled forward. As the ceiling came lower still, Quint was forced down onto all fours. He emerged a moment later through an opening little bigger than a fromp hole, head bent and on his knees.

Looking round, he found himself in a great open courtyard covered, like everything else, in a thick layer of snow. At one side, running parallel to the West Wall, was a long avenue of poles, with horizontal branches that criss-crossed each other to create a sort of aerial maze. These were the tilt trees, where the knights academic-in-waiting and squires practised riding skills with their prowlgrins.

Ahead rose the white walls of the Lower Halls, and behind them, rising higher still, the ancient façade of the Upper Halls, with its ornately carved timber beams and lintels. At the western end of the Upper Halls, looming above the whole academy, was the magnificent Gantry Tower, now just a misty outline against the snowy sky. It was here that the young knights academic practised lowering themselves on their prowlgrin mounts, in preparation for their storm-chasing voyages.

Around Quint, his fellow squires – all still down on their knees – had formed themselves into a line. In front of them, despite the early hour and the bitter cold, the entire Knights Academy had turned out to greet the new arrivals.

On one side stood the squires of the Upper Halls, in short cloaks and white tunics. And how confident and self-assured they looked, thought Quint. Next to them, their teachers – the high professors – regarded the new squires benevolently. These were the finest scholars in the academy, destined some day, each and every one of them, for high office in the other academies of Sanctaphrax. Linius Pallitax himself, Quint knew, had once been a high professor in the Knights Academy, before joining the School of Mist.

On the other side of the snowy courtyard, in a great untidy throng, stood the academics-at-arms. Dressed in helmets, breast-plates and long black robes – and carrying a bewildering array of weapons – these were the members of the Knights Academy charged with the duty of protecting the sacred rock. Highly trained and well-equipped, the academics-at-arms were rugged individualists who took their orders directly from the Most High Academe.

Beside them, standing to attention in rigid ranks, were the gatekeepers, keys hanging from their thick, studded belts. Ignoring the scornful looks they were getting from the academics-at-arms, they stared sullenly ahead, the logworm badges on their tunics startlingly red against the snowy backdrop. Recruited from Undertown, and under the direct control of the Hall Master of High Cloud, the gatekeepers were well aware how much all the other academics despised them. Their captain, Daxiel Xaxis, stood stiffly to attention at their head, his hard, chiselled features betraying no emotion.

Directly in front of the kneeling squires, and completing the hierarchy of academics, stood the thirteen knights academic-in-waiting. They were all in the full armour – complete with glinting array of pipes, valves and dials – that Quint recognized from Linius's funeral ship. Each one of them had the visor to his helmet firmly shut.

Thronging the courtyard, at a respectful distance from the squires, high professors, academics-at-arms, gatekeepers and knights academic-in-waiting, were the massed ranks of hall servants, hushed and expectant. Ostlers, stable-hands and byre-gillies from the Hall of Grey Cloud rubbed shoulders with forge-hands, timber-workers and lectern-turners from the other halls. Servants from the barracks which housed the academics-at-arms mingled with stew-cart tenders from the Eightways refectory. All – no matter what their status – had their eyes fixed firmly on the kneeling squires in front of the Gates of Humility.

A hush fell, as four figures made their way across the courtyard. They came to a halt immediately in front of Quint and his companions. And as the academy looked on, they introduced themselves to the squires, one after the other.

'I am Arboretum Sicklebough,' snapped the first, an aged, mottle-skinned tree goblin, dressed in deep green robes and clutching a gnarled walking stick in both hands. 'Hall Master of Storm Cloud.'

'I . . . I . . . er . . . I am . . . Philius . . .' mumbled an aged figure in full knight academic armour, his startlingly blue eyes testifying to time spent in the Twilight Woods on stormchasing voyages. 'Philius Embertine. Hall Master of . . . of . . .'

'White Cloud,' said the figure next to him, a sharp-featured professor in a short grey cloak, who was carrying a tilderleather whip. 'Whilst I,' he continued, 'am Fenviel Vendix, Hall Master of Grey Cloud.'

The last of the four professors of the Knights Academy stepped forward. He was tall, with a thick white beard and stern, unsmiling features. His long cloak was of finest woodweave, edged in quarm fur, and he held an ornately carved staff with intricate markings and calibrations inlaid in blackwood and Edgewater pearl.

'I am Hax Vostillix,' he announced in a deep and sonorous voice, stroking his beard with a jewelled hand as he spoke. 'Hall Master of High Cloud.'

He strode along the line of kneeling squires, their shoulders and heads covered in a thin layer of snow.

'You have entered the Knights Academy through the Gates of Humility on your knees, young squires,' he said. 'In the Lower Halls, you shall learn woodcraft, forgecraft, prowlgrin husbandry and navigation. Some of you are destined for the Upper Halls to become high professors and perhaps even, Sky willing, Knights Academic. The rest of you shall become academics-at-arms and dedicate yourselves to the protection of this great floating city of ours. Whatever your destiny, young squires, I promise you one thing . . .'

The Hall Master of High Cloud raised his staff high above his head.

'None of you shall ever go on bended knees before anyone again. Squires of the Knights Academy, arise!'

·CHAPTER FIVE·

THE HALL OF STORM CLOUD

The deep, resonating sound of the dawn gong rippled through the Hall of Storm Cloud. It was four hours in the morning. Quint groaned and rolled over in the small sleeping closet. In the closet directly beneath him, he could hear Phin still softly snoring.

They, together with the other young squires, had been studying woodcraft in the Hall of Storm Cloud for three months now, under the short-tempered tutelage of Arboretum Sicklebough, the irascible tree-goblin hall master. Some said that it was his aching joints born of barkfever that made Sicklebough so crabby and stern. Others, that it was staying up most nights betting – and losing – on fromp fights at the Viaduct Steps which gave him such a foul temper. Whatever it was, Quint had never seen the mottled-skinned tree goblin in a good mood.

'You there! Squire Splinter-Finger!' he would snap in

the woodworking theatres below the Central Staircase. 'Call that a ship frame? A sick fromp could do better! Do it again!'

'Squire Blunt-Saw! I've seen ironwood stumps with a better finish than that. This isn't a mast, it's an eyesore! Do it again!'

Even in Quint's sleep, he heard Arboretum Sicklebough's rasping voice. Do it again! Do it again! And for what? To make a scaled-down model of a sky ship – perfect in every detail.

'I wouldn't mind,' Phin had joked as he fiddled to fit tiny deck planks to his model, 'if I was half a stride tall and could actually sail in the thing!'

Unfortunately, the sharp-eared hall master had overheard him.

'One fine day!' he'd barked, rapping Quint's friend over the knuckles with his gnarled cane, 'you'll find yourself turning turvey over the Twilight Woods in a half-wrecked stormchaser, and the only thing between you and a living death in the forest below will be your intimate knowledge of sky-ship construction. Now, remove that decking, and do it again!'

The ratbird gave a sleepy squeak as it stretched its leathery wings and settled back down on the perch of its small cage in the corner of the sleeping closet. Quint sat up and pushed open the doors. Above him, below and on either side, other doors were opening, and the sleepy faces of his fellow squires were appearing. Tonsor Wexis, his fat face puffy with sleep, yawned and knocked on his neighbour's doors. Quiltis Wistelweb's head appeared, his black hair sticking up like an enraged fromp's.

'What do you want?' he demanded.

'Dawn gong!'

'Already?'

'Yes, pass it on.'

Soon, the dormitory closet ladders were full of squires in various states of undress climbing down to the floor below, capes, barkscrolls and satchels clasped in their arms. Quint reached the floor and pulled on his cape, before realizing that someone was missing. He called up to one of the closets, high above his head.

'Phin! Phin! You'll be late!'

Phin's curly-haired head appeared. 'Late?' he yawned. 'Late for what?'

'For the storm test, stupid!' yelled Quint.

'Earth and Sky!' Phin exclaimed, disappearing inside his closet, and reappearing half-dressed moments later. 'Of course! It's today, isn't it?'

Phin shinned down the dormitory closet ladder to Quint's side.

'To the woodworking theatres!' he proclaimed, hurrying off towards the spiralling Central Staircase, with Quint at his heels. 'And let's just hope old Barkface is in a good mood for once!'

They raced down the staircase, jostling and being jostled by the other squires as they went, and through the high doorless archway below into the woodworking theatres.

There, amongst the aromatic piles of wood shavings, were high workbenches and tall backless stools, tool-chests and lug-barrels and long, extendable racks. Heavy vices attached to the sides of the tables clamped the squires' skycraft models firmly, while suspended on hooks from ropes and chains there hung great logs in various stages of carving.

Over by the walls was the wood itself, in towering stacks and of every shape, size and variety, as well as the great, exotic machines especially designed to fashion it. There were stipple-ridgers, plank-benders, turning-lathes and corrugated buzz-saws; eyelet-piercers and balk-strimmers, rivet-ties and adjustable planes ... and the whole lot was illuminated with large, spherical lamps that bathed everything in pools of creamy light.

Most of the other squires were already at their work-benches by the time Quint and Phin arrived, and the atmosphere was tense. Everyone knew that the time for theory and calculations was over. Their rigour was about to be put to the test. After weeks spent shaping the bows, erecting the masts, working on the deck/hull-weight ratio, hand-stitching the miniature spider-silk sails and securing the rigging, the day had come at last for the young squires to see how well their model sky ships would fly.

For today was the day of the storm test.

Wishing Phin good luck as he made for his work-bench, Quint crossed the woodworking theatre to his own bench, where his model craft was clamped rigidly, yet delicately, in a heavy vice.

It was a classic stormchaser, just like the one that had taken Linius's body down to the Stone Gardens. It had a single mast, a high bow and a sleek, pointed prow. The rudder was polished lufwood and the hull and decking, bloodoak planks no thicker than Quint's finger. The rock-cage in the centre of the vessel contained a polished ball of buoyant sumpwood to simulate a flight-rock, and the flight-weights which dangled beneath the hull-rigging were made of leadwood, meticulously fashioned through many a long night.

Quint stroked the blood - oak hull and traced a finger lovingly over the gossamer-thin spider-silk sails. You had to hand it to the irritable old tree goblin, he thought. Under his tutelage, every single squire had learned all about how a sky-craft worked and fitted together. Today, at last, they were going to find out whether that knowledge had been put to good use.

'Not bad,' came a sneering voice to Quint's left. 'If you want a skycraft for hauling ironwood to Undertown, that is. Still, what can you expect from the son of a sky pirate?'

Vilnix stood at his own workbench, smiling maliciously at Quint. Perhaps because he felt inferior to the Sanctaphrax-born and bred squires and wanted to deflect attention away from himself, Vilnix never missed an opportunity to needle Quint as another outsider. What was more, he had heard Vilnix boasting to Quiltis Wistelweb that his father was a powerful leaguesman who lived in a sumptuous palace in the Western Quays. Quint had said nothing because he actually felt sorry for Vilnix who, despite his boasting and attempts to suck up to his fellow squires, was liked by nobody.

'This, on the other hand,' said Vilnix pompously, tightening a hull-weight on his own model, 'is a *real* stormchaser.'

Quint looked across at Vilnix's bench. He had to admit that when it came to model-making, Vilnix was far better than anyone else in the class. The ship he had designed and fashioned had subtle innovations, like a retractable nether-mast and double hull-weights which not only added to its capabilities, but also enhanced its beauty. Even Arboretum Sicklebough had seemed impressed.

'Not bad, Pompolnius. Not bad,' he had snapped. 'But let's see how she sails before congratulating ourselves, shall we?'

And now at last that time had come.

'Good morning, squires!' A thin, peevish voice cut through the theatre. The frail-looking tree goblin made his way to the centre of the hall, his gnarled walking stick *tap-tap-tapping* as he went. He looked round at the squires, his dark, hooded eyes betraying nothing of what he was thinking – although if the latest gossip was to be believed, the number of gold pieces he'd lost on a fromp fight the previous night must have been high on his list of concerns.

'Take your models and follow me to the Storm Chamber!' he barked.

The squires did as they were told, chattering excitedly to one another while they removed their sky ships from the vices and carried them carefully across to the neighbouring theatre. As they approached the great pump-bellows – huge concertina-shaped leather sacks with tapered pipes emerging from them – the roar of the wind they were making grew louder, and the air filled with the smell of pinewood smoke.

'That's it, that's it,' said Arboretum Sicklebough, taking up his position on a podium above the pumping bellows where he could watch everything that was happening. 'First of all, observe the movement of the air,' he told them, and pulled on a lever to his side. 'And mark it closely.'

Immediately, a streak of grey-white smoke was released into the airstream which, as the bellows pumped, showed the swirls and eddies of the shifting air. Quint noticed how it dipped in the middle, then spiralled off to the left before whirling round and round in the centre, like water pouring down a plughole.

Sicklebough closed off the lever. The smoke stopped. 'Right,' he said. 'Let the storm test commence!'

The squires assembled in a large circle round the edge of the chamber, holding their precious models by the fingertips of their outstretched left hands. With their right hands, they carefully adjusted the hull-weights and sail settings.

Quint looked across the Storm Chamber to where Phin was battling with a stubborn studsail, his brow creased with concentration. Looking up, he caught Quint's eye and smiled weakly. Quint set his hull-weights high, to compensate for the down-draught at the edge of the miniature storm, but gave his mast extra topsail for the eddying winds closer to the centre.

He touched the talisman around his neck for good

luck, and hoped that he hadn't made a mistake in his calculations – a mistake that would lead to his mast being snapped off at the last moment. Just then, a sly elbow dug into his ribs, knocking him off balance.

'Sorry, didn't see you there,' said Vilnix, smiling unpleasantly.

He was standing next to Quint, attaching an extra staysail to his retractable nether-mast and adding neben-hull-weights below as a counterbalance. Quint bit his tongue.

'Make your final adjustments and prepare to launch!' Sicklebough's voice rang out above them.

Quint looked at the model in Vilnix's hand. It was a beautiful craft, certainly, but Vilnix had completely misread the pinewood smoke. If he launched the sky ship with the sails set as they were, the extra neben-weights would cause it to turn turvey the moment it reached the centre of the Storm Chamber.

Quint wrestled with his conscience for a moment. Should he keep quiet? Let Vilnix humiliate himself after all his hard work? He didn't like Vilnix, but still . . .

'Your neben-weights,' Quint whispered out of the corner of his mouth.

'What?' said Vilnix, a startled look in his eyes.

'Your neben-weights,' Quint repeated. 'You've mis-set them. They'll wreck your ship. If you just take them up three notches . . .'

'I'm not falling for that,' sneered Vilnix. 'I know your sort, sky pirate's brat!'

Quint turned away.

'Launch!' Sicklebough's voice rang out.

As one, the squires released their sky ships into the swirling air at the centre of the Storm Chamber, where they darted and dipped like stormhornets at dusk.

Above their heads, Arboretum Sicklebough craned his thin neck forward and narrowed his eyes as he assessed the performance of each of the twenty-two miniature sky ships. Several were torn to shreds within moments.

'Faulty hull construction, Squire Wexis!' barked the tree goblin.

A moment later, his irritated voice rose up above the sound of the storm winds a second time.

'Split rudder, Mendellix. That'll teach you to skip lathe-practice!' And Quint grimaced as his friend Phin's sky ship shattered in mid air.

The others hovered at odd angles, buffeted by the savage winds of the miniature storm, until Sicklebough signalled for their makers to haul them back in by tugging on their anchor ropes. After several minutes, only Quint and Vilnix's sky ships remained, sailing ever closer to the centre of the swirling storm.

Of the two, Vilnix's model was faring far better, its nether mast allowing it to ride the worst of the down-draught. But Quint's stormchaser was holding its own – despite its tiny mast bending alarmingly. He could hardly bear to look.

All round him, the squires clasped their own battered models and held their breath. Vilnix, at Quint's side, stared at his own beautiful model, a look of triumph on his face.

Suddenly, Vilnix's craft reached the centre of the storm. For an instant, it hung there in the air. The next, the neben-weights abruptly flew up in the air and dragged the tiny ship upside down, like a fighting fromp on the end of a chain. With a loud *crack*, the retractable mast snapped, and the ship hurtled downwards, smashing to smithereens on the ironwood floor below.

A gasp went round as Quint's ship reached the centre of the storm, where it hovered gracefully and effortlessly in classic, stormchasing style.

Sicklebough pulled hard on the lever by his side, and the bellows wheezed to a halt. Quint pulled his craft back towards him with shaking hands before glancing over at Vilnix.

'I'm sorry, Vilnix,' he said. 'I did try to warn you . . .'

He stopped, shocked at the look of pure hatred on the squire's face.

'You think you're so clever, Quintinius Verginix,' Vilnix rasped, spitting the words out. 'But I'll show you. Just you wait and see . . .'

·CHAPTER SIX·

THE HALL OF WHITE CLOUD

Sigbord smiled as he turned the breast-plate over in his great paddle-like hands. 'Excellent,' he said. 'Beautiful workmanship. I haven't seen anything like it since the old days back in the Deepwoods.'

The forge throbbed with heat thrown out by the glowing furnaces and the pounding of the foundry hammers. Spedius Heepe looked at the Captain of the Treasury Guard, a greedy glint in his eyes.

'You just can't get quality like this in Undertown,' Sigbord continued, shaking his head. 'Not for love nor money,' he added, running his fingers over the stylized emblem of the bloodoak that had been picked out in burnished copper on the breast-plate's front.

'Yes, I thought you'd appreciate that, as an old Deepwoods goblin yourself,' said Spedius, pushing his wire-framed spectacles up over the bridge of his nose. 'Old hammerhead design, I believe. Isn't that right,

Clud?' He paused, and frowned. 'I said, isn't that right, Clud?'

The huge mottled goblin turned from the convoluted tangle of pipes and gauges that spread across the walls and ceiling of the forge like metallic tarry-vine.

'That's right, Spedius,' Clud Mudskut growled, a lop-sided, gap-filled grin crossing his lumpen face. 'Though what would a weedy little Undertown scroll-scratcher like you know about old hammerhead designs, eh?'

Spedius gave a thin, high-pitched laugh and climbed to his feet. Short and slight, the bespectacled armourer barely came up to the mottled goblin's waist, but he reached up and slapped his colleague heartily on the back.

'Only what you tell me, Clud, you old Deepwoods metal-basher. Only what you tell me.'

The two armourers laughed heartily, Spedius's shrill giggle mingling with Clud's rumbling guffaw. Sigbord waited for a moment, then cleared his throat noisily.

'Yes, well,' he said, placing the breast-plate carefully down on the scroll-strewn desk, 'beautiful workman-ship, as I say. But if I know you two I'm going to have to pay handsomely for it.' His stroked his stubbled jaw. 'Shall we say fifteen gold pieces?'

Spedius Heepe stopped laughing and his small, dark eyes narrowed behind the wire-framed spectacles. 'Come come, Captain Sigbord,' he said, 'you can do better than that.' His mouth set in a thin, hard line beneath his sharp, twitching nose. 'Clud here has spent the best part of a week on this breast-plate, just so that you'd look your best for Treasury Day.' He paused thoughtfully, and when he spoke again his voice was little more than a whisper. 'Shall we say, *fifty* gold pieces?'

'Fifty!' Sigbord exploded, the heavy rings in his ears clinking as he shook his head. 'Why that's . . . that's . . .'

He fell still. The breast-plate was indeed magnificent and he *did* want to look his best on Treasury Day. It was the day when all of Sanctaphrax celebrated the overthrowing of the earth-scholars by the sky-scholars – with a little help from a band of loyal flat-head goblins. Now the descendants of those goblins stood guard over the treasury and its precious store of stormphrax, with Sigbord standing proudly at their head.

'I don't have that sort of money,' he growled.

'Then perhaps we can come to some other arrange-ment?' said Spedius, with a tight little smile.

'Such as?' said Sigbord, picking the breast-plate up and stroking its polished surface.

'A trade,' said Clud with a grin.

'Precisely,' added Spedius. 'You, my dear captain, have keys to the Treasury Chamber.'

'A couple of shards of stormphrax,' growled Clud, his face suddenly serious.

'In return for this magnificent breast-plate . . .' Spedius folded his arms.

'Out of the question!' stormed Sigbord, raising the armour as if to fling it across the forge.

'And five more like it,' finished Spedius.

Sigbord hesitated.

Stormphrax was sacred, so sacred that it was considered blasphemy for anyone, save the Knights Academic and the Treasury Guardians – the Professors of Light and Darkness – even to cast their gaze upon it. The glowing crystals, so heavy in absolute darkness, were the priceless reward that lay at the heart of great storms; a glittering prize which the Knights Academic risked their lives for on their valiant quests. Certainly no furnace masters would ever be granted access to it. Yet Sigbord knew that, even though it was strictly forbidden, there were many in Sanctaphrax desperate to get their hands on it, to experiment with it, to unlock its fabulous secrets . . .

'A couple of shards?' he growled.

'Tiny little shards,' grinned Spedius. 'Who's to know, Sigbord? It'll be our little secret, and just think how magnificent you and your lieutenants are going to look . . .'

*

'Stope . . . ! Stope . . . !'

The small, wiry grey goblin stirred in the nest he'd made for himself out of rags and straw, in the furthest corner of the forge.

'Stope!' Clud Mudskut's voice boomed, rattling the forge pipes and setting the gauges quivering.

'Coming, Furnace Master, sir,' he called back, scrabbling to his feet and rubbing his eyes.

'There you are,' the mottled goblin growled as Stope approached the central furnace, where the pipes from all directions converged.

He grasped the young goblin by the collar of his shabby tunic and lifted him off his feet. Stope found himself staring into the furnace master's mottled face, which was inches from his own.

'Listen up, whelp,' growled Clud. 'That breast-plate you made for me . . .'

'Y . . . yes,' stammered Stope.

'You're to make five more before Treasury Day.'

'But . . . but that's only a week away . . .' Stope protested. 'There isn't time . . .'

'Then you'd better *make* time, my dear young forge-hand,' came Spedius Heepe's wheedling voice from below, 'or you'll find yourself back in Undertown next Dumping Day!'

Stope shuddered. Like so many before him, he'd left the dark and dangerous Deepwoods to seek a better life in Undertown, only to find squalor and misery awaiting him. A friendly basket-puller had taken pity on the starving grey goblin and smuggled him up to Sanctaphrax, where he'd knocked on the first door he'd come to and claimed 'Sanctaphrax Sanctuary'.

According to the ancient laws of the great floating city, any who made it up to the rock and claimed sanctuary had to be taken in, so long as they were prepared to work as unpaid servants. After a year, they could be thrown out on 'Dumping Day' if they hadn't given satisfaction. Stope had been taken in by the Hall of White Cloud, where he'd proved himself a skilled forge-hand and quick learner. But despite this, he knew that the furnace masters, Clud and Spedius, could throw him out any time they chose.

'I'll do it,' he croaked.

Clud released his grip, and Stope slumped to the floor.

'That's a good forge-hand,' smiled Spedius, turning to go. 'Oh, and Stope ...' The smile froze on his thin, pinched features. 'Not a word of this to anyone, understand?'

The heat of the central furnace took Stope's breath away, despite the heavy tilderleather visor he wore. He checked the ventilation gauze and the temperature setting. The blue-grey metal ingot was now white-hot in the heart of the furnace, ready to be beaten out into a curved sheet on the great anvil beside him. Stope grasped the fire tongs with gloved hands and carefully removed the glowing lump of metal.

It was almost midday, but Stope was far too busy to notice the time. Day and night, he'd worked in the armoury forge, snatching sleep only while he waited for the furnace to reach forging temperature. Two gleaming breast-plates, each exquisitely tooled with bloodoak designs, sat on the polishing bench in the corner, but they were not enough. And time, as Stope knew, was running out. He raised a hammer and brought it down on the ingot.

Clang!

A shower of sparks flew into the air.

Clang! Clang! Clang!

The metal began to take shape beneath his blows, thinning and curving as its glow turned from white to orange, to a fiery red.

'Such a pleasure to watch a craftsman at work,' came a cracked, ancient-sounding voice.

Startled, Stope looked up.

An aged knight academic in full armour stood before him. His white hair fanned out like a halo around his lined face, as his startlingly blue eyes sparkled in the furnace light.

'Hall Master!' Stope exclaimed, lowering his hammer and lifting his visor.

'Please,' said Philius Embertine, raising a gauntleted hand. 'Don't let me stop you. You must be the forge-hand my furnace masters told me about . . .'

The young grey goblin blushed. 'My name's Stope, sir, and I'm proud to serve the Hall of White Cloud.'

'I'm sure you are, my lad,' said Philius, his blue eyes twinkling. 'And by making these fine breast-plates, you are rendering a service far greater than you can possibly know . . .'

'I . . . I . . .' Stope stammered, unsure what to say.

'Ah, Hall Master,' came Spedius's voice as the furnace master suddenly appeared through the tangle of forge pipes. 'Sigbord has agreed to your little deal, and you can take delivery as soon as Clud and I finish these breast-plates . . . With young Stope's help, of course.'

Behind him, Clud scowled at Stope.

Philius turned and Stope saw a look of vague befuddlement fall, like a veil, over his ancient features.

'Good . . . good . . . You've made an old knight very happy . . .' he mumbled distractedly. 'Just thought I'd look in on you . . . I'm on my way to . . . to the Armour Hall . . . to lecture . . .'

Spedius smiled. 'Of course you are,' he said smoothly.

'If you'll permit it, Hall Master, my forge-hand here can guide you there.' He looked round. 'Stope!' He clicked his fingers and motioned that the youth should lay down his tools and take Philius by the arm.

Quickly removing his visor and gloves, Stope did as he was bid, and escorted Philius out of the forge.

'Most ... most obliging ...' mumbled the old knight academic as they shuffled out. 'So easy to ... lose ... one's way.'

With the hall master's heavy, gauntleted hand resting on his shoulder, Stope made his way from the forge, up a half-flight of stairs and down a long hallway. He could hear the rasping breath of the old professor close to his left ear, and feel its warmth. And glancing

behind him, Stope caught him looking about – through the windows, along the adjoining corridors and at the name plaques on the doors they passed – without the faintest hint of recognition.

As they approached the Armour Hall, the sound of the rowdy squires echoed back along the hall. Bored with waiting, they were laughing and joking and teasing one another. Stope wondered how poor old Philius Embertine – someone who could no longer even find his way around his old academy hall – managed to conduct lectures at all.

Just then, Stope heard a hissed, 'Here he comes,' followed by the sound of scurrying footsteps and scraping wood.

He peered in through the small, circular window in the door. The squires had all scrambled to their seats, and were perched on their jutting study-ledges, slates balanced on their laps and legs dangling. Seizing the handle, Stope pulled the door open and ushered the professor in.

'Er ... Good afternoon ... Knights of ... er ...' he muttered, his voice soft and quavering.

'Good morning, Professor Embertine, sir,' the squires chanted back from the study-ledges.

The hall master clanked across the room to the raised podium at the front, apparently oblivious to the whispers that hissed round the high, vaulted ceiling. He took his place at the lectern beside an ancient-looking suit of armour, suspended from a rickety frame.

Stope turned to go. He was exhausted and knew he

had to get back to the forge to have any hope of finish-
ing the breast-plates. But it felt so cool in the corridor
beside the half-opened door compared to working at the
furnaces, and besides, the hall master – whom he'd only
ever glimpsed from a distance at meal times in the
Eightways – intrigued him. A moment or two wouldn't
make any difference, he told himself.

Up on the podium, the hall master seemed to be gear-
ing himself up for the lecture. He was swaying gently, to
and fro, to and fro, and staring straight ahead of him.

'Um . . . Um . . . Right . . . um . . . yes . . . So where were
we?' He looked at the hanging suit of armour as if half
expecting the answer to come from it. 'I . . . um . . .'

Stope looked around at the group of squires. Some of
them he recognized.

There was that fat one with the pudding-bowl haircut.
Always in trouble he was. What was his name? Tonsor?
Yes, that was it. Tonsor Wexis. And there, next to him, the
brown, curly-haired one who was always making jokes
– Belphinius Something. And Someone Wistelweb . . .
And . . . Oh, yes, on the ledge just above him was the
young squire who'd noticed that Stope had burned his
arm that one time, and brought him hyleberry salve.
Stope wouldn't forget his kindness.

Quint was his name. He wasn't like the other squires
– Sanctaphrax born and bred, confident of their place in
the world and with no time for others. No, Quint seemed
to notice and care about the servants and hall attendants
and even had time for a lowly forge-hand with a burnt
arm. But then he was the son of a sky pirate captain, or

so they said. He had flown on a sky ship high above the Edge.

What things he must have seen! Stope marvelled. What adventures he must have had! No wonder he wasn't like those sons of academics, with their heads in the clouds. Quint had actually flown *above* the clouds!

Stope smiled dreamily. From the Armour Hall came the sound of the hall master's ancient voice.

'Ah, yes . . . Now we come to the flange release of the light-meter, to be calibrated in twilight, here.' There came a soft tapping sound as the hall master pointed out a lever below a dial on the breast-plate with a long stick of polished lufwood. 'Connected to the equalizing pipes, both exterior . . .' – *Tap! Tap! Tap!* – 'and interior' – *Tap! Tap!* – 'and regulated by the sumpwood oil gauge, which in turn . . .' – *Tap!* – 'leads to the shoulderguard and bracing handles . . .' *Tap! Tap!*

All round the hall, the squires were attending to the lecture with varying degrees of concentration. Some scribbled down notes on their slates, some frowned and nodded earnestly, while some, Stope thought, seemed barely able to keep their eyes open.

'And of course, at this juncture, note also the clever design of the gauntlets,' Philius was saying. 'The fingers are banded for maximum manoeuvrability . . .' – *Tap! Tap! Tap!* – 'while the locking sprocket, here . . .' – *Tap!* – 'ensures that a tight grip can be maintained effortlessly for as long as the wearer requires . . .'

As he intoned the details he knew by heart, the old knight's words flowed smoothly – all uncertainty, wavering and confusion gone. Outside, soothed by the sonorous rhythm of his speech, Stope's eyes began to droop and his head to nod.

CHAPTER SEVEN

THE EIGHTWAYS

'Moving on to the leg brace and knee protectors . . .'

Before Philius Embertine could expound further, the lunch gong sounded in the distance and the squires – those who were still awake, that is – let out a collective sigh of relief.

'. . . Um . . . that will be . . . all for today,' the hall master mumbled. He lay down his lufwood cane and shuffled out.

Yawning and stretching, the squires climbed down from the study-ledges and, in groups of twos and threes, followed him from the hall.

'Did you understand any of that?' asked Phin, scratching his head before replacing his cap.

'Most of it,' said Quint. 'You see, it's all about deflecting the energy of the lightning charges. The knight has to be insulated from the effects of twilight through the filters in the . . .'

'No, sorry,' said Phin, grinning. 'You've lost me. But there's one thing a lecture from old Iron Breeches does give me.'

'What's that?' asked Quint, gathering his barkscroll notes and returning them to his satchel.

'A healthy appetite,' laughed Phin. 'Come on, let's get to the Eightways before they empty the stew-cart without us!'

They left the Armour Hall and Phin strode off down the hallway. Quint was about to follow him when he noticed a figure slumped beside the doorway. He leaned down and tapped the sleeping goblin on the shoulder.

'Stope? Stope?' he said, then paused. 'It *is* Stope, isn't it?'

The grey goblin stirred, shuddered, and opened his eyes.

'Squire Quint!' Stope leaped to his feet. 'I must have dozed off! How long have I been sleeping? What time is it?'

'Calm down,' said Quint. 'It's lunchtime. The gong's just sounded.' He looked at the young goblin more closely. 'Stope, you look terrible . . .'

'I must get back to the armoury!' he said, and turned to go.

'Not so fast,' said Quint firmly and grabbed his arm. 'First you need a plate of stew and a hunk of barley bread. Come, you can sit next to me on the lower benches.'

Stope allowed Quint to lead him towards the Eightways. The mention of stew had made his stomach gurgle with hunger, and he felt too weak and tired to resist. At the end of the hallway, they entered a circular corridor with eight large doorways cut into its inner

wall. They made their way round, past the Hall of Storm
Cloud and Hall of Grey Cloud entrances, to the White
Cloud entrance, where the Winter Knights and other hall
servants jostled impatiently for the doors to open.

As they approached, Spedius Heepe and Clud
Mudskut exchanged glances, and glowered at Stope.
Vilnix Pompolnius stepped out of the crowd and stuck
his face into Quint's.

'Who's your little friend?' he sneered, gesturing to
Stope. 'Making friends with Sanctaphrax sanctuary-
slaves now, are we?'

'At least I *have* friends,' said Quint icily, and pushed
past Vilnix, whose face seemed to drain of colour at his
words.

Just then, the sound of bolts being drawn filled the
corridor as, one by one, the doors to the Eightways were
pulled open by the gatekeepers.

First the hall masters entered and crossed the circular
chamber to sit at the high table, followed shortly after by
the knights academic, stern and silent, who joined them.
Then, in complete contrast, the rowdy academics-at-
arms came bursting in through the second entrance;
with the squires of the Upper Halls entering by the third
doorway, laughing and joking, and jostling one another
to find seats at the middle tables. Finally, with a surge of
bodies, the four Lower Halls doorways were filled with
squires, servants and hall attendants, who fanned out
across the lower benches, perching on them like roosting
ratbirds fleeing from a storm.

The great chamber of the Eightways was filled with

clamour and conversation as, all around at the different tables, the various groups in the Knights Academy – from ostlers who worked in the prowlgrin roosts of the Hall of Grey Cloud and lathe-turners from the wood-working theatres of the Hall of Storm Cloud, to lectern-keepers from the Hall of High Cloud – engaged in uproarious debate and gossip.

Only the thirteen knights academic-in-waiting at the high table sat silently. They stared ahead of them, as if in contemplation of the stormchasing voyages to which they'd dedicated their lives.

Quint and Stope found a place next to Phin on the lower benches next to a noisy group of lectern-keepers. Above them, Hax Vostillix, Hall Master of High Cloud, resplendent in purple robes with marsh-pearl embroidery, stood up and beat the table with his staff.

The Eightways fell silent.

'From Sky we come, to Sky we shall return,' he intoned in his deep, sonorous voice. 'Though we partake of the produce of the Earth, may it be only to nourish the Sky in our hearts.'

'Sky in our hearts!' echoed the massed voices of the Knights Academy.

As if in answer, the eighth door of the chamber clanged open. There was a blast of icy air and a flurry of snow-flakes, and two huge grey hammelhorn bulls entered, pulling an enormous sealed cauldron on wheels, complete with a glowing brazier suspended from its undercarriage. Behind them lumbered the kitchen master, a massive cloddertrog in a pristine white apron and tall, conical hat, with twenty mobgnomes in white tunics in tow, baskets piled high with loaves of barley bread on their heads.

'Fresh from the Great Refectory, from a grateful Sanctaphrax!' boomed the huge cloddertrog. 'Come and get it while it's hot!'

At this, the occupants of the lower benches and middle tables surged forward, and the mobgnomes began tossing barley loaves over their heads. Meanwhile the gatekeepers, in their white tunics and red logworm badges, barged through and collected special tureens, which they delivered to the high table. As the squires jostled forward, Quint glimpsed Vilnix staring up at the knights academic and hall masters as they were served their stew, a look of greedy envy on his face.

'Come on!' shouted a lectern-keeper just in front of them. 'What's the hold-up? We're starving back here!'

Up ahead, the cloddertrog kitchen master was panting with effort, sweat pouring down his flabby face as he wrestled with the heavy metal tap on the side of the cauldron. It seemed to be stuck.

He strained at the tap-handle.

Nothing happened.

Grunting with effort, he tried again. Still, the handle would not move.

'Damn and blast you to Open Sky!' the kitchen master shouted, and seized the tap-handle with both hands. He tugged with all his might, straining until the muscles in his arms and neck bulged and the veins at the side of his head began to throb. Yet for all that, the tap would not turn. 'It's no good,' he muttered. 'It's stuck fast.'

A low groan of disappointment passed back through the waiting crowd as everyone craned their necks to see what the problem was. The groan became a mutter, which rose in volume until everyone was roaring with a mixture of anger and hunger.

'Nourish the Sky in our hearts! Nourish the Sky in our hearts! . . .'

The kitchen master turned, his face red with rage and bellowed loudly.

'Forge-hand! Is there a forge-hand here?'

His voice echoed round the Eightways above the sound of the impatient chanting and, for a moment, the noise subsided as everyone looked about them.

Vilnix dug Quint in the ribs with a bony elbow.

'What about your little friend?' he shouted in his ear. 'He's a forge-hand, isn't he?'

'Let him through! Let him through!' shouted the lectern-keepers as the crowd parted to allow Stope to approach the stew-cart. Vilnix gave him a vicious shove in the back for good measure.

'Sir?' said Stope, as he approached the red-faced cloddertrog.

'I swear I don't know what you lot do all day in that armoury,' the cloddertrog complained. 'Maintenance of the stew-cart is *your* responsibility. You tell your furnace masters that! Too busy lining their own pockets to care, no doubt . . .'

Stope tried to ignore the kitchen master's tirade as he kneeled at the tap and traced a finger along the pipe leading to the cauldron.

'Well?' demanded the cloddertrog as all round the hall, the hungry demands for food once more began getting louder.

'The tap joint's sound,' Stope began, 'and the pipework isn't showing any sign of damage . . .'

'So, what's wrong with it?' stormed the cloddertrog. 'If the tap isn't faulty, why won't it turn?'

Stope felt along the pipe. 'I'm not sure, but it could be . . .'

'Oh, I don't have time for this!' roared the cloddertrog to a mixture of cheers and jeers. He stuck his great head beneath the tap and peered up into the spout. 'It's broken, I tell you!'

Stope gave the pipe a hefty thump. '... An air-lock – nothing to do with bad maintenance at all ...'

From inside the great stew-pot there came a series of loud gurgles and plops.

'Broken,' the cloddertrog repeated. 'Thanks to you lot in the armoury ... *Aargh!* Cloppl-plobbl ...'

A sudden rush of steaming stew came gushing out of the tap and hit the cloddertrog full in the face. He staggered backwards, whimpering loudly, and fell heavily to the floor.

'Plobbl ... Stop it!' he wailed. 'Shut the tap off ... Now!'

Stope wrestled with the tap, but the cloddertrog had twisted it so violently that the tap was now jammed open. All he could do was stand back as the stew continued to pour over the cloddertrog and onto the floor.

The crowd gave a loud groan and, giving up on the rapidly emptying stew-cart, they turned and grabbed loaves of barley bread, before returning to the benches and tables. The hefty cloddertrog clambered to his feet and strode towards Stope, his face dripping with stew.

'You forge-hand moron!' he bellowed. 'You over-baked halfwit! You did that on purpose!' And he grabbed Stope in one of his huge fists, raised him high up off the ground and shook him about, like a prowlgrin pup with a rag.

'Put him down!' shouted Quint, outraged.

'Put him down?' roared the cloddertrog, his voice getting louder. 'I'll put him down, all right!' and with that, he tossed Stope to the ground, where he skidded across the pool of spilled stew. He unbuckled his heavy leather belt, pulled it from his waist and swung it round his head. 'And then I'll give him a hiding he won't soon forget!' he bellowed as he lunged at Stope.

But Quint was too fast for him. As the cloddertrog leaped forwards, he seized the heavy brass buckle of the belt and yanked it hard to one side. Caught off balance, the cloddertrog skidded on the stew, lost his footing and crashed to the ground once more. Quint stood above him, the belt now in his own hands.

'Now unless *you'd* like a hiding you won't soon forget from a squire of the Knights Academy,' he said, his eyes blazing with anger, 'you'll thank Stope here for trying to help, and get this mess cleared up!'

The cloddertrog gave a whimper. 'I've got nothing

against you squires,' he pleaded, suddenly craven and subservient. 'It's just them that don't do their jobs properly, that's all . . .'

Quint snorted and tossed the belt down beside him. 'Come on, Stope,' he said. 'Let's leave the kitchen master to do *his* job properly.'

And with that, as the cloddertrog set to work on the spilt stew with a shovel, bucket and mop, the pair of them made their way from the Eightways.

'That's the second time you've helped me, sir,' said Stope as he and Quint entered the circular corridor.

'Is it?'

'Yes, sir,' said Stope. 'You got me that hyleberry salve, sir. For the burn on my arm . . . And it worked a treat, by the way, sir.'

'Glad to hear it, Stope,' said Quint. 'But don't keep calling me "sir". I'm not a day older than you.' He smiled. 'Call me Quint.'

Stope grinned from ear to ear. 'Oh, thank you, sir,' he said. 'I . . . I mean, Quint. And if there's anything *I* can do for you, then . . .' He stopped.

Quint followed Stope's gaze.

There, coming out of the hall master's entrance just up ahead, their backs towards them, were Philius Embertine and a knight academic. The pair of them were deep in whispered conversation. Quint and Stope exchanged puzzled looks. This certainly wasn't the doddering, confused old hall master they both knew.

' . . . And there are rumours, Philius, old friend,' the knight academic was saying, 'that Hax Vostillix is having the Great Library watched.'

'You are the finest knight academic of your generation, Screedius, and like a son to me,' the Hall Master of White Cloud replied, his voice steady and firm. 'But not even you can protect me if Hax decides to show his hand. He has powerful allies.'

'You mean the gatekeepers? They're nothing but a bunch of jumped-up lackeys,' the knight academic replied scornfully.

'Maybe so,' said Philius. 'But those jumped-up lackeys are well-armed, thanks to my greedy furnace masters, and looking for trouble.'

'Then the knights and high professors will be happy to oblige them!' Screedius replied gravely.

Philius Embertine shook his head. 'That could be just what Hax wants us to do,' he said. 'No, we must bide our time. I know it's hard, Screedius, but you must trust me on this, I still have work to do . . .'

Their voices faded as they continued down the corridor. Quint turned to Stope. 'Well that was very strange,' he said. 'I've never heard Philius Embertine talk that clearly about anything but armour before.'

'I have,' said Stope, his brow wrinkling into a puzzled frown. 'Earlier today, when he talked to me in the armoury. He's not as foolish as he looks, you know.'

Quint broke into a broad smile and clapped the grey goblin on the shoulder. 'He's not the only one!' he laughed.

CHAPTER EIGHT

TREASURY DAY

After a brief respite, snow was once again falling on Sanctaphrax. Roofs, turrets, bridges and balustrades were all piled high with great pillow-like drifts which, as the snowflakes settled, grew higher and higher, and more unstable. In the end, a light gust of wind or a white raven's flapping wing was all it took to upset the snow's precarious balance and send it tumbling down through the air. All round Sanctaphrax, the *flupp flupp flupp* of the packed snow hitting the ground could be heard – followed, on occasions, by the muffled cries of unwary passers-by.

Of course, these weren't the only sounds to be heard in Sanctaphrax. As always, there was the curiously ethereal music of the great floating city – from the percussion and timpani of the meteorological instruments clashing and clattering, to the reedy pipe-like sounds of the wind whistling through narrow gaps and gullies.

With the snowfall, however, not only was the music more subdued, but now there were new sounds. The eerie chiming of countless giant icicles, the muted plash of footsteps tramping through the snow and, loudest of all, the constant grating and grinding of the massed ranks of shovels. Armies of underlings from the academies and labourers from Undertown were working around the clock to keep the streets and squares of Sanctaphrax clear. Under the watchful eye of flat-head goblin guards, they worked in teams, shifting the snow along from the centre of the city, down avenues and roads, until they reached the edge, where it was dumped over the side.

'Put your backs into it, you lot!' barked a stocky flat-head, a fur-lined hood crammed down over his hairless head. 'Gotta clear all this lot away before the procession arrives.'

The rag-tag collection of trogs and goblins said nothing. Heads down and thick mist billowing from their mouths, they continued the arduous, if not impossible, task of removing all the snow from Mosaic Quadrangle, even as more was falling from the dark-grey sky above.

'Blooming ridiculous,' a mobgnome complained to his neighbour, an old, bow-legged tusked goblin. 'Procession! I mean, I ask you! In this!' He straightened up and swung his arm round in a wide arc.

'Snow on Treasury Day,' the tusked goblin commented, as she shuffled forwards. 'Beggars belief, dunnit?'

'You can say that again,' said the mobgnome, resuming his snow-clearing. 'I remember last year. Beautiful blue sky and hardly a breath of wind. And the year before that, a slight shower, but there's never been snow before – not on Treasury Day.'

'And now look at it,' grumbled a lumbering cloddertrog to their left. 'You'd think they'd cancel it, what with all this weather 'n' all. Or at least postpone it . . .'

'Ooh, can't do that,' came a voice from behind them. The mobgnome, the tusked goblin and the cloddertrog turned to see a shabby woodwaif, a stiff broom in his spidery hands, shaking his head grimly. 'First day of the second moon when it's in its third quarter. That's Treasury Day. Always has been and always will be. It's tradition, and you can't change tradition . . .'

'Which is where we lot come in,' the mobgnome muttered. 'Shovelling and sweating . . .' He looked up at the sky and brandished a fist. 'Snow, snow and more snow, curse the sky!'

'Curse the sky?' muttered the cloddertrog. 'That sounds like earth-scholar talk to me . . .'

'So what if it is,' said the mobgnome hotly. 'Those earth-scholars knew a thing or two, if you ask me . . .'

A gasp went round the small group, followed by an uneasy silence. Such talk was bad enough in the current atmosphere of Sanctaphrax, where earth-scholars were considered blasphemers and infidels, but on Treasury Day – the day set aside to commemorate their overthrow – it could result in the gravest of punishments.

A flock of white ravens flapped overhead, camouflaged by the falling snow, but cawing so raucously that no-one could fail to notice them. The snow shovellers looked up.

'There, listen to that,' said the mobgnome. 'The white ravens are as unhappy as we are.'

'It's the cold,' said the woodwaif.

'The cold?' the cloddertrog laughed. 'But they've got feathers to keep 'em warm, ain't they?'

The woodwaif smiled indulgently. 'I mean the effect the cold's having on the Stone Gardens,' he said. 'Normally, the rocks down there grow slowly. It takes years before they're buoyant enough to break away from their rock stacks. And those there white ravens, they can tell, just by sitting on 'em, when a rock is nice and ripe and ready to float.'

The others nodded. Everyone knew how the great flock of snowy birds would rise up, squawking loudly in their Chorus of the Dead, to announce to the academics of

Sanctaphrax that it was time to harvest the
buoyant rocks.

'These days, though,' the
woodwaif continued, 'the
poor creatures don't
know whether
they're coming or
going. It's so cold
that the rocks are
ripening too quickly –
breaking away
from the stacks
and flying off,
they are, when
they're still small. If this weather keeps up, there'll be no
rocks left to harvest, you
mark my words.'

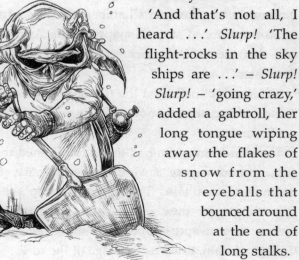

'And that's not all, I
heard ...' *Slurp!* 'The
flight-rocks in the sky
ships are ...' – *Slurp!*
Slurp! – 'going crazy,'
added a gabtroll, her
long tongue wiping
away the flakes of
snow from the
eyeballs that
bounced around
at the end of
long stalks.

'Ay,' said the tusked goblin. 'I've got a brother on a sky pirate ship holed up in the boom-docks. His stone pilot refuses to fly until the weather clears up.'

'I don't blame him. After all, half a dozen league ships have gone missing this month already,' added the mobgnome.

'And if flight-rocks are going crazy, then ...' – *Slurp!* – 'what in Earth and Sky's name is going to happen to the biggest buoyant rock of all?' asked the gabtroll.

For a second time, the group gasped as one. The next moment – as if in response – the great Sanctaphrax rock gave an almighty lurch, sending them all sprawling. The cloddertrog lost his footing and ended up headfirst in the heap of snow they were shovelling.

'If the great rock gets much colder,' said the woodwaif, his huge, diaphanous ears fluttering ominously, 'the Treasury Chamber will need a fresh load of stormphrax to stop it snapping the Anchor Chain, and that means a stormchasing voyage sooner rather than later!'

'Oi! You lot!' bellowed the flat-head overseer. 'You're being paid to shovel snow, not gossip like a gaggle of goblin matrons!'

The cloddertrog climbed to his feet, joined the others and, without saying a word, the work-party resumed its monotonous task. They were outside the Mosaic Quadrangle by now and, at the flat-head's barked orders, they swept, scraped and shovelled on past the College of Rain, towards the edge of the rock.

'Watch out below!' bellowed the cloddertrog as they pushed the great heap of compacted snow off the floating rock. Not that his warning would have done much good if a hapless Undertowner had been walking along as the huge ball of snow crashed down. Luckily no-one was hurt – this time . . .

Back in Sanctaphrax, the Mosaic Quadrangle was filling up with academics who, despite the weather, had turned out to witness the annual spectacle. They stood, shivering and stamping their feet: professors, apprentices, servants and squires, their usual robes now lined with fur or stuffed with rags, depending on their status, to keep out the penetrating cold.

All round, academic hoods and headgear now sported ear-flaps and mufflers of extravagant size and design. A bunch of junior academics from the Institute of Ice and Snow sported huge turbans wound tightly round their heads, while the under-professors of the School of Sleet favoured shaggy hammelhornskin snow-caps, complete with tinted goggles and fromp-fur handwarmers. Most exotic of all were the 'furnace bonnets' – specially designed headpieces that comprised a miniature sumpwood burner and heated ear-muffs.

The square had only recently been cleared, yet the snow was falling so quickly that it had already obscured most of the ornate mosaic pattern of concentric circles and zigzag lightning bolts once more. From the southern end there came the sound of tramping feet as a line of squires in smart, ankle-length cloaks and polished silver helmets – chaperoned by a phalanx of gatekeepers in their familiar logworm-emblazoned white tunics – marched in strict formation into the square.

Word of their appearance went round the crowd in loud whispers, as the onlookers nudged one another and pointed.

'It's the squires from the Knights Academy, look!'

'Sky preserve 'em!'

'Gonna need all the knights academic we can get for stormchasing if this cold weather persists.'

From the middle of the front rank, Quint stared straight ahead and tried to concentrate on keeping in step. Behind him marched the squires from both the Lower and the Upper Halls, plus the hall servants, and behind them, the knights academic-in-waiting, marching stiffly in their gleaming armour and attracting looks and whispers from the crowd.

Phin was beside him, head high and back straight, with Tonsor, Quiltis and Vilnix completing the rank. Out of the corner of his eye, Quint could see Vilnix's dark, mistrustful eyes scanning the crowds, a curious expression – a mixture of contempt and malice – distorting his sullen features.

Quint tried to ignore him. It felt good to be out of the academy after so many weeks penned up inside, and although the burnished silver helmet was heavy and uncomfortable and the long cloak threatened to trip him up at any moment, Quint felt his heart swell with pride as they marched towards the corner of the quadrangle.

It was all so very different from the first time he'd witnessed the ceremony a year earlier.

On that occasion, he'd watched it from the sidelines with Maris. The two of them – pupils of the Fountain House school – had mingled with the other onlookers, and no-one had given them so much as a second glance. Now, however, as a squire from the Knights Academy, Quint was to stand to attention beside the pyramid-shaped entrance to the treasury tunnel, with all eyes on him.

He felt a sudden twinge of guilt when he thought of Maris down below in Undertown, missing all this. Next to him, unaware of his friend's thoughts, Phin was smiling now with a mixture of delight and pride, a lock of unruly hair tumbling from beneath his helmet to cover one eye.

'Academy, halt!' came Hax Vostillix's deep voice from the back. 'Form ranks!'

The squires turned about and lined up beside the treasury tunnel entrance, hall by hall, and to Quint's dismay he realized that now, instead of being in the front rank, he was at the back and having to peer over the shoulders of the squires from the Upper Halls to get a view.

Behind him, the crowd jostled and pushed at the squires' backs as they, too, craned their necks to see. Just then, Quint felt a tug on his cloak, which he brushed away – and then another, more insistent this time.

'Master Quint,' came a voice. 'It is you, isn't it? Master Quint!'

Looking round, Quint found himself staring at a familiar figure. Short and roly-poly with a small rubbery nose and chapped lips, she was dressed in a heavy fur-lined coat and a familiar frilly mob-cap. But if Quint hadn't looked into that smiling face with its twinkling eyes, then the small lemkin crouched on her shoulder, its striped tail twitching, would have been enough for him to recognize her instantly.

'Welma!' he cried, and fell into the motherly woodtroll's warm embrace. The lemkin screeched loudly and began jumping up and down, tugging at its leash. Quint grinned. 'And Digit,' he said, and tickled the small creature behind its ears. 'How are you both?'

'All the better for seeing you, Master Quint,' said Welma, speaking over the *kha-kha-kha-kha* sounds of the chattering lemkin. 'Oh, but it's all been a bit of an upheaval,' she went on quickly, as Phin and Tonsor looked round to see what was going on. 'Tweezel and I have taken rooms at the top of an iron-monger's run by a nice pink-eyed goblin family. Tweezel's been selling tinctures and potions up at the Viaduct Steps, and I . . . oh, a bit of cleaning here and there, taking in washing. Nothing too taxing. Just enough to make ends meet . . .'

'And Maris?' said Quint, aware that the squires of the Upper Halls in front were now looking back over their shoulders.

'That's why I'm here,' said Welma, urgently. 'That hard-faced cousin of hers, Dacia, never lets her out of her sight . . .' Her face creased up with distaste as she uttered the name. 'But I managed to have a few words with her when they visited the market-place last week,' she said, reaching inside the folds of her coat. 'She told me not to worry, and to give you this.'

She pulled out a scrolled letter, and Quint saw his own name written on the front in Maris's familiar angular writing.

'Is that all she said?' he asked.

Welma nodded and pushed the letter into his hands. 'There,' she said, 'now I'd best be off. Before any of these fine squires here have something to say about a scruffy old woodtroll engaging in conversation with the likes of you, a future knight academic.' She smiled and winked, and quickly squeezed his hands in her own. 'Earth and Sky love you,' she whispered, and slipped back into the crowd before Quint had time even to wish her farewell.

'Who was that?' Vilnix sneered. 'Your old nursemaid?' He sniggered. 'Worried that her little darling will catch a cold out here in the snow . . .'

'Shut up, Vilnix,' said Phin, turning on him angrily.

Quint grabbed his arm. 'Forget it, Phin,' he said. 'He's not worth it.'

'I say, you chaps,' came a voice from the rank in front. It belonged to a squire from the Upper Halls who had turned and was facing them. He was tall and gangly with slightly protruding teeth and small oval spectacles. 'I don't suppose you could keep it down a bit, because the jolly old ceremony's about to start and you wouldn't want to miss it, now would you?'

Vilnix snapped to attention, while Phin looked down at his feet, blushing furiously and scowling. Quint smiled apologetically.

'Sorry, an old friend of mine was just wishing me well,' he said.

'I quite understand,' said the Upper Hall squire with a smile. 'You're the new lot, aren't you?'

Quint and the others nodded.

'Hope to have some of you chaps joining us in the Upper Halls soon. Raffix Emilius,' he said. 'Pleased to meet you.' The squire stuck out a thin, bony hand.

Quint took it and winced at the surprisingly strong grip. 'Quint Verginix.'

'Well, Quint,' said Raffix Emilius, 'here come the treasury guards, so if you and your chums stand on tiptoe, you might just glimpse the tops of their heads.

My, my, what splendid breast-plates they're wearing!' he added, turning round to face the front once more.

As he did so, there came a loud fanfare and all eyes fixed themselves on the entrance to the treasury tunnel, where an ornately decorated carriage had just come to a halt. It was drawn by an even more ornately decorated prowlgrin, with a jewel-encrusted harness, a flapping purple plume and a swaying umbrella of gold and black that was keeping the falling snow at bay.

On either side, it was flanked by four enormous flat-head treasury guards, resplendent in identical armour, the silver bloodoaks on their breast-plates gleaming in the snowy light. One of them opened the carriage door and bowed low as a small professor in dark grey robes and a string of spectacles and eye-glasses round his neck, clambered out. As tradition demanded, the twin Most High Academes, the Professors of Light and Darkness, had sent their deputy – the 'Next-Most High Academe' – to enter the treasury tunnel and venture into the dangerous stonecomb.

Following the prescribed ritual, the academic hammered hard with his stave – one, two, three times – on the door, which was opened by the Captain of the Treasury Guard, Sigbord, himself. He, too, wore a magnificent breast-plate, which he showed off to the crowd by puffing out his chest as he gestured grandly to the Next-Most High Academe and his guard to enter. And as they all disappeared inside, a tumultuous roar went up and cries of *Trust the skies! Trust the skies!* echoed round the Mosaic Quadrangle.

The heavy ironwood door to the treasury tunnel slammed shut with a dull clang and the crowd stood for a moment in silence and then turned to go. There was none of the jollity and laughter that Quint remembered from the year before.

The celebration of the day when the Sanctaphrax rock was first weighted down with stormphrax was usually a raucous, joyful affair. But with the snow falling and the temperature dropping swiftly as the light failed, the atmosphere was sombre. The academics trudged back to their schools and academies, eager to escape the biting wind and swirling snow.

'Academy! Dismissed!' came Hax Vostillix's loud command, and as the ranks of squires broke up, Quint saw the Hall Master of High Cloud in a robe of pure white tilderfur standing in front with the other hall masters on either side of him. Behind them, like statues, stood the knights academic-in-waiting, the visors to their helmets closed, giving them a mysterious and distinctly sinister air.

'Treasury Day banquet at evening gong in the Eightways!' Hax was announcing over the heads of chattering squires. 'Don't be late!'

He strode from the Mosaic Quadrangle, which was now covered by a thick coating of snow, followed by Arboretum Sicklebough, Philius Embertine and Fenviel Vendix, the Hall Master of Grey Cloud. The knights academic-in-waiting fell in behind them and marched stiffly off.

'Well,' said Raffix Emilius, adjusting his spectacles, 'we have the rest of the afternoon off, my dear squires.

Might I suggest a diversion?'
He kneeled and picked up a
handful of snow. 'Upper
Halls against the Lower!'

With a loud cheer, the
squires raced to opposite sides
of the Mosaic Quadrangle and
began scooping up snow.
Suddenly, the air was full of
flying snowballs as squire
pelted squire in the greying
snowy light.

'Watch out, Phin!' yelled
Quint as his friend took three
direct hits on the chest.

'Watch out, yourself!'
laughed Phin, bending to
scoop handfuls of snow –
and being hit full in the face.

'Charge!' shouted Quint,
running towards Raffix and
the Upper Hall squires.
'Phoarrr! Uggh! Phhwl!'

A hail of snowballs sent
him sprawling to his knees,
helpless with laughter, but
not before the squires of
the Lower Halls had sur-
rounded their Upper Halls'
colleagues. And all round the

quadrangle the whoops and cries rang out as they pelted them to a standstill.

Finally, wet through and exhausted, the squires made their way back to the Knights Academy, laughing and joking and in high spirits.

'I like your style, Quint Verginix,' said Raffix Emilius, slapping Quint on the back as they rounded the corner of the College of Rain. 'That was quite a fight you and your chums put up.'

'Thanks, Raffix,' said Quint, trying to stop his teeth from chattering. 'You didn't do too badly yourself.'

'I shall allow you to call me Raff,' said the Upper Hall squire with a laugh, 'since I now consider us to be friends. And that goes for you too, Phin.'

'I'm honoured, Raff,' said Phin, bowing low with mock solemnity, 'and you can save me a place in line for the stew-cart while you're about it!'

'That reminds me!' said Quint, quickening his step. 'It's almost evening gong. We'd better hurry if we don't want to be late for the banquet!'

That evening, as the crowded tables and benches of the Eightways resounded to the laughter and songs of the squires celebrating Treasury Day, Quint shared a banquet of roast snowbird and tilder pie with his three friends. Phin, always with a ready smile and an encouraging word, sat next to him, complimenting the grey goblin, Stope, on the fine workmanship of the breast-plates he'd made for the treasury-guards.

'Sssshh!' Stope said, smiling delightedly.

'That's all meant to be a secret! I didn't mean to say anything, Squire Phin! Honest!'

'To the finest forge-hand in the Academy!' Phin toasted Stope with a tankard of woodale.

On the other side of him, Raffix, the Upper Hall squire, joined in the laughter. 'If only I'd known what good company you keep down here on the lower benches, I'd have joined you sooner. Here's to you, Stope!' He raised his tankard.

'Thank you, Squire Raff, sir,' beamed Stope, raising his tankard in reply.

Quint smiled and raised his tankard to join the others. 'Here's to all of us!' he grinned.

In the far corner, hunched over his wooden platter, Vilnix Pompolnius glared over at the happy group of squires. They all thought they were better than him – all of them, even that little upstart forge-hand. He could see it in their eyes. Especially the sky pirate brat, Quint.

Well, he'd show them. He'd show *all* of them.

He had avoided that stupid snowball fight organized by the snooty Upper Hall Squire . . . Raff! What a ridiculous name.

Vilnix smiled to himself. Instead of throwing snow-balls like an idiotic young'un, he'd visited the Viaduct Towers – or rather, one viaduct tower in particular. The one with a vulpoon skeleton hanging outside. And a very useful little trip it had turned out to be.

He patted his pocket and then raised his tankard of woodale with a sarcastic sneer.

'Here's to all of you!'

·CHAPTER NINE·

THE HALL OF GREY CLOUD

Quint couldn't sleep. Outside, an icy wind howled through the turrets and towers of Sanctaphrax like an angry white-collar wolf, rattling windowpanes and threatening to tear shutters and awnings from their hinges. He was inside his dormitory closet and should have been warm and snug. But even though he'd pulled the lufwood door tight shut and drawn his snowbird-down quilt up over his head, Quint could still feel the cold draught which was sweeping up the central staircase.

Light and airy, the buildings of the great floating city had not been built to withstand such intense winter cold. Unable to stop shivering, Quint abandoned his attempts to sleep before the dawn gong sounded and, bleary-eyed, began to pull on his clothes.

He was slipping his arms into the long-sleeved tunic when he first heard something rustle. He paused. The rustling stopped. It was probably just the little ratbird, he thought.

Leaning forward in the darkness, he fumbled for his lamp, lit it, and held it up. But the creature was still fast asleep in her cage, her head tucked under a furry wing. Puzzled, Quint hung the lamp back on its hook and started dressing again – only to hear the rustling once more. This time he realized where the sound was coming from.

He reached into the side pocket of the tunic – and groaned. There, still rolled and fastened with a black spider-silk ribbon, was Maris's letter, unopened and unread.

'Earth and Sky,' he muttered. 'How *could* I?'

From the cage there came a soft, questioning trill. Quint looked round at the tiny ratbird whose beaklike snout was now poking out and sniffing the air.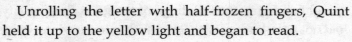

'Oh, Nibblick,' said Quint as he pushed a small piece of barley bread through the bars. 'I forgot all about Maris. Fine friend *I* am!'

Unrolling the letter with half-frozen fingers, Quint held it up to the yellow light and began to read.

Dear Quint,

It is so cold down here in Undertown that, as I write this, I can hardly stop my hands from shaking. My guardian, Heft, is so mean that he only allows one fire to be lit a day, and that is a small one in his and Dacia's personal apartments. The rest of us – Grewlock the cook, the little mobgnome maid who cries the whole time, Pule the old goblin butler and me – all have to freeze!

I know I shouldn't be ungrateful, but, oh, Quint, it's so miserable and boring down here. My room is small and poky and has bars at the window. Heft and Dacia are so security conscious that they keep practically every door in the place locked! I swear they even lock my door at night. I'm sure I've heard a key in the lock after I've turned the lamp out. Where on earth do they imagine I'm going to run off to?

The only good thing about my room is the view it has of the market-place in Western Quay Square. Most days I wave to Welma from my window, and sometimes I call down to her – but I have to be careful because Dacia considers such behaviour unbecoming to the daughter of a High Academe.

I miss Father so much, Quint, and our old life up in Sanctaphrax. What adventures we had! Down here, Dacia never allows me out of her sight, and all I seem to do is sit here in my room or stand beside her chair when boring old leagues-men and their wives come to visit. I have to curtsy, and only talk when I'm spoken to – which is practically never – and listen to Heft rattle on and on . . .

You wouldn't believe the stories he tells, Quint. From the things he says, you'd think he was Father's most trusted friend, and that Father never did anything without consulting him first. It's all just boasting, of course, and completely untrue, but I know that if I say anything he'll lose his temper and fly into one of his rages – rages he usually takes out on the servants.

Just the other day, he flew into a terrible tantrum and all

because I wouldn't sign some silly barkscroll he waved under my nose. Father told me never to sign anything without reading it first, and I told him so. He got very angry and red in the face, but I wouldn't give in, so he stormed off and told Dacia that I wasn't to leave my room for a week! He's nothing but a big bully!

But listen to me! Moaning on! How are <u>you</u>, Quint, up there in your Knights Academy? I bet you'll look splendid in your squires' robes on Treasury Day! Do you remember last year? It seems so long ago now. Don't forget me, down here, Quint, and try to drop me a line sometime when you're not too busy.

I must stop now, because the Leaguesmaster is coming to visit, and Heft is insisting that I be there – still, at least I'll get to stand next to the fire and warm up a bit!

I'll slip this letter to Welma in the market-place the next time old fromp-face lets me go out!

Your friend,

Maris

Quint rolled the letter up and carefully tied the spider-silk ribbon. He didn't like the sound of Maris's guardians one little bit. He looked at the ratbird nibbling on the barley bread.

Should he send word to his father? he wondered.

He reached for his tilderleather satchel with its barkscrolls and ink-pot, then hesitated. After all, what would he say? Maris isn't allowed out much? Her guardians are too mean to heat their apartments properly? They keep their doors locked?

Perhaps he should wait – go down and see Maris and

her guardians first, before worrying his father. In the meantime, he'd send Maris a nice long letter full of news, to cheer her up . . .

Tap! Tap! Tap!

'Hey, Quint! Are you awake?' It was Phin's voice, calling up from the sleeping closet below.

Quint leaned over and opened his door, an icy gust of air making his teeth chatter. 'I w-was . . . j-j-just . . . about to write a l-l-letter . . . before th-the dawn gong . . .' he said, shivering uncontrollably.

Phin climbed out of his sleeping closet and onto the dormitory ladder. He was clad in three sets of robes and had a large untidy turban wound round his head.

'Do you like it?' he asked Quint with a laugh. 'I got it from an ice-scholar the other day. It certainly keeps the cold out!'

'*I* like it,' smiled Quint, 'but I'm not sure the Hall Master of Grey Cloud is going to.'

Phin's face fell for a moment. 'Of course,' he said. 'We start in the Hall of Grey Cloud today!'

Below them, the sound of the dawn gong drifted up the central staircase.

133

'You'll have to write that letter of yours later, Quint,' he said, smiling again. 'If Fenviel Vendix is as strict as they say he is, we don't want to keep him waiting!'

Twenty minutes later, after a hurried breakfast of hammelhornmilk and semmelseed cakes in the Eightways, Quint and Phin joined the group of squires milling about in front of the entrance to the Hall of Grey Cloud. From behind the tall, narrow doors, the low grunts and piercing squeals of prowlgrins could be plainly heard, and Quint felt a shiver of excitement. After all the dry, theoretical work of sky-ship construction and sail-setting, and the endless hours of armour naming, now, at last, they were about to work with living, breathing creatures.

Ever since entering the Knights Academy, Quint had taken every opportunity to watch the prowlgrins being exercised by their grooms and knights-in-waiting in the Inner Courtyard. Despite the restricted space, they were so fast and so agile, and he'd marvelled as they leaped high into the tilt trees that stretched in an avenue across the paving stones, always elegantly poised and perfectly balanced. Now, at last, he was going to get the chance to ride a prowlgrin himself.

The doors opened slowly, their heavy hinges protesting, and a warm blast of scented air filled the corridor outside. A deep expressionless voice from within barked a single command.

'Enter!'

Quint took a deep breath and followed the other squires through the doorway and into the Hall of Grey Cloud. The smell that greeted them was unmistakable –

straw, both damp and dusty, mingled with the musty odour of chopped meat, while underneath, the sweet, earthy smell of prowlgrins themselves pervaded everything. Occasionally, when he'd been lying in his sleeping closet, Quint had caught a whiff of the place. But now, walking through the tall arched doors, the mix of scents was intoxicating.

Before him, situated at the top of tall, square pillars which stretched the length of the hall at regular intervals, were the prowlgrin roosts. There were pegs hammered in from the bottom to the top for the ostlers and grooms to scale – on occasions also used by those old or weary prowlgrins that were unable to leap up from the ground. Halfway up were great metal byres, stuffed with straw and used to catch the prowlgrin droppings. Above these, extending both to the left and the right, all the way up to the high vaulted ceiling, were thick, horizontal roost 'branches'.

And there, perched upon them, were the roosting prowlgrins themselves.

The great hall thronged with grooms, ostlers and farriers, byre-gillies and stable-hands, all hurrying about their business. Some were pushing wheelbarrows of straw; some were lugging buckets of water, or offal, or the dark, pungent grease that was used to massage the creatures' joints. Some were leading their prowlgrins outside for their daily exercise. Some were mucking out. Everywhere there was feverish activity, endless coming and going and unfamiliar noises.

The squires stumbled across the hay-strewn floor in a

daze, unable to take it all in. Some way in front of him, Quint noticed Vilnix's lip curl with disgust as a stable-hand brushed past, a gently steaming offal bucket in his hand.

'Halt!'

The low, expressionless voice rang out again. The squires snapped out of their daze and quickly formed a line, backs straight and eyes front. From beside a roost pillar, the tall angular figure of Fenviel Vendix, Hall Master of Grey Cloud, stepped out. His small eyes narrowed as he surveyed the squires, one by one, stopping when he came to Phin.

His mouth set into a thin line and his eyebrows furrowed as he eyed the squire's untidy turban for a moment. Then he pointed his long riding crop at Phin's rapidly reddening face and slashed the air.

'Yes, sir,' said Phin, snatching at the turban. 'At once, sir.'

He unwound it and held it out. Fenviel's eyes glittered, and for one horrible moment Quint thought he was about to strike his friend with the crop.

Beside him, Vilnix sniggered, and instantly Fenviel turned his gaze on him. Vilnix straightened up and wiped the smile from his face. Beads of sweat glistened on his forehead as the hall master approached and stared intently into the squire's face. For a moment there was utter silence. Then, from above, there came a strange mewling cry. Fenviel turned from Vilnix, whose knees were now trembling, and pointed his riding crop at the roost pillar.

'Climb!' he barked.

The order seemed to cut through the tension and the squires sprang to life, climbing the roost pillar in groups. Up on one of the branches, a smiling groom greeted them and motioned for them to spread out around him.

'Welcome, Squires,' the gnokgoblin smiled and looked them up and down. 'For many of you, your time in the Hall of Grey Cloud will be the most rewarding part of your training. For others, the most arduous.'

The squires listened to him closely.

'For here,' the gnokgoblin went on, tapping the side of his head, 'it is not enough to rely on this. You must use *this*.' He placed his hand on his chest. 'Your heart.'

Quint found himself nodding. To his left, Vilnix tutted impatiently.

'Now, if you look down at the nests,' the gnokgoblin told them, 'you'll find your new charges waiting to greet you.'

Quint looked down at his feet. There, nestling in a cradle of compacted straw that hung down from the branch on which he stood, was a prowlgrin egg. It was soft and jelly-like. Inside it, just visible through the translucent membrane, was the blurry shape of an infant prowlgrin. The small creature let out a muffled cry and, with its tiny claws, began scratching and scraping at the egg-case from within. Quint gasped and kneeled down to take a closer look.

Along the branch, all the other squires did the same, looks of wonder and amazement on their faces as they examined the nests at their own feet – all, that is, except Vilnix, who leaned down awkwardly and regarded the hatching egg with shock and disgust. Suddenly, one by one, the egg sacs burst with a gentle popping sound and the tiny prowlgrin pups leaped free and high into the air.

'Catch!' came Fenviel's barked command from below.

With his heart in his mouth, Quint stuck out both arms as his pup sailed up over his head.

'*Oof!*'

A moment later, he let out a sharp breath – a mixture of relief and wonder – as the prowlgrin pup landed with extraordinary poise and delicacy on an outstretched arm, and its tiny yet powerful legs gripped on tightly as if it were a branch.

'Amazing!' gasped Phin.

'Incredible!' 'Awesome!' the other squires, their newly-hatched charges clinging to their arms, all agreed.

'Not so tight!' Vilnix rasped at the glistening pup gripping his arm. 'You filthy little beast.'

Quint stared at his own prowlgrin pup in awe. Its fur was damp and sticky and its eyes were still closed, but its balance was perfect. And as it shifted its grip with its powerful toes, it let out thin mewling cries. Quint smiled with delight and was about to tickle it under its chin when the pup's huge eyes snapped open. Instantly its gaze focused on Quint's, and the pair of them stared at one another in rapt wonder.

'You're beautiful,' Quint breathed, 'aren't you, boy? Now what shall I call you?'

'No names!' came Fenviel's barked order from behind him.

Startled, Quint jumped, and the prowlgrin gave out a sharp yelp.

'No, sir. Sorry, sir,' he mumbled.

'Right, young squires,' said the gnokgoblin groom cheerfully. 'Clean them up, like so . . .'

He grabbed a handful of straw and began rubbing the prowlgrin pup on the squire's arm next to him. Quint and the others followed suit with their own pups, and soon the branch was filled with the sound of tiny prowlgrin purrs.

'Then give them some morsels . . . Just a little, mind . . .' He dangled a fromp giblet above the pup, who gave a tiny leap and snatched it from his fingers. 'Take a handful from the offal bucket,' commanded the groom, 'and pass it along.'

'Good boy,' smiled Quint as his pup gobbled down the bloody scraps. 'Good boy!'

The prowlgrin pup licked its lips and settled down on his arm. Down the line, he could hear Vilnix complaining.

'This is disgusting . . . I think I'm going to be sick.'

Fenviel fixed him with one of his terrifying stares and Vilnix quickly shut his mouth.

'Introduce the pups to the branch!' commanded the groom. He demonstrated by kneeling and allowing the prowlgrin on his arm to hop off, onto the roosting branch, where it settled down sleepily.

The squires all did as they were told, with Vilnix giving an audible sigh of relief as his prowlgrin let go of his arm.

'They will need feeding every hour, day and night, for the next three weeks,' announced the groom with a rueful smile. 'So I suggest you snatch what sleep you can, and work together! You'll find offal buckets and arm protectors below.'

Fenviel Vendix strode across the branch and permitted himself a small smile as he began to climb down the roost pillar.

'Good luck!' he barked.

As the weeks passed, Quint often thought back to that first morning in the Hall of Grey Cloud. It had all seemed so chaotic then. Yet, the longer he remained there, the more he realized that beneath the apparent disorder, the prowlgrin stables were highly organized and meticulously run.

For a start, he discovered that the prowlgrins were not allowed to perch in any old place. Each one of them – old and young, large and small – was assigned a special spot on a specific roost pillar.

The half-dozen pillars to the left of the hall, for instance, were home to those prowlgrins that were kept for work purposes – riding, carrying, pulling, transporting – with the roost pillar on the extreme left reserved for the finest, strongest male beasts which had been selected for breeding. Further to the right, where he and the other squires were busy raising their pups, were the brood-prowlgrin roosts.

It was here that the pregnant females laid their eggs in nests carefully constructed from straw chewed over and over in their great mouths. Their task over, they retreated to the upper branches and sat – purring and grumbling – while their pups were fussed over and fed by Quint and his companions.

'In the wild,' said Tuggel, the gnokgoblin groom, 'the young fend for themselves as soon as they hatch. But here in the hall' – he laughed cheerfully as Vilnix scowled – 'they've got you lovely young squires to mother them!'

The first three weeks had been the hardest, with none of the squires getting anywhere near enough sleep. Phin and Quint had shared their tasks, taking it in turns to muck out and do the feeding, and had managed well. Now their pups were half-grown, young, sleek and powerful. Quint would spend hours every day, brushing and currying the young creature until its bright orange fur gleamed like burnished copper. He filed its claws, polished its teeth, oiled its paws and rubbed herbal liniments into its joints.

'You'll be a knight's prowlgrin one day, won't you, boy?' Quint cooed as he combed the growing fringe of fur beneath its chin. The pup gazed back at him with its big yellow eyes, mewling and purring contentedly. 'The biggest, strongest and most magnificent prowlgrin of all in the knights' roost pillar!'

Quint gazed across at the grand roost pillar situated at the centre of the Hall of Grey Cloud. It was in its thick, jutting branches that the thirteen mighty 'stormchaser' prowlgrins perched – each one the chosen mount of a knight academic-in-waiting. Unlike the lesser prowlgrins in the other roost pillars, these prowlgrins had names – Felvix, Borix, Demquix ... They had all been trained with one aim in mind – to travel with their masters to the Twilight Woods on stormchasing quests.

Along the branch from where Phin and Quint's pups were roosting, Vilnix was doing less well. His pup was a sad, thin creature with rheumy eyes and patchy fur. Quint suspected that if it wasn't for Vilnix's neglect, the pup would have been as fit and healthy as their own. But, true to form, Vilnix was having none of it.

'It's not my fault,' he'd storm. 'The stupid creature won't feed properly! Besides, how am I meant to look after it all on my own? You lot help each other ... It's not fair.'

It was true, Quint realized. The other squires had teamed up and helped each other. The thing was, Vilnix was so unpleasant and rude, nobody had wanted to work with him. Now he seemed to sleep half the time and often forgot to feed the poor animal. Quint had taken pity on it and, whenever he could, would haul an extra bucket of offal up to the branch to feed Vilnix's pup.

It was on just such an occasion when it happened.

Three months had passed and Quint awoke in his dormitory sleeping closet, his back aching and his arms sore from stablework. He didn't need the dawn gong to wake him up any longer. No matter how tired he felt, just the thought of the pup waiting for him was all he needed to send him hurrying to the Hall of Grey Cloud.

But on that particular morning, the moment he had climbed the roost pillar and stepped onto the branch, he knew that something was wrong.

The prowlgrin pups were skittish and agitated, and above them the brood-prowlgrins were whinnying and snorting. Quint struggled along the branch with two laden offal buckets. The first, he hooked onto the branch at the feet of his prowlgrin pup, who bent down and guzzled greedily at the bucket's contents. He was about to hook the second offal bucket for Phin's pup when his gaze wandered along the branch.

There, slumped on its side, its breathing coming in laboured bursts, was Vilnix's pup. It looked terrible, its eyes sunk deep into its sockets and its ribs showing. Quint approached and kneeled down, and stroked the poor creature's patchy fur.

'There, there, boy,' he said gently. 'Here, try some of this.'

The pup's nostrils quivered and a dull, glassy eye swivelled to meet Quint's gaze. With a grunt of effort, the pup hauled itself unsteadily to its feet and opened its mouth. Carefully, Quint scooped the steaming offal onto the prowlgrin's lolling tongue. The pup flicked it back and swallowed greedily. Quint scooped up some more.

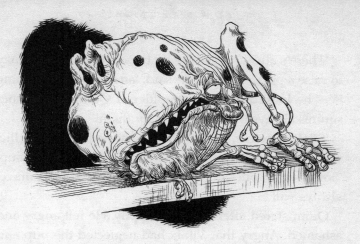

'You're starving!' he muttered angrily. 'Just you wait. I'll give that Vilnix Pompolnius a piece of my mind . . .'

'Vilnix Pompolnius,' came a low voice, and Quint looked up to see Fenviel Vendix standing over him, a look of fury on his face. 'Vilnix Pompolnius!'

Quint reddened. 'Please, sir, it's probably not his fault . . .' he began, not wanting to get another squire into trouble.

'Starving!' barked the hall master, clenching the riding crop and striding back across the branch.

Above him, the brood prowlgrins yelped and growled, as if sensing his displeasure. From down below there came barked commands, and moments later Quint found himself surrounded by grooms and byre-gillies.

'It's all right, lad, we'll take over from here,' said one of the grooms as they gently lifted the pup from the branch.

'We'll take him to the old'uns' roost and feed him up, don't you worry,' said another, and shook his head as they shuffled back along the branch.

'There's always one in every bunch, too stupid or lazy to raise a pup,' the first one said, 'and the amazing thing is' – he looked over his shoulder at Quint – 'the other squires always try to cover up for them!'

'Stick together, don't they?' snorted a byre-gillie, scooping up an armful of hay and following the group. 'Sort things out amongst themselves. Always have, always will.'

Quint stared after them unhappily. He felt angry and ashamed. Angry that Vilnix had neglected the pup and that he hadn't stopped him; ashamed that he'd covered up for him – *and* that he'd been found out. He turned and made his way miserably out of the Hall of Grey Cloud and towards the central staircase.

Outside, a fierce wind continued to buffet the Knights Academy and whistle through its corridors. Quint pulled his cape around his shoulders and climbed slowly up the spiralling stairs. Halfway up, he bumped into Phin, his hair sticking up and his clothes dishevelled.

'Quint! There you are. You'll never guess what,' he babbled excitedly. 'Fenviel Vendix just came storming into the dormitories and hauled old Vilnix out of his closet by the scruff of the neck. Hopping mad he was about how he'd been treating his prowlgrin! Somebody must have told on him! Do you reckon it was one of the grooms? Tuggel, maybe? Or one of the byre-gillies? They all hate him, you know. One thing's for certain.' He grabbed Quint's arm and steered him back down in the direction of the Eightways, from which the smell of freshly baked semmelseed cakes was wafting. 'It couldn't have been a squire.'

'What's that?' said Quint, numbly, a hollow in the pit of his stomach.

'I said,' Phin repeated earnestly, 'it couldn't have been a squire, Quint. After all, we squires stick together, don't we?'

·CHAPTER TEN·

SCREEDIUS TOLLINIX

A hushed stillness hung over the Hall of Grey Cloud as Quint walked through it that cold, overcast evening. Most of the roost pillars were empty and those that weren't had exhausted prowlgrins draped across their branches, fast asleep and softly snoring. Apart from them, the only sounds came from the central roost, where the magnificent stormchasing prowlgrins grumbled and purred, and from the nursery pillars, where the soft mewling cries of the most recently hatched pups trembled in the chilly air.

Not that the Hall of Grey Cloud was any different from the rest of the Knights Academy or, for that matter, from the towers and walkways of Sanctaphrax beyond. The stranglehold of deepest winter had still not relaxed its grip. Every day, as the ice-storms and blizzards blew in from Open Sky, the great floating city was wrapped up in a fresh blanket of smothering snow. Once, Sanctaphrax had been a city of sounds, but no longer. Now, after the howling roar of the latest storm abated, the ice froze the music of the towers, and the drifts of fresh snow muffled the sounds in the streets.

Quint reached the foot of a roost pillar, beside which a crackling brazier burned with a fierce purple light. There were squat, black braziers of burning lufwood at the foot of each roost pillar, with several more clustered together at the centre of the hall. They had been installed at Fenviel Vendix's insistence after several in the prowlgrin flocks had developed hacking coughs. The blazing stoves took the chill off the roosts above, but with the bitter cold seeping through every crack and crevice of the hall, the lufwood logs they burned had to be constantly replenished.

'Warm enough, I hope, you bouncing sacks of guts!' came a bitter sneering voice.

Quint turned to see Vilnix coming towards him. Dressed up against the cold in thick leggings, heavy boots, a tilderfleece and a down-filled waistcoat, his movements were stiff. Dragging a cart laden with logs with one hand, he shook a fist at the roosting prowlgrins high above him with the other. When he noticed Quint, he stopped and narrowed his eyes suspiciously.

'Oh, it's you again,' he said. 'Come to pamper that prowlgrin of yours, I suppose.'

Quint glanced up at the branch above where, three from the end, his pup – now a half-yearling and almost fully grown – nestled drowsily. With its magnificent orange coat and thick, glossy chin-mane, Quint would have known the creature anywhere. It stood a good stride taller than its companions and was, Quint felt sure, destined for the central roost one day.

'No, he's fine,' he said. 'Aren't you, Tash?' He smiled. 'It's you I came to find, Vilnix. I thought you might like a little help.'

Ever since the neglect of Vilnix's own pup had come to light, Fenviel had assigned the squire to stove duty. 'Logs,' he'd ordered simply in his low, expressionless voice, and strode away – but every squire could tell the depth of the hall master's displeasure from the angry welt that ran the length of Vilnix's left cheek. Even now, weeks later, it was still raised and red from where Fenviel's riding crop had struck. And even though it had been an unfortunate accident, every time Quint saw it, he felt a sharp pang of guilt for having landed a fellow squire in trouble.

Vilnix shrugged and stepped away from the log cart. 'Be my guest,' he said grudgingly, and went over to lean against the roost pillar.

Quint rolled up his sleeves and began to unload the logs and stack them as close to the glowing brazier as he dared. Quint had lost his mother and five brothers in a terrible fire and now, despite the burnished metal that encased the blazing logs, the flames still made him shudder.

'I was wrong about you,' said Vilnix, stretching lazily. 'You're not like those other stuck-up squires. Tonsor. Stupid, grinning Phin. They're all the same . . .'

'Phin's a friend of mine,' said Quint quietly, opening the stove door and gingerly throwing a log inside.

'They do whatever that brute, Fenviel, barks at them,'

Vilnix went on, ignoring him. 'But you, Quintinius, you're different. *You* can tell that I'm being picked on by the hall master, just because my prowlgrin fell sick. I mean, it's simply not fair!'

Quint bit his lip and continued feeding the brazier with logs until it glowed brightly and the roost branches above filled with appreciative purrs. He'd heard it all before. Every evening when he came to lend a hand, Vilnix would trot out the same old story . . .

'Why me?' he said, his voice high-pitched and indignant. 'It's because I'm clever. Yes, that's what it is. I might not be Sanctaphrax born and bred, but I'm smarter than them. All of them. And *my* mentor is the Professor of Darkness – one of the twin Most High Academes no less – and they hate me for it!'

His stare hardened, and Quint knew what was coming next. He busied himself with another log.

'Why, if I ever find out who told on me to the hall master, I'll . . . I'll . . .' Vilnix slapped the roost pillar with the flat of his hand, his face white with a mixture of rage and self pity.

'Yes, well,' said Quint quickly, feeling his own face flush bright crimson. 'Why don't you let me finish the other stoves while you get a spot of supper at the Eightways. It's hammelhorn steaks tonight, I think.'

Vilnix paused for a moment. 'No, you're not like the others,' he said, turning and sloping off, his bony shoulders hunched. 'I won't forget, Quintinius. I won't forget.'

It took four more trips to the log store before all the stoves were replenished and blazing brightly. Quint's back ached from hauling the heavy cart back and forth. With a sigh, he propped the wretched contraption against one of the cluster of stoves that heated the central roost, and slumped wearily to his haunches – which is where, moments later, Raffix Emilius, the Upper Hall squire, found him.

'Not covering for that miserable, sour-faced squire again, are you?' he said, shaking his head with disbelief. 'Why do you do it, Quint?'

'Oh, Vilnix isn't that bad,' Quint said, climbing to his feet.

'No?' said Raffix, sounding doubtful. 'From what I understand, he deliberately starved a pup. No wonder Fenviel lost his temper. If it had been up to me, I'd have thrown him out of the academy.' He frowned. 'What I don't understand though, Quint, old chap, is why you insist on doing his punishment for him.'

'Squires should stick together,' said Quint quietly.

'Everybody knows that, Quint, but it doesn't mean having to do another fellow's punishments . . .'

'You don't understand, Raff,' said Quint, blushing. 'The thing is . . .' He scanned the hall about them, to make sure they couldn't be overheard. 'I let it slip that Vilnix was neglecting that pup. Fenviel heard me and stormed off. That was when he struck him with that riding crop of his.'

Raffix winced. 'Yes, well, that was rather unfortunate, but the miserable squire undoubtedly deserved it.' He shook his head. 'Still, you being an honourable squire and all, I can see why you feel the need to help him . . .'

Raffix put a hand on Quint's shoulder as they walked back through the hall.

'Leave this with me, Quint, old chap. I'll have a word with the hall master. See if he can't ease off on Vilnix a little – and then you can stop doing his chores for him and concentrate on prowlgrin riding. Talking of which ...' The Upper Hall squire's face broke into a broad smile. 'I don't suppose you'd care to join me in an evening gallop?'

Quint spun round excitedly. 'In the Inner Courtyard? You bet! I'll just go and saddle up Tash!'

Raffix's eyebrows shot upwards. 'Don't let Fenviel catch you calling him that,' he laughed as Quint hurried back to the roost pillar. 'No names, remember!'

Just then there came a whole lot of noise from the far end of the hall. There was grunting and wheezing, heavy footfall and urgent commands.

A moment later, the tall doors burst open and, under the supervision of a rowdy band of goblin grooms and stable-hands, each one dressed in heavy boots, fur-lined hats and over-smocks of finest hammelhorn leather, a long column of exhausted-looking prowlgrins appeared. They tramped inside, whinnying and snorting. Orange, black, brown, grey, piebald and skewbald – there was even an albino in amongst them, with snow-white fur and huge pink eyes. The one thing they all had in common was that their fur was steaming, with thick swirls of mist coiling up off their backs.

These were the flocks returning from the giant tread-mill on the West Landing. All day, they had been patiently trotting on the huge ironwood wheel, powering it as it winched a vast log burner up and down the surface of the Sanctaphrax rock. As the burner moved, so it came close to the rock face, warming the chilled stonecomb within and helping to make the great floating rock less buoyant.

Quint reached the roost pillar and hurriedly climbed it. All round him, he could see the roost branches of the other roost pillars filling up as the tired creatures leaped up to them with the last of their strength.

Soon, the flocks working on the giant treadmill on the East Landing would also return. The giant log burner suspended from that side of the rock balanced the effect of its counterpart, and consumed whole

tree-trunks at the same prodigious rate. There would, however, be fewer prowlgrins returning from the East Landing, since a pair of giant tree fromps had been brought up from Undertown to aid them in their labours. Even so, with their arrival, the prowlgrin roosts would be full again.

'Hello, Tash,' grinned Quint as he patted his prowlgrin tenderly on its quivering nostrils. 'Did you miss me? Time to stretch those legs of yours!'

He swung the tilderleather saddle onto his prowl-grin's back, and the creature gave a whinnying cry of excitement in reply.

Already the squeals and barks of the second group of returning prowlgrins could be heard approaching the hall. Their daily labours done, they were looking forward to their rest on the heated roost branches. In fact, it was the source of that heat – the braziers Fenviel had installed – that had given the Professors of Light and Darkness the idea for the giant log burners that now glowed day and night on either side of the great floating rock.

It wasn't, however, a permanent solution. It could never be, for the giant log burners needed huge quantities of timber to do their work – timber that had to be shipped in from the distant Deepwoods. And in this perilously cold weather, that was no easy task.

League ships (and the occasional sky ship of an enterprising sky pirate captain intent on undercutting the leagues' prices) landed at the boom-docks constantly, where they unloaded their cargoes of timber logs.

Lufwood and lullabee burned best, the latter filling the air with eerie strains of music, but the leaguesmen liked to carry the denser leadwood too, in an attempt to counter the extreme buoyancy of the chilled flight-rock. There were few accidents on the incoming journeys. The return flights, however, in the unloaded sky ships, were a different matter entirely, with several vessels losing control and soaring off into Open Sky.

From the boom-docks, the logs were transported on the backs of flat wagons. They were driven by mobgnomes and cloddertrogs, and drawn by teams of hammelhorns through the snowbound streets of Undertown to Anchor Chain Square. There, each day at dawn, the log burners were lowered and replenished before being winched up to resume their vital task.

Quint watched the latest returning prowlgrins climb wearily up to their perches, while the ostlers and stable-hands rushed about, delivering buckets of refreshing water and nourishing offal.

'Come on, Tash,' he urged, jumping into the saddle and twitching the reins. 'Let's go and find Raffix before it gets too crowded to move.'

With a low growl, Quint's prowlgrin hopped down to the floor a dozen strides below. It landed soundlessly beside the glowing brazier and, at Quint's tugged command, headed towards the central roost pillar. There they met Raffix – who was sitting on the tall, dark brown prowlgrin that *he* had raised from a pup – and the pair of prowlgrins loped off on powerful legs to the far end of the hall, where high doors led to the Inner Courtyard.

Quint had thought that the hall itself was cold, despite the braziers, yet as he led his prowlgrin out through the doorway, the blistering icy air struck him like a vicious slap in the face. It was so cold it snatched his breath away, leaving his nostrils stinging and his eyes watering.

Bathed in moonlight and shrouded in the latest fall of snow, the Inner Courtyard resembled a vast blank barkscroll. On the far side, a row of tall posts ran along the curve of the West Wall, stopping just short of the low entrance to the Gates of Humility. At irregular intervals up the central trunk were thin horizontal branches of varying strength, which criss-crossed from one post to the next, creating a thicket of timber. These were the tilt trees, on which the abilities of the ablest prowlgrin and rider could be tested to the limit.

'Catch us if you can, old chap!' Raffix shouted, and urged his mount forward.

In an instant, prowlgrin and rider sped across the blanket of snow in huge bounds, leaving a spattering of churned-up footprints in their wake.

Quint leaned forward, braced his legs in the stirrups and gave two small twitches on the reins. Beneath him, he felt the force of the prowlgrin's mighty legs as it kicked off from the ground in a huge leap. The West Wall seemed to dip, then rise up like a flapping curtain as they sailed towards it, the air rushing past Quint's ears with an exhilarating roar.

Then, as suddenly as they had launched off, they landed again, softly yet firmly, on a gently yielding branch, and the sound of tinkling icicles filled the air. Just ahead, higher up in the branches, the black shape of Raffix's prowlgrin rose in the moonlit air.

'Trust the leap!' Fenviel Vendix's barked instructions sounded in Quint's head as he squeezed the flanks of his prowlgrin with his knees. In answer, it leaped forward and on through the maze of criss-cross branches, seeming hardly to touch them with its powerful yet sensitive feet. 'But remember to duck!'

Whoosh!

A branch whizzed past, a hair's breadth from Quint's face. Then another, and another, as he rolled in the saddle, this way and that, like a giddy fighting fromp.

'Ooooh!'

On his prowlgrin's final leap, a jutting branch – supple as a sapling – sprang back and caught Quint full in the chest, plucking him from the saddle. Before he knew it, he was tumbling down to earth. His fall was broken by the maze of branches – each one grasping at him, only to bend back and pass him down to those below.

'Ooooh! Ooooh! Ummmph!'

He landed in a flurry of snow at the foot of the last tilt tree. Perched high in the branches above, his prowlgrin looked down at him, head on one side and a great plume of mist billowing up from its flared nostrils. The next moment, Raffix landed beside him, sitting upright in the saddle and with the reins of his prowlgrin held nonchalantly in one hand.

'I say, bad luck, old chap! You almost made it that time. Very last tilt tree caught you out.' He let out a cry of laughter and pointed to the wall beside Quint. There, half obscured by snow, were the Gates of Humility. 'Back where you started, I see!'

'Yes, yes, very funny,' Quint said, scrambling to his feet and dusting the powdery snow from his tunic. 'I just need a bit more practice.'

'Well, you carry on, old chap,' laughed Raffix, with a tug on his reins. 'I'll save you a hammelhorn steak. Whether you eat it or apply it to your bruises is up to you!'

With that, he bounded back towards the Hall of Grey Cloud in a flurry of snow.

'Here, Tash! Here, Tash,' Quint called to the prowlgrin high in the tilt tree above him as loud as he dared.

Just then, from behind him, there came a heavy wheezing sound, accompanied by odd clicks and whirrs. Quint spun round. And there, looming above him, blotting out the moonlight and throwing him into shadow, was the figure of a knight academic in full armour, sitting astride a magnificent black prowlgrin. From behind the visor, Quint could see two glittering eyes boring into his own.

'Explain yourself, squire!' a deep voice boomed from inside the visor as the silvery moonlight created a halo round the helmeted head, so bright that it made Quint shield his eyes with trembling fingers.

'I . . . I . . .' he began.

'You called to that prowlgrin by name!'

'Y . . . y . . . yes,' admitted Quint, looking down at his feet. Above him, his prowlgrin gave a whinny.

'You are aware, are you not, that naming a prowlgrin is the sole right of a knight academic-in-waiting?'

Quint nodded miserably. In front of him, the huge black prowlgrin stamped its foot as if to emphasize its master's point. On its bridle the name *Vanquix* was picked out in silver letters.

So this must be the great Screedius Tollinix himself, thought Quint, with a sinking feeling in the pit of his stomach. Screedius Tollinix, the finest knight academic in the academy, as harsh on himself as he was on others.

'It's just that I raised him from a pup, sir. He's always had this line of fur around his mouth. That's why I call him Tash, sir. But it's only a nickname . . .'

'Silence!' the voice behind the visor boomed. 'Have they taught you nothing in the Lower Halls, squire? We are sky-scholars here. These creatures are of the earth. Naming is an honour we sky-scholars bestow on them only when they rise to the highest rank, to serve our purpose in sacred stormchasing! Anything else smacks of earth-scholarship. Do you understand?'

Quint nodded glumly.

A gauntleted hand reached up and snapped open the visor catch. Slowly, the visor rose and Quint found himself staring into a stern but by no means unkindly face.

'You are young,' Screedius said, his voice less angry now, 'and you have admitted your mistake. But you must understand that prowlgrins here in our venerable academy exist only to serve us. We tolerate them because we need them. Even noble Vanquix here.' He patted the black prowlgrin affectionately. 'It is to the sky we look,' Screedius continued, his intense eyes boring into Quint's. 'To await the day when we are called to serve Sanctaphrax.'

'You mean, stormchasing . . .' Quint whispered.

The knight-in-waiting nodded. 'Indeed, and there's a storm coming all right, young squire,' he said. 'I can feel it. Why else are we plagued by this eternal winter? There is a Great Storm brewing, perhaps even the Mother Storm herself. A storm that I've been waiting for all my life. I shall be ready and waiting for it as it passes over-head. And when I am chosen . . .' He hesitated. '*If* I am chosen, then I shall not let Sanctaphrax down.'

There were twelve other knights academic-in-waiting in the towers that ringed the academy, but surely, Quint thought, Screedius would indeed be chosen. After all, everybody knew he was the finest of them all, didn't they? Quint looked into the knight's face. He seemed to have forgotten he was standing in front of him, for his eyes had a strange faraway look in them.

'I shall chase the Great Storm,' Screedius continued in a low voice, as if to himself, 'penetrating to its still centre, and journey with it on into the heart of the Twilight Woods. There, at the moment the lightning strikes, I shall lower Vanquix and myself down from the stormchaser in our body-harness to recover the bolt of sacred storm-phrax, even as it buries itself in the forest floor. Then we shall return to Sanctaphrax in triumph . . .'

His face was flushed and his eyes burned with fiery intent.

'I shall not fail. I *shall not fail!*'

With those words, Screedius Tollinix lowered his visor once more, tugged on Vanquix's reins, and the pair of them headed across the frozen courtyard. Back towards the lonely tower they went, high above the western end of the Upper Halls.

In the twelve adjacent towers, the other knights were

also waiting, just like Screedius, to prove themselves, Quint thought. And perhaps, one day, he – Quintinius Verginix – would join them. If he did, then one thing was certain. He wanted the prowlgrin in the tilt tree above him to be by his side.

'Here, boy!' he called. 'Here, boy!'

Three weeks later, Quint woke to the sound of the dawn gong with a strange sense of foreboding. It was as if his time in the Hall of Grey Cloud had been but a dream. Outside, the skies were heavy with dark grey stormclouds and a light snow shower was beginning to fall.

The other squires were also subdued that morning. Today was the last day in the Hall of Grey Cloud and the greatest test lay just ahead. Quint tried to clear his head of the vision of Hax Vostillix and the Hall of High Cloud. After all, he told himself later, as they all lined up to await the arrival of Fenviel Vendix, the Hall Master of Grey Cloud himself had seemed strict and frightening on that first day. Yet now, despite his stiff manner, Quint and all the other squires saw him almost as a friend.

All, that is, except Vilnix Pompolnius. For even though, at Raffix's prompting, Fenviel had tempered his punishments, Vilnix still hated the hall master with a passion.

Fenviel Vendix appeared, cutting short Quint's day-dreaming, and the squires snapped to attention. The hall master started far to Quint's right, and proceeded to make his way along from the end of the line, pausing to shake hands with the squires, one by one, as he went.

Quint felt a shiver of excitement mixed with pride. In taking them by the hand and looking them in the eyes, Fenviel was according the young squires great respect. It had been tough in the Hall of Grey Cloud, but they had made it, and the hall master was proud of his young charges. Above them all, their prowlgrins – each one hand-raised from the egg – sat on their roost branches, looking down.

Fenviel stopped at Quiltis, shook hands, and moved on. Then at Tonsor, repeating the process. And on to Phin, who was standing next to Quint. Staring ahead, yet observing the procedure as best he could out of the corner of his eye, Quint saw the angular academic bend stiffly forward and clasp Phin by the hand. He nodded curtly and Quint thought he detected the hint of a smile playing at the corners of his mouth.

The next moment it was his turn.

He looked up to see Fenviel gazing back at him. There was a softness about his expression that surprised the youth, and when he shook his hand, the grip was firm and reassuring. He nodded. Quint nodded back, his heart almost bursting with the pride he was feeling.

Not a word was spoken as the hall master passed on down the line.

Half a dozen squires on from Quint, at the end of the line, Fenviel arrived at last in front of Vilnix Pompolnius. The youth's face was ashen white, and he was staring ahead defiantly.

Fenviel looked into the youth's eyes and held out his hand.

Vilnix's lip curled almost imperceptibly, but the effect was as shocking as if he'd hit Fenviel with his own riding crop. Unable to forgive the hall master, Vilnix kept his hand clenched at his side. The two of them faced each other, motionless, for what seemed like an eternity.

Finally, the hall master turned and left.

As soon as he was gone, the squires let out a collective breath and the line broke up into excited huddles of friends congratulating each other. Only Vilnix was left alone, and he slunk off behind a roost pillar.

'Quint! Phin!' Raffix's voice rang out. 'Look who I've brought to congratulate you on completing your time in the Hall of Grey Cloud!'

The squires turned to find Stope the forge-hand beaming with delight, standing next to the tall Upper Hall squire.

'Stope!' cried Quint and Phin together, and they both grabbed the grey goblin's hand excitedly. When they had finished laughing and joking and slapping each other on the back, Quint took Raffix to one side.

'I just wanted to say thank you, Raff, for having a word with Fenviel.' He smiled ruefully. 'Vilnix didn't seem that grateful, but it certainly made *my* life a lot easier!'

'Don't mention it, old chap,' laughed Raffix. 'After all, it's Vilnix who should be thanking me, not you. You only let his name slip to the hall master. He, on the other hand, practically starved a prowlgrin pup to death.'

From behind them came a sharp hiss, and Quint turned round to see Vilnix glaring at him from behind the roost pillar. His face was whiter than ever, his eyes blazing and the fading scar on his cheek flushed with colour.

'*You* told on me?' he snarled, spitting the words out. 'I won't forget, Quintinius. I won't ever forget!'

·CHAPTER ELEVEN·

THE HALL OF HIGH CLOUD

The Lecture Dome of the Hall of High Cloud was every bit as impressive as Quint had heard. Considered by many to be the finest work that the renowned architect, Flux Cartius, had ever designed, it was a masterpiece, more splendid than the domed Great Hall which stood at one end of the Central Viaduct, and in design ranking alongside the elegant Mistsifting Towers. As he and his fellow Lower Hall squires filed in, Quint realized – and not for the first time – just how privileged they all were to be members of the Knights Academy.

They made their way along one of the ornately carved flying-jetties to the buoyant benches, which floated at the ends of delicate silver chains. As they did so, Quint craned his neck back to gaze up at the clear dome far above his head.

Built above the northern wing of the Knights

Academy, the great glass construction spanned the air with the lightness and delicacy of a nightspider web. Each bowed strut was fashioned from a slender length of leadwood, steam-curved and slotted into place to form great interconnecting arcs. Then the whole structure had been glazed with the finest crystal ever to have been produced in the glass foundries of early Sanctaphrax.

Each flawless pane had been hand-cut and individually polished; some were tinted, and all of them had been etched with detailed calibrations by which the size, speed, shade and billow of the clouds passing overhead could be calculated.

Sadly, the original foundries had long since disappeared, taking most of their manufacturing secrets with them – though their legacy lived on in the various viaduct schools dedicated to glass-blowing. The difference between the original panes of glass and those which had been replaced due to weather damage was all too plain to see. It was, Quint thought, the difference between homespun and spider-silk, between woodgrog and winesap – between the merely adequate and the absolutely outstanding.

'Watch out,' Phin said, his voice hushed yet urgent as he grabbed at Quint's sleeve.

Even though he'd spoken barely above a whisper, Phin's warning rang out around the Lecture Dome. Alarmed, Quint looked down to find that they'd reached the end of the jetty and that below him the golden walls of the lower half of the hall curved down to form a vast bowl. It was, he thought, like being in the middle of a huge, hollow egg.

Because it was a place for lectures, it was essential that the professors who spoke there could be heard without having to raise their voices. The Lecture Dome fulfilled this requirement perfectly, for the acoustics of the egg-shaped hall were as crystal clear as the glass dome that encased it. Even the most hushed and tremulous whisper uttered from the magnificent buoyant lectern could be heard perfectly in every part of the hall.

'Hall Master of High Cloud . . .'

'Important speech, I heard . . .'

'. . . about the weather . . .'

'And about time!'

Phin's whisper was not alone. The domed hall was filled with voices, both soft and loud. Academy lecturers and professors, dressed in long dark gowns and ceremonial conical hats, filled the gantries that curved around the walls. Visiting academics from the School of Light and Darkness, the College of Cloud, the School of Mist, the Academy of Wind, and all the other more prestigious institutions in Sanctaphrax packed the visitors' balconies above. And squires – from both the Upper and the Lower Halls – filed through the entrance halfway up the golden wall, out along the flying-jetties and onto the buoyant sumpwood benches bobbing about in the air just beyond.

'Hold it steady,' said Quint, as he climbed gingerly onto the floating bench, joining Phin and Tonsor, who were already sitting down and preparing to adjust the leadwood weights that dangled below it.

All round the great domed lecture theatre, the procedure was being repeated as the squires took their places on the benches – in twos, threes; sometimes even in fours – and fiddled with the weights until they were hovering effortlessly in mid air.

The sumpwood seats were so sensitive that once equilibrium had been reached, the slightest movement was enough to make the bench rise gracefully up, or descend, or drift off in any desired direction. And that was what they did, rising and falling as their occupants vied with each other to get the best position, floating above, below or in front of the Grand Lectern.

'Careful!' Phin said urgently as a bench shunted past, knocking them momentarily off balance.

Its sole occupant, Vilnix Pompolnius, glared back at them. 'Just stay out of my way,' he snarled before turning away.

Ignoring him, Quint readjusted the balance-weights, and they rose higher to get a better view of the lectern.

Just then, Hax Vostillix appeared at the entrance to the hall, with the captain of the gatekeepers, Daxiel Xaxis, grim-faced at his side. The hall master was dressed in robes of finest spider-silk, trimmed with lemkin fur and embroidered with marsh-gems and mire-pearls. In his hand, he carried a long, carved staff of black thornwood, which he raised to silence the hall as he made his way along a flying-jetty towards the Grand Lectern.

At the end of the jetty, Daxiel Xaxis stepped forward and steadied the buoyant lectern for his master.

Hax Vostillix climbed onto it, leaned down and expertly adjusted the hanging-weights. The lectern slowly floated out into the great open void of the hall. Then, when he was satisfied that it was hovering just where he wanted it – at the very centre of the Lecture Dome, and high enough to require everyone to lift their heads to see him – Hax straightened up, looked around and raised his staff once more for absolute silence.

'Members of the Knights Academy . . .' he began in his deep, resonant voice, made even deeper and more impressive by the acoustics of the lecture hall.

The high professors, academics-at-arms and knights academic crowding the gantries round the walls acknowledged

him by bowing their heads. The three other hall masters – Philius Embertine in his armour; small, stooped Arboretum Sicklebough the tree goblin, and Fenviel Vendix, who was standing stiff and upright, gripping his prowlgrin crop – bowed from their own ornate gantry.

'Esteemed visitors from the seven schools . . .'

Hax's gaze fell on the visiting academics in the balconies, who smiled and bowed obsequiously. Hax returned their smiles, and as he bared his teeth, a look of wolfish triumph passed across his face, only to vanish a moment later as he gripped the lectern and turned his gaze upward.

Before the proceedings had got underway, Hax had ordered the cleaning of the glass. All traces of snow had been swept off and every smear and smudge wiped away. Now, as he looked up through the spotless dome, his eyes grew wide. And as he did so, every eye in the Lecture Dome followed his gaze.

'Fellow sky-scholars, observe the cloud formations,' Hax boomed, and the floating benches clustered round the Grand Lectern bobbed and swayed as the squires leaned back and stared at the dome. 'Mark them well. Note the mist density, the swirl-factor and above all, the rate of billow . . .'

Quint stared at the ominous grey clouds that filled the sky above the dome and attempted to read the complicated mosaic of calibrations and symbols etched into the glass panes. Around him, the lecture hall was filled with whispers as the academics watched the skies and muttered their own calculations under their breath.

'Three strides, eight, settling cursive . . .'

'Mist sight, one tenth by slow drift . . .

'Quantain, septrim, anodeflit . . .'

Hax's deep voice rang out. 'The clouds are in the process of forming an anvil. There is no doubt. I have done the calculations. But that is not all.' He nodded up at one of the visitors' balconies. 'Our friends from the School of Mist inform me that these clouds are laden with sourmist particles.'

A collective gasp rose up from the watching academics, mingled with cries of 'Thank Sky!' and 'Open Sky be praised!'

'That's right,' Hax continued triumphantly. 'The clouds now blowing in from Open Sky herald a Great Storm!'

The lecture hall broke into wild cheering, with squires and professors alike throwing their hats into the air and the academics-at-arms rattling their swords and beating their breast-plates. Up on the hall masters' gantry, Quint could see that the three hall masters had been joined by a knight academic – none other than Screedius Tollinix, who was excitedly shaking Philius Embertine's hand.

Hax raised his blackthorn staff for silence. Quint returned his attention to the buoyant lectern and was startled to see a look of barely suppressed rage on the Hall Master of High Cloud's face.

'Remember the Great Purge,' he roared, staring around the gantries, 'when the taint of earth-scholarship was banished from this great floating city of ours! And remember also the reason why we sky-scholars were driven to act! Our sacred rock was threatening to break free, just as it is today. And where did the earth-scholars look for salvation?'

He paused, his eyes blazing.

'To the Deepwoods! *Pah!*' Hax spat the words out, his face contorted with hate. 'They wouldn't listen to us sky-scholars. We told them that only the sky could save us. And we were proved right! With sacred stormphrax born of the Great Storm brought to the treasury, Sanctaphrax was saved! You see, my dear sky-scholars . . .'

Hax dropped his voice, and stared down at the lectern, his sunken eyes glittering from beneath a furrowed brow.

'I believe that the sky was testing us then, just as it is testing us now. With the Great Purge of earth-scholarship, we sky-scholars rose to that challenge. But now, as a Great Storm approaches, and with the Sanctaphrax rock once more in peril, we must have the courage to act decisively again!'

The gantries were now buzzing with whispers and mutters, and beside Quint, Phin nudged him in the ribs.

'Hey, Quint,' he whispered. 'Look at Vilnix. He's hanging on Hax's every word.'

Quint looked down at the solitary squire on the floating bench just below. Vilnix's hands were gripping the arms of his seat with white-knuckled intensity and a twisted grimace contorted his features.

'Who does he remind you of?' Phin chuckled.

Quint looked from the squire to the hall master at the lectern, and back again. 'Hax Vostillix,' he murmured.

It was true. Vilnix had the same look of barely

suppressed hatred and resentment on his face as Hax himself.

'Except without the beard and fancy robes,' giggled Phin.

'Earth-scholarship lives on!' Hax roared, his voice laden with venomous hatred. 'The earth-scholars might not be out in the open where we can see them any longer, but they are still there; skulking in the corners, waiting at every opportunity to tempt sky-scholars from their sacred studies. Why, they have even infiltrated the Knights Academy itself!'

At that, cries of 'No!' and 'It can't be true!' filled the air.

'It *is* true, my dear sky-scholars,' Hax broke in. 'Here in this great academy of ours, earth-scholars are infecting the minds of our young squires!'

Whistles and boos rang out now, along with shouts of anger from the crowded gantries. Hax smiled, clearly pleased with the effects his words were having on the academics.

'So long as even one earth-scholar remains in our midst, then the taint of earth-scholarship remains upon us.' Hax's eyes took on a steely glare. 'The old Most High Academe failed to raze the Great Library to the ground, despite my pleas and petitions. To this day, that symbol of earth-studies' folly remains standing. Filled, as it is, with the misguided endeavours of generations of earth-scholars from the past, it serves only to inspire the fools and traitors of the present to pursue their evil studies. And I tell you this,' he added, pausing once again. 'If we do not act now, as the sky tests us and our great floating city for a second time, then there will be no future for Sanctaphrax.'

Again the crowd – whipped up into a mixture of fury and indignation – reacted violently. They bellowed and bawled and shook their fists, their faces contorted with rage. Vilnix, Quint noticed, seemed to shouting louder than anyone else. His eyes were narrowed and his face was white, while his whole body was racked with spasms of hatred.

Quint had to turn away. His father, Wind Jackal, had warned him about the power of crowds and the danger of rabble-rousers, and told him to steer clear of those who allowed themselves to lose control in this way. Besides, the old Most High Academe was Linius Pallitax, Maris's father. Quint could never betray the memory of someone he knew that, for all his faults, only ever meant to do good.

No, Linius hadn't destroyed the Great Library. And why? Because he had believed in the sanctity of knowledge, because he had understood how much their forebears might teach them and, yes, because he had believed that the way forward for Sanctaphrax was for earth- and sky-scholars to work together. And having known Bungus Septrill – the wise and valiant High Librarian of the Great Library, who had sacrificed his own life to save Maris and himself down in the stonecomb – Quint knew that Linius had been right.

Unfortunately, judging by the shouts of the academics all around, he seemed to be the only one – although looking up, he did notice that the three hall masters in their gantry were silent and grim-faced.

'Look at the sky!' Hax was declaiming, his staff raised and his robes flapping. 'It is testing us! Are you ready to rise to the challenge, like those valiant sky-scholars who went before you?'

For a second time, all eyes looked upwards. Through the spotless glass, the late afternoon sky was already growing darker now that the sun had set. Unusually for a lecture at this time of day, however, the lamps had not been lit, so that when Hax pointed, the assembled academics could see that a new front of heavy dark clouds was rolling in from deepest Open Sky, beyond the Edge.

'Yes!' the academics roared in reply.

'Then we must purge the Knights Academy of earth-scholarship, once and for all!' Hax boomed.

'Yes!' 'Yes!' 'Yes!' the academics roared back.

Feeling increasingly uneasy, Quint shifted in his seat.

The next moment, he realized he wasn't the only one to be doing so. The three hall masters were on their feet and turning to go, only to find their way blocked by gatekeepers in long white capes.

'Stay where you are!' Daxiel Xaxis shouted at the hall masters.

Hax permitted himself another wolfish grin of triumph. 'Arboretum Sicklebough, Hall Master of Storm Cloud . . .' he said, his voice low and menacing. 'Do you deny your earth-scholar sympathies?'

'Of course I do!' snapped the tree goblin. 'This is an outrage!'

'Do you deny possession of these barkscrolls from the Great Library?' Hax held up two well-thumbed barkscrolls with evident distaste.

'They're just treatises on

fromps,' protested Sicklebough. 'On their care and training. Harmless enough. Everybody knows my interest in
fromp fighting . . .'

'Harmless?' roared Hax, slamming his fist down on
the lectern. 'Harmless? When it has led you into gambling debts you cannot hope to pay, and forced you to
neglect your studies! See how the stain of earth-scholarship taints even the finest amongst us!'

Arboretum hung his head in shame. 'I never meant it
to go so far. I just had a run of bad luck. Thought if I read
up on the little beasts . . .'

'You are a disgrace to the Knights Academy!' Hax
roared, before turning his gaze on a grim-faced Fenviel
Vendix. 'Ah, yes, Fenviel Vendix,' he said. 'Hall Master
of Grey Cloud . . .'

Fenviel returned Hax's gaze, his fist tightening round
his riding crop.

'Do *you* deny your earth-scholar sympathies?'

'I do,' barked the hall master.

'Do you deny that you value the life of one of your
prowlgrins – a beast of the earth – above that of a young
squire of the Knights Academy?'

'I deny it!' barked Fenviel.

Hax motioned to Vilnix Pompolnius, who rose
unsteadily from his floating bench, the look of triumph
on his face mirroring that of the Hall Master of High
Cloud.

'You deny beating this young squire with that earth-
scholar's whip of yours in full view of his comrades
because a puny prowlgrin pup failed to thrive?'

Fenviel's face drained of colour, and the prowlgrin crop trembled in his fist.

'See how earth-scholarship has fed a vicious temper, leading a hall master to violently attack a squire over a creature of the earth. A squire! The very future and hope of us all!' Hax appealed to the academics, who called out, 'Shame!' 'Shame!'

'You, too, are a disgrace to the Knights Academy!' Hax roared above their cries.

'Enough of this!' The voice of Philius Embertine, Hall Master of White Cloud, rang out surprisingly power- fully for the usually befuddled and dazed old knight. 'I must protest!'

'Ah, the great Philius Embertine, Hall Master of White Cloud, so we come to you.' Hax's voice was suddenly soft and full of sorrow, and he shook his head, grimac- ing, as if in pain.

A deathly hush had fallen on the academics on every side of the lecture hall. Everybody knew that the old knight academic was the most famous living member of the academy, despite his absent-minded ways. After all, he had completed not one, but two stormchasing voy- ages, single-handedly ensuring the stability of the great rock for years to come – until the harsh, neverending winter had struck and changed everything.

Quint stared at him uneasily. Surely the old Hall Master of White Cloud was beyond reproach, he thought. Wasn't he?

'Even you,' Hax growled, 'are not immune from the curse of earth-scholarship.'

'What . . . what do you mean?' Philius seemed uncertain and confused once more.

'It is more in sorrow than in anger I have to report that a gross breach of the laws of Sanctaphrax has been committed,' Hax went on. 'The Most High Academes are as saddened as I am. Whether it was the extreme dangers and privations of his epic voyages, or the effects of the Twilight Woods, Philius Embertine's reason has clearly deserted him . . .'

'Nonsense! He's as sane as I am!' Screedius Tollinix cried out as he stepped forward, his eyes blazing with anger. 'This must be some misunderstanding . . .'

'I wish it were,' said Hax sadly. 'Oh, how I wish it were. But before you jump to your mentor's defence, my brave young knight, perhaps you ought to listen to the facts. It seems that the Hall Master of White Cloud instructed his furnace masters, against their will, to bribe the treasury guard to steal stormphrax from the treasury. Perhaps it was the desire to have in his possession that which he'd suffered so much for; to see a sacred shard of stormphrax one last time before he died. Who knows? Perhaps he even intended to return it to the treasury.' He shrugged and shook his head. 'Who can tell what thoughts went through that poor addled head of his . . .'

'But it's not like that at all!' stormed Philius Embertine, staggering towards the gantry rail. 'You don't understand . . .'

'Oh, I understand perfectly clearly,' replied Hax, his voice suddenly harsh and rasping. '*This* tells me everything I need to know!'

He held up a crisp new barkscroll for all to see.

'Captain Sigbord's signed confession obtained just this morning, after a little persuasion by Daxiel Xaxis here,' he said, with a flourish. Hax Vostillix was clearly enjoying himself. 'And with the willing co-operation of your own furnace masters, Spedius Heepe and Clud Mudskut. Your private chambers were searched and a shard of stormphrax in a light-casket was discovered. This, I might add, was witnessed by the Most High Academes, who were as shocked as I was!'

'If you'd just listen for a moment . . .' wheezed Philius, falling to his knees, his face as grey as his ancient armour.

'Also amongst your personal effects were barkscrolls from the Great Library, great piles of them – all written by earth-scholars. No wonder you finally lost your reason.'

'You're a fool, Hax Vostillix,' gasped the old knight academic. 'A blind fool. Those scrolls hold . . . the answer . . . to . . .'

'Silence!' roared the Hall Master of High Cloud, and levelled his staff at the gantry. 'You, Philius Embertine, are a disgrace to the Knights Academy! Gatekeepers! Take him away! Take them *all* away!'

The gatekeepers sprang forward, their swords drawn, only to be confronted by Screedius, his own sword unsheathed.

'Screedius Tollinix, knight academic-in-waiting!' Hax's voice boomed out from the buoyant lectern. 'Before you defy my orders, I must remind you of one thing.'

Screedius turned to Hax, his eyes blazing. 'And that is?' he snarled.

'A Great Storm is approaching, and Sanctaphrax has need of the talents of her finest knight academic. Think carefully before you make your next move.'

Screedius glared at the hall master, then down at the slumped figure of his friend, Philius Embertine. The old knight looked up and searched his young colleague's face as if reading his thoughts. Then, slowly, he nodded his head. Screedius turned, sheathed his sword, and stepped aside as the gatekeepers led the three hall masters away.

'Fellow sky-scholars, the Purge has begun!' announced Hax Vostillix. 'Sanctaphrax *shall* be saved!'

On the floating bench, Quint looked down miserably as the lecture hall resounded to the cheers of the academics. Being a member of the Knights Academy didn't seem to feel quite so good any more.

·CHAPTER TWELVE·

THE WINDCUTTER

The mechanism of the great telescope screeched in protest as the Professor of Darkness attempted to adjust its focus.

'It's no good, my friend,' he called down from the glass-domed roof of the Loftus Observatory to his colleague, the Professor of Light, who was peering up at him from the foot of the ladder. 'Frozen practically solid. It's all I can do to turn the blasted thing.'

He rapped a knuckle against the shaft of the great brass telescope and, getting up from the padded seat, began to climb back down the ladder.

'I don't like it, old friend,' his colleague began, the moment the Professor of Darkness had rejoined him. 'The sourmist particles certainly denote the arrival of a Great Storm, but these cloud formations . . .' He shook his head. 'Too compact, far too little drift, and I for one am not at all convinced by the mist density . . .'

'Neither am I, dear friend,' the Professor of Darkness agreed. 'Neither am I. Yet no such doubts seem to afflict our esteemed colleague, the Hall Master of High Cloud. Every school and academy seems to be hanging on his every word.'

'That,' said the Professor of Light grimly, 'is the power of rabble-rousing. He's got half the academics in Sanctaphrax looking in their sleeping closets for earth-scholars, and the other half convinced of the imminent arrival of this Great Storm of his . . .'

'And in the meantime, he can do what he likes,' added the Professor of Darkness with a heavy sigh. 'I thought our dear friend Linius Pallitax, Sky rest his soul, had put an end to these absurd sky- and earth-scholarship divisions.'

'Talking of which,' broke in the Professor of Light, as the two Most High Academes made their way down the long spiralling staircase of the Loftus Observatory, the tallest tower in Sanctaphrax, 'how *are* the hall masters?'

'*Ex*-hall masters, dear friend,' replied the Professor of Darkness. He sucked in air noisily through his teeth. 'Well, Fenviel Vendix has taken to hanging about at the treadmills on the West Landing. Can't bear being parted from his beloved prowlgrins, I imagine – but Hax has threatened to set his gatekeepers on him if he should ever show his face in the Hall of Grey Cloud again. Arboretum, poor chap, has fled to Undertown in complete disgrace. It seems his gambling debts were far bigger than anyone realized, and he owes money everywhere. Several of the viaduct schools turned particularly nasty over it, I understand.'

'And Embertine?'

'Ah, yes, poor Philius. It's really so very sad,' said the Professor of Darkness. 'He's taken to his bed, still protesting his innocence. They say he's fading fast and not even Hax is hard-hearted enough to throw him out. But it's a bad business,' he muttered as they reached the bottom of the tower. 'A bad business all round.'

'And I'll tell you this,' said the Professor of Light, as they stepped out into a blizzard of snowflakes, 'Hax Vostillix might seem like the saviour of Sanctaphrax right now, but if he's wrong about this Great Storm, the academics will turn on him quicker than the Chorus of the Dead at a funeral.'

You hardly ever saw the Hall Master of High Cloud in the great Lecture Dome these days, thought Quint, leaning back against the padded cushions of the floating bench.

Beside him, Phin's head was drooping over a tattered barkscroll, which was covered with spots and smudges of black ink.

Poor old Phin. Quint smiled. He just didn't seem to be

able to get the hang of cloudwatching at all.

'I mean to say,' he'd whisper to Quint – protesting as loudly as he dared, given the tell-tale acoustics of the egg-shaped hall. 'If I'd wanted to stare at the sky all day long, I'd have stayed at the Academy of Wind. At least you could talk there!'

'*Sssshh!*' Quint would hiss in reply. 'Someone will hear.'

That 'someone', they both knew, was Vilnix Pompolnius, hovering high above the others, a solitary figure on a floating bench all to himself. The other squires now shunned him completely, not only in the lecture hall, but also in the Eightways *and* the dormitory closets.

Not that the sour-faced young squire seemed to care. He was too busy sucking up to Hax Vostillix on those rare occasions when the hall master made an appearance in the lecture hall; or snooping about, eavesdropping on the conversations of the other squires when he wasn't. Indeed, many of them were so convinced that Vilnix was spying on them, searching for signs of earth-scholar sympathies, that they refused to say a single word in his presence. Quint wasn't as certain, but even he thought it best to watch what he said, just in case.

Every day, high professors from the Upper Halls came down to the domed hall to deliver lectures, and the squires' heads were filled with new equations and fresh formulae, each one more complicated than the one before. Using the sectors and lines etched into the glass dome, they learned of ocular swirls, eddies and flows, drift measures and drizzle patterns. Then, with the long complicated lectures over, they would switch from theory to practice. The high professors would set them navigational problems – everything from mist-shift and billow-swell to graded transits and hover feints. Most afternoons, the only sound to be heard was a faint scratching, as the squires scribbled furiously on their barkscrolls.

There was no let-up. From dusk till dawn they laboured, and often late into the night – so that they might examine the effects of darkness on the increasingly turbulent cloud formations coming in from Open Sky.

Although Phin often grew bored and restive, beside him, Quint found himself swept up in the beauty and mystery of the sky. Some days, it was all he could do to drag himself away from the mesmerizing spectacle unfolding through the crystal panes of the great dome. Yet as he studied the cloud formations, day after day, nagging questions and uncertainties began to drift through his mind, as dark and ominous as the clouds above – until one afternoon, he could help himself no longer.

At the end of a long lecture on low cloud clusters given by High Professor Graydle Flax, Quint raised his hand.

'Please, Professor Flax,' he began. 'There's something that's been bothering me ... It's about the Great Storm ...'

Around him, several of the squires suppressed

nervous giggles, and Phin gasped. Questions were only permitted if a high professor specifically asked for them. Graydle Flax turned from adjusting the buoyant lectern's weights and stared at the squire, his mouth set in a tight, grim line.

'The mist density of the anvil formations seems far too great,' Quint said. 'And, according to my calculations, there's insufficient drift to denote the arrival of a Great Storm. I mean, I know I'm only a Lower Hall squire, but . . .'

'But nothing, squire!' a voice boomed across the lecture hall. 'How dare you question the considered judgement of the Hall Master of High Cloud?'

The buoyant benches clattered and buffeted each other as the squires upon them turned to see Hax Vostillix standing on a flying-jetty at the entrance to the lecture hall. His face was drawn and tired, and the spider-silk robe was so creased it looked as though the hall master had slept in it.

'Professor Flax,' he barked, outraged, 'what kind of lecture are you running here, where squires are allowed to shout out whatever comes into their heads?'

He swept along the jetty and, brushing the high professor aside, stepped onto the buoyant lectern, which rose back into the air.

'Now, who amongst you can correct this impudent youth?' he demanded, and glared round at the squires in front of him.

'Please, Hall Master Vostillix, sir,' Vilnix's thin, ingratiating voice sounded from behind Quint's back.

'As you've already made clear, the increase of sourmist particles in the air shows the build-up of a Great Storm beyond any doubt. And the anvil formations – despite the masking effects of snow and ice – herald its imminent arrival, Sky be praised!' His eyes narrowed. 'To believe otherwise is earth-scholar talk!'

His voice sank to a low hiss as he uttered the words 'earth-scholar talk', and Quint flinched as he heard them, wishing he hadn't spoken out. The former hall masters weren't the only ones who needed to watch their step in this new charged atmosphere.

'Excellent, young Pompolnius! Excellent!' Hax enthused, 'a Great Storm *is* imminent!' Yet as he spoke, the anxious, fretful look on his face showed that even he was having doubts. 'Squires, dismissed!' he barked. 'And you, Quintinius Verginix . . .' Hax fixed Quint with an icy stare. 'The high professors tell me you are clever.' His eyes narrowed. 'Far too clever, I trust, to be taken in by earth-scholar lies . . .'

'N . . . n . . . no, sir,' stammered Quint. 'I . . . I mean, yes, sir . . .'

'Just watch what you say in future!' The hall master yanked the lectern round and descended to the jetty, then stormed out.

Quint was just about to return to his studies, when he caught Professor Flax's eye. There was a faint smile playing on the high professor's thin lips and, before Quint could look away, he winked at him. Clearly Quint wasn't the only one with doubts about the Great Storm.

*

High in his tower in the Knights Academy, Screedius Tollinix rose, crossed to the window and threw it open. Outside, dark clouds in anvil formations billowed across the sky, but at least the blizzard of the past three weeks seemed to have abated.

His green eyes scanned the sky, noting every detail. His nostrils flared. There was definitely sourmist in the air, and stronger than ever. Yet, something wasn't right. Was it the cloud density, or the lack of cloud drift? He shook his head. Even though he couldn't put his finger on it, something was causing the uncomfortable feeling in the pit of his stomach.

Screedius wished he could talk to his friend, Philius Embertine, the old knight academic. *He* would know what this baffling weather meant . . . But that was impossible. Philius was delirious in his quarters in the Hall of White Cloud, calling out to his long-dead prowlgrin and reliving his famous stormchasing voyages over and over in his poor, fevered imagination.

No, Screedius had to trust in Hax Vostillix whether he liked it or not. Hax claimed that a Great Storm was imminent and every fibre of the knight academic's being wanted to believe he was right.

He turned away from the window and began the long slow task of buckling himself into his armour, the same ritual that he repeated every day. First the underquilting, then the inner pipework – tightening valves, securing joints. Now the leg-armour, joints greased, clips checked; then the arms – elbow guards, shoulder arches. Next the great breast-plate and backplate, smooth and polished, bedecked in outer pipework and glass-capped gauges. And finally the heavy helmet, lifted into place and firmly secured.

As he lowered the visor, Screedius could hear the sound of his own breath roaring in his ears. And, seen through the eye-plates of twilight-refracting crystal, the world outside turned the colour of golden wood-honey.

He was ready now to descend the three hundred and seventy-two steps of the tower and climb into the saddle of Vanquix, oiled, groomed and waiting for him in the Inner Courtyard. Then it was a short gallop to the Great Hall at the far end of the Central Viaduct, where he would wait for the bell to toll.

Three weeks had passed since the twin Most High

Academes had knighted him with the great curved ceremonial sword. A tap on each shoulder and suddenly he was a knight academic-in-waiting no longer, but instead, a fully-fledged knight academic!

Yet the waiting went on. Hour after hour, day after day. For three long weeks he'd dressed in his armour and waited at one end of the viaduct, while his stormchaser – the *Windcutter* – waited for him at the other. And still the Great Storm had not come.

Arriving at the Great Hall and urging Vanquix inside, Screedius raised his visor and permitted himself another look at the sky. He checked the drift and swirl of the towering anvil clouds. Perhaps today *would* be the day . . .

'I'm ready,' he whispered to the sky, his breath a long, wispy plume of mist, 'whenever you are.'

Out of nowhere, there came a sound, the like of which no-one in the great floating city of Sanctaphrax had heard before – but one that none would ever forget.

It began as a low rumble, more a vibration in the freezing air than an actual noise. The ink-pots and bone-handled quills rattled across the desk-tops of the floating benches, causing the squires to reach out and grab them, before they fell and smashed on the curved walls below.

Then, as the sky rapidly darkened, the rumble turned into a roar. It was coming from above them, out of the depths of Open Sky. Louder it grew, and louder, clattering round the egg-shaped lecture hall like an invisible caged beast.

Quint trembled and clapped his hands to his ears.

Rising in pitch now, shifting from a roar to a shriek to a piercing wail, it sounded as if a thousand sky spirits were laying siege to the towers of Sanctaphrax, which bent and quivered before them. And as the rasping, screeching sky-howl climbed to its terrible crescendo, so the ground trembled, the buildings shook, and in every college and school of the frozen city academics fell to their knees and called for the Sky to protect them . . .

And then – just as Quint thought he could bear it no longer – something happened. Almost as suddenly as it had arisen, the sound simply died away and the bruised air was left throbbing with silence.

Hax Vostillix burst into the great lecture hall, wild-eyed and dishevelled, and stabbed a finger towards the dome. Quint looked up, and saw a huge anvil-shaped cloud billowing across the sky, churning and curdling everything around it.

'The Great Storm!' the Hall Master of High Cloud cried out in triumph, and let out an unhinged cackle. 'It has come! Sky be praised!'

At the same moment, echoing through the hallway, came the sound of a distant bell tolling.

'It's the Great Hall bell!' someone exclaimed.

'They're ringing the Great Hall bell!'

All at once, the Knights Academy exploded in a flurry of frantic activity. Doors slammed, voices were raised, and from every corner there came the tramp of running feet as the professors and squires, the gatekeepers, academics-at-arms and hall-servants alike all dashed down stairs and along corridors. Cloaks and capes were grabbed, caps with furry ear-flaps were pulled down over heads, snow-goggles were put into place. And as the vast multitude surged towards the magnificent double doors, which burst open with a loud *crash*, the tolling bell grew louder still.

Swept along with the rest were Quint and Phin, hurriedly wrapping scarves around their necks and tucking in their quilted vests.

'What's wrong, Quint?' Phin asked above the babble of voices. 'The Great Storm has arrived. Aren't you excited?'

The next moment they burst out from the end of the corridor, like a cork from a bottle of shaken winesap, into the windlashed, snow-covered cityscape beyond. The colour was extraordinary – a malevolent ochre-tinged wash tainting the thick snow; and there was a curious odour to the air. Sour, burnt, almost like toasted almonds.

'It's just that ... The stormcloud ...' Quint began, struggling to keep up with Phin as he peered up at the swirling sky above. 'There's something not quite right . . .'

Impelled along the snow-filled streets, their booted feet crunching in the frozen snow, Quint and Phin continued on to the foot of the Viaduct Steps. From every corner of Sanctaphrax, hundreds and thousands of others joined the throng, streaming from the buildings on all sides and converging.

Past the East Landing they went, the creak of the turning treadmill filling the air as the prowlgrins and giant fromps inside it tramped on and on, endlessly raising and lowering the log burner suspended below. Into the bottleneck between the Minor Academies and the Loftus Observatory – grunting with effort as they forced themselves through – and on towards the great squares which afforded the best views of the magnificent viaduct.

'Over here, Quint, old chap!' came a voice.

Quint glanced round to see Raffix, his head swathed in a tilderskin hat with thick ear-muffs, standing on a raised plinth waving his arms.

He and Phin struggled towards him, their elbows gouging a route through the dense, surging crowd. As they got closer, Raffix leaned towards them with an arm outstretched and, one after the other, pulled them up on the plinth beside him. As Quint squeezed in beside Phin, he turned – and gasped. For there, high up in the air, secured to the side of the Loftus Observatory was a sky ship.

A stormchaser!

'What do you think of her?' said Raffix.

'She's magnificent,' said Quint, awestruck by the beauty of the sleek vessel.

'She's called the *Windcutter*,' Raffix went on, and smiled wryly as the icy wind plucked at the ear-flaps on his hat. 'A fine name for a stormchaser! And here comes her master!'

Just then, from the other end of the Central Viaduct there came a fanfare of tilderhorns. A moment later, high up, just beneath the towering glass dome, the balcony doors flew open. And there, resplendent in shining armour, sat Screedius Tollinix, knight academic, astride his black prowlgrin, Vanquix.

At the sight of the knight and his prowlgrin, the entire crowd erupted with whoops and cheers, which grew louder and more frenzied as the pair of them made their way slowly along the top of the viaduct. They looked so magnificent that, for the moment, Quint forgot his misgivings about the huge cloud that was fast approaching.

With Vanquix and Screedius more than halfway across the viaduct, the sky was looking more threatening than ever. The wind had grown stronger too and, as the crowd stared up at the valiant knight and his prowlgrin mount, so thick feathery flakes of snow began to tumble down out of the sky.

Screedius approached the sky ship, tethered at the far end of the viaduct. He was met by the excited figure of Hax Vostillix, whose white beard was flapping wildly in the wind.

'The Great Storm is approaching!' he screamed as the sky blackened overhead.

Screedius raised his visor and turned his green eyes upwards. The anvil-shaped stormcloud was moving swiftly, and the suggestion of a swirl was beginning to spin it. But its formation was dense, and no tendrils of lightning flickered in its depths. Instead, the eddies of snow seemed to be getting thicker.

'What are you waiting for?' screamed Hax, almost beside himself with anxiety and excitement. 'It is a Great Storm. You must not let it get away!'

Screedius turned his intense gaze on the Hall Master of High Cloud and spoke, his low voice almost lost in the swirling snow-filled wind.

'I shall not fail.'

With those words, Screedius tugged at his reins and Vanquix leaped from the viaduct and landed on the deck of the sky ship. The crowd, shielding their eyes from the falling snow, cried out in jubilation. And their cries grew more excited still as Screedius dismounted and began raising the sails, one by one. First the mainsail, then the sky- and studsails – each one flapping and billowing as the wind caught it. Finally, the loudest cry of all went up as Screedius loosed the tolley-rope and, with a sudden lurch, the *Windcutter* soared up into the turbulent air.

'Skyspeed!'

'Return safely!'

'Sky protect you!'

The words of encouragement and well-being were whipped away on the lashing wind, and it is doubtful whether Screedius Tollinix heard anything as he struggled to control the sky ship. Battling with the billowing sails while at the same time trying to maintain control of the dangerously buoyant flight-rock, he circled the Loftus Observatory, before setting off into the heart of the storm as it passed overhead and sped on over Undertown and on towards the Mire.

Quint felt his heart racing as he watched the sky ship grow tiny in the raging maelstrom. It looked so fragile, so flimsy. The sails flapped, the flight-rock burners flared on and off and, in the crowd all round him, there were murmured prayers and benedictions, with the more suspicious of those in the crowd fingering the charms and amulets which hung around their necks.

For a second the *Windcutter* could be seen clearly, sideways on against the mass of turbulent cloud. The next, it disappeared inside. All eyes in the crowd stared unblinking at the spot where the sky ship had entered the storm, but there was nothing more to see as the Great Storm continued inexorably towards the Twilight Woods, with the knight academic and his faithful prowlgrin at its centre.

'Sky protect you, Screedius Tollinix,' Quint murmured. 'Sky protect you.'

QUODE QUAN DC
QUERIDC

CHAPTER THIRTEEN

THE BARKSCROLL LETTER

'Are you all right, Quint, old chap?' called Raffix. He was looking up at his friend from the base of the plinth, a puzzled expression on his red, wind-lashed face.

Already, the crowds on the Viaduct Steps were thinning out as the academics, servants and all the other onlookers hurried back to the warmth and shelter of their schools and academies.

'I hate to interrupt your daydreaming,' Raffix persisted, 'but it's getting rather chilly out here. Or hadn't you noticed?'

Quint turned, realizing with a jolt that Raffix was right. While he had been standing there, staring out at the distant horizon, a fresh blizzard had blown in from Open Sky and the icy air was once again thick with snow.

'I'm sorry,' said Quint, brushing the gathering

snowflakes from his shoulders and jumping down from the plinth. 'It's just that I can't get this nagging thought out of my head . . .'

'And what thought is that, my dear fellow?' said Raffix.

The two of them linked arms and, leaning against one another for support, began trudging back through the snow-clogged streets towards the Knights Academy.

'The thought,' said Quint, as they caught up with Phin, who was battling to pull a pair of snow-goggles down over his cap, 'that Hax Vostillix might be wrong. That what we just witnessed wasn't really a Great Storm at all.'

'He'd jolly well better not be wrong!' said Phin hotly. 'After all, he's just sent the finest knight academic in all of Sanctaphrax to chase the wretched thing!' He grimaced with irritation. 'Blast these wretched goggles! Why won't they fit?'

'Here, you've got them all tangled up,' said Raffix, coming to his aid. He tugged at the ear-flaps of Phin's cap, pulling them free, then turned back to Quint. 'But you've certainly got a point, old chap. There are quite a few in the Upper Halls who also have their doubts about this Great Storm of Hax's. The thing is, the treasury needs stormphrax so desperately that they're prepared to hold their tongues and go along with him.'

They were approaching the East Landing, where the treadmills worked day and night hauling the vast log burners up and down the surface of the great rock. The steady *tramp tramp tramp* of the prowlgrins marching endlessly round and round in the great wheel was all but lost in the howling, snow-filled wind.

With their heads down and their thick cloaks flapping, the three squires hurried past as fast as the thick snow would allow. None of them wanted to acknowledge the awful truth about the great floating rock.

Already the freezing winter weather had made it so buoyant that the Anchor Chain was stretched taut. It creaked and cracked constantly, as if about to snap at any moment. The vast log burners warmed the rock as best they could, but they were fighting a losing battle. The icy winds which blew through the stonecomb were threatening to freeze the heartrock at its core – and if that happened, then no amount of chains or burners could prevent the great rock from breaking free and disappearing into Open Sky for ever.

No, the only hope for the floating city was stormphrax, and everyone in Sanctaphrax knew it. Only that sacred substance – a small cupful of which weighed more than a hundred thousand ironwood trees when placed in the absolute darkness of the treasury – could provide the necessary counter-balance to the increasing buoyancy of the rock. It was little wonder that, despite any individual doubts or reservations, the crowd had reacted with such joyous enthusiasm to the departure of the knight academic on his stormchaser.

'And Screedius is just the first,' said Raffix darkly. They were opposite the School of Mist now, wading through the drifting snow as they approached the North Gate of the Knights Academy. 'Every knight academic-in waiting in the Thirteen Towers will get sent, you mark my words. Hophix, Dantius, Queritis . . . Hax will have them all off chasing after every single snow flurry and blizzard on the merest off-chance that it'll turn out to be a Great Storm. And the funny thing is . . .' He paused.

'The funny thing?' whispered Quint.

They nodded to the burly gatekeeper as they slipped through the high entrance of the North Gate.

'The funny thing is, they'll all go,' said Raffix with a smile. 'All the knights *and* all the squires promoted to replace them. Every last one of them.' He smiled rue-fully. 'Even me.'

'But why?' said Quint. 'I mean, if you doubt Hax . . .'

'Because, my dear chap, this is the Knights Academy,' Raffix replied. 'We were born to stormchase.' They had reached the foot of the staircase which led to the Upper Halls. 'And one of these days . . .' he called back, as he set off up the stairs, 'old Hax might just get it right.'

Outside in the driving snow, a hunched figure turned the corner of the School of Mist and hurried towards the Knights Academy. The woodtroll matron, her skirts flap-ping and bonnet held in place with a mittened hand, slipped and skidded over the icy cobblestones. Beneath her feet, the slush – created by the passing of so many boots over the settling snow – was freezing into sharp, jagged peaks that cracked and crunched, and threatened to turn her ankle with every step she took.

'Am I too late?' she wheezed to the burly guard, his white hooded cape bearing the red logworm insignia of the gatekeepers. 'Have I missed the young squires?'

''Fraid so, mother,' laughed the gatekeeper, his deep voice muffled by the long scarf wound round his face. 'Far too chilly for the little darlings to stay out long. Might catch their death of a cold. We gatekeepers, on the other hand, we can freeze out here for all they care . . .'

He stamped his heavy boots on the frozen ground and shivered theatrically.

'I don't suppose . . .' began the woodtroll, peeling off her mittens and rummaging in a tilderleather purse, 'that you could see to it that squire Quintinius Verginix of the Lower Halls gets this?'

She held out a rolled barkscroll in a shaking hand.

'Did you say Quintinius Verginix?' came a thin ingratiating voice, and the woodtroll matron turned to see a wiry youth peering down at her.

'It seems I was mistaken, mother,' the gatekeeper said. 'This will be the last of the little darlings – young Vilnix here is always the last one in. Browsing in the viaduct schools again, were we?'

'Mind your own business!' snapped the youth. 'And it's Squire Pompolnius, to you, gatekeeper, and don't you forget it!'

The gatekeeper guffawed behind his scarf and gave a sarcastic bow. Ignoring him, Vilnix reached out and snatched the barkscroll from the woodtroll matron's hand.

'I'll see that he gets it!' he said, with a quick, wolfish flash of his teeth, before darting away through the gates.

'Tell him, Welma and Tweezel send their best wishes . . .' the woodtroll called after him uncertainly.

There was something about the youth's thin, pinched face and shifty eyes that disturbed her – yet he wore the robes of a squire of the Knights Academy, and seemed to know Quint. Besides, since she couldn't hand the letter to the young master in person, she had no choice *but* to trust him. In front of her, the gatekeeper swung the heavy gates shut again and folded his arms.

'I'd hurry along, mother, if you intend to get back to Undertown this afternoon,' he said. 'What with all this heavy snow, they're talking of closing the hanging-baskets.'

Welma gasped. 'Ooh, I can't afford to get stuck up here,' she said and, bidding the gatekeeper a hasty 'good-day', she hurried away in the direction of the East Landing.

As Vilnix strode along the central corridor, lightly patting the little bulge in his inside pocket as he went, he permitted himself a rasping chuckle. How it amused him that the ridiculous old woodtroll had entrusted the barkscroll to his care. Up until that point, it had been a cold, miserable, unsatisfying afternoon, his studies inter-rupted by the preposterous ritual of sending off old 'brass-breeches' in that swanky sky ship of his.

Oh, and how the other squires had cheered and hollered, and waved their arms in the air like demented fromps. Fools, the lot of them!

Vilnix smiled to himself.

Stormchasing! It was all they ever talked about, those pampered Sanctaphrax-born and bred squires. But he, Vilnix Pompolnius, would show them! Reaching the end of the corridor, he turned right, surreptitiously patting the scroll once more as he did so.

Ahead of him, several squires exchanged looks and stepped aside to let him pass. They all hated him, he knew that – but one day Vilnix would make them fear him as well. One day, he would look down on all of them, because he – plain old Vil Spatweed, knife-grinder from Undertown – would be Vilnix Pompolnius, Most High Academe of Sanctaphrax.

He thrust out his jaw and his face took on a look of twisted pride.

He would become Most High Academe because he had what it took to make it to the very top – cunning, malice, treachery and deceit. And he knew this for a fact, because these were just the things it had taken to survive in the fetid sewers of Undertown.

The drunken grey waif who'd found him as a baby and raised him in a sewer tunnel in the boom-docks had taught him to pick locks and pockets almost as soon as he could walk. He'd shown real talent, and before long he'd left the pathetic old creature snoring in its hammock and set up on his own as a knife-grinder.

He was the best – everybody knew it. Every goblin with a grudge, every cloddertrog on the warpath, every waif assassin, knew to come to him to have their sickles sharpened, their axes honed or their daggers given a razorlike edge.

But even back then, Vilnix had known it wasn't enough. He had wanted more, much more. He was fed up with others telling him what to do – he wanted to be the one in control, in charge. In short, he wanted power. Then the Professor of Darkness had dropped that telescope of his and the rest, as they say, was history.

It was his mentor, the professor, who had given him his name.

'Vil Spatweed,' he'd mused, as the pair of them had sat opposite one another in the professor's study. 'An excellent name for a knife-grinder, but not, I'm afraid to

say, quite right for a future knight academic.' He stroked
his beard thoughtfully. 'Vil,' he said at last. 'The short-
ened form of Villox, Vilfius and Vilnix . . .' He frowned.
'Now, there's a name to conjure with . . . Vilnix . . .'

'Pompolnius,' the youth had said.

It was the name of one of the leaguesmen in the
Western Quays who had met an unfortunate end at the
point of a dagger, sharpened to perfection just the week
before by the best knife-grinder in Undertown.

'Vilnix Pompolnius it is,' the Professor of Darkness
had said, nodding in agreement. 'A scholar could go a
long way with such a name.'

To the top, Vilnix had thought as he smiled back
respectfully. To the very top.

Being sponsored through the Knights Academy was
the first step on that ladder. The moment he met the
other squires, he was immediately confident that he
could outdo the lot of them – all, that is, except
Quintinius Verginix. He frowned. What *was* it about that
particular squire that got so under his skin?

Was it because he was sponsored by the Professor of
Light? Or that he, too, had been born in Undertown?

Vilnix's lip curled with contempt. Those weren't the
reasons at all. He was the pampered son of a famous sky
pirate – and as for his mentor, in Vilnix's mind, the
Professor of Light was no match for his own Professor of
Darkness.

No, there was something else about Quint that
enraged Vilnix – something he couldn't quite put his
finger on . . .

He had reached the Central Staircase by now and, roughly brushing aside several squires coming down, he strode purposefully up the circular stairs.

True, Quint had scuppered his chances to shine throughout the Lower Halls. In the Hall of Storm Cloud, he'd ruined his model sky ship. And then, how he had sucked up to Philius Embertine in the Hall of White Cloud, *and* made such a fuss over that forge-hand, Stope. And worst of all, the way he'd pretended to be his friend in the Hall of Grey Cloud, only to betray him to Fenviel Vendix.

Vilnix rubbed his fingers lightly over the raised scar that ran the length of his left cheek, and permitted himself a wry smile.

Still, that had actually worked out pretty well in the end, he remembered, with Vendix banished from the academy and he, Vilnix, becoming the favourite of Hax Vostillix . . .

But no, none of these things could explain the cold hatred for Quint that gripped his heart.

At the first landing, Vilnix paused. Down the corridor to his right was a gaggle of his fellow-squires, laughing at some joke or other. Phin, Tonsor, Quiltis . . . When they saw him, they stopped and moved away.

Well, the joke was on them, thought Vilnix, with a bitter little smile. While they cold-shouldered and ignored him, he had been paying each of them particular attention. The gaunt young squire had discovered that there were all manner of ingenious little potions on offer in the viaduct schools. You just had to know where to look.

Quiltis Wistelweb had never managed to work out why the notes he worked so hard on kept disappearing

– but then why *should* he suspect the ink in his ink-pot was to blame? And Belphinius Mendellix; why *would* he question the reason he kept oversleeping. Surely it couldn't be the little pouch stuffed into the lining of his pillow, could it? And as for Tonsor, no matter how many times he'd washed his robes they'd remained annoyingly itchy – but then the soap couldn't have anything to do with it, could it?

And then there was that very special vial he had, sealed with green wood-wasp wax and kept hidden away. The one that Vilnix was saving . . .

He reached the bottom of the dormitory ladder and smiled to himself. Cunning, malice, treachery and deceit – yes, that was what it took to get to the very top. Quickly, he climbed the rungs of the ladder, opened the doors to his sleeping

215

closet and crawled inside. Then, having lit the lamp and made himself comfortable on the mattress, he pulled the barkscroll from his inside pocket and untied the ribbon – slowly, deliberately, and savouring every moment.

He'd thought long and hard about what he was going to do to Quint. Disappearing ink, drowsy-herb pouches and itching-soap were all very well for the others, but Quint deserved something better – something altogether nastier. Vilnix had even been toying with the idea of his special vial . . . But no, that was to be used only as a last resort.

And now this barkscroll letter had quite literally fallen into his hands. He felt sure it would be good. Just *how* good, he couldn't wait any longer to find out. With a soft cackle of amusement, he unrolled the barkscroll and held it to the light.

Dear Quint, he read. *Thank you for the lovely long letter you sent. It was so good to get all your news. Your friend Stope gave all eight scrolls to me in the market square, hidden inside a beautifully wrought lullabee burner that he said he'd made himself. I told Dacia that I'd bought the burner in the market-place, and she didn't think any more about it. So you see, your plan worked. How clever of you both!*

I liked Stope as soon as I saw him, and I like him even more now that I have read your letter – and how beastly those furnace masters are to him. They sound like real woodhogs! Your other friends sound nice, too. Phin and Raffix . . . Oh, how I hope that one day I'll get to meet them all.

You won't forget me, will you, Quint, when you're a high and mighty knight academic up there in your beautiful floating city? I can hardly believe I've just written 'your'

216

*floating city, when once I thought of it as 'my' floating city.
Yet it seems so far away now . . .*

*Still, it was lovely to hear how well you're doing. I'm sure
you will be one of the squires sent up to the Upper Halls. But
even if you're not, Quint, it is a great honour to be an
academic-at-arms, so you mustn't be too disappointed.*

*I'm sorry the hall masters you liked are in disgrace –
especially poor Philius Embertine. He was a great friend of
Father's and I'm so sad that he is ill. Hax Vostillix always was
too proud for his own good, at least that's what Father used to
say. Which brings me to the point of this letter.*

Vilnix glanced involuntarily towards the little door of
his sleeping closet, just to make sure that no-one had followed him up the ladder and was, even now, peeking
through the gap. Then, shifting round where he sat, he
pulled the lamp a little closer.

*You know I told you how Heft and Dacia, my so-called
guardians, were always pestering Father for favours because
he was the Most High Academe, and they were related? Well,
it seems that a tilder doesn't change its stripes!*

*Heft's latest trick was to try and get the Professors of Light
and Darkness to make him Master of the Treadmills on the
East and West Landings. I know this, because he forced me to
sign the barkscroll that he sent to them. You should have seen
it, Quint! Heft went on about how they owed it to the
guardian of Linius Pallitax's only child to make sure that he
could look after her in the manner to which she was accustomed.*

*If they only knew that I'm locked up in an icy room all day,
and hardly ever allowed out!*

Well, of course, the professors were having none of it. They wrote back and told Heft politely that, while I had their express permission to visit Sanctaphrax any time I liked, no special favours could be accorded to my guardian. And what's more, that reports of Heft's cruelty to the hammelhorns he owned in Undertown showed he was not to be trusted with any creatures, especially the prowlgrins and giant fromps working on the treadmills.

That last bit really made Heft mad! He said that he'd get even with the twin Most High Academes if it was the last thing he did, and then he locked me in my room as if it was all my fault! Though not before muttering something about his good friend, Daxiel Xaxis, and how it was time to teach those high and mighty academics a lesson . . .

Isn't Daxiel Xaxis the Captain of the Gatekeepers? And doesn't he work for Hax Vostillix?

Heft is up to something, Quint, I'm sure of it. And whatever it is, it has something to do with that Knights Academy of yours.

Meanwhile, I'm stuck in this freezing room without even my little lemkin for company. I'll try to get this letter to Welma somehow. Please think of me, Quint, and write soon,

Your friend, Maris.

P.S. I think that squire, Vilnix Pompolnius, sounds horrible! But perhaps you're right, and he is just lonely and insecure and needs a friend. You try to see the best in everyone, Quint. That's what makes you such a good friend.

The colour drained from Vilnix's face. 'Horrible?' Lonely and insecure?' he muttered. 'Needs a friend?

At last, the exact reason why he hated Quintinius

Verginix so much was beginning to dawn on him. It wasn't that he was such a goody-goody, or sucked up to the professors, or even that he was best friends with the snooty daughter of none other than Linius Pallitax himself.

No, what Vilnix really hated; what he loathed with a fury that even now was clenching his stomach into knots and made his heart thud sickeningly in his chest, was the fact that Quint felt sorry for him. That he returned his hatred with pity!

Pity!

The insolence! The nerve! How dare he?

Tears of fury sprang to Vilnix's eyes. He hadn't come this far to fall for the oldest trick in the book. Friendship was for failures and weaklings. Where there was friendship, there was betrayal . . .

Slowly, Vilnix began tearing the barkscroll into very small pieces. And with each rip, he felt a little better, until a broad grin was plastered across his face – and the barkscroll letter was little more than sawdust on the tilderwool blanket.

'So, Quintinius Verginix,' Vilnix said, his voice a rasping whisper. 'You want to make friends, do you?'

·CHAPTER FOURTEEN·

THE FORGER

Ferule Gleet drew his grubby, paint-spattered robes of 'viaduct' blue tightly round his thin, angular body and shivered. It was freezing in the cluttered tower of the School of Colour and Light Studies, and had been for so long that the cold seemed to have seeped through his pores, chilling him to the marrow and making his joints stiff and painful.

But then, thought the old academic, he was no worse off than anyone else. It was freezing everywhere in Sanctaphrax these days.

It didn't help, of course, that several of the tiny diamond-shaped panes of glass in his leaded windows were cracked or missing completely, allowing the icy wind to whistle through the gaps; nor that the fire in his lufwood stove had gone out hours earlier. He'd run out of logs to burn, and given the exorbitant price of wood these days, it would be a while before he could afford to buy any more to light a new one.

He sighed, and rubbed his hands together, the fingerless gloves he was wearing rasping softly.

The trouble was, every last bit of timber was needed for those great burners which had been suspended from the East and West Landings. All that was left for the academics to keep themselves warm were chippings and splinters, and assorted fragments of bark that made more smoke than heat. Why, only the other day, Ferule had been so desperate he'd actually burned several wood panels that he'd prepared for portraits.

It was madness, he knew, for without wood panels to paint on, he'd lose his livelihood. But he was desperate. Then again, wasn't that exactly what they were doing with those huge log burners – desperately burning timber in order to buy time for the Knights Academic to find stormphrax?

Ferule crossed the studio to the window and rubbed the jagged patterns of frost from the glass. He put an eye to the small circle he'd made, like a spy at a keyhole, and peered out.

No stormchasing voyage today, he noted, as he surveyed the yellowy grey, snow-filled sky. It was far too cold. Mind you, he thought, that didn't always stop them. Sighing wearily, he sat back down at his easel and shook his head.

It had all seemed so promising when Screedius Tollinix had set off aboard the *Windcutter*. Now there was a *real* knight academic for you! The finest in the academy . . .

Yet that had been three long months ago and, despite the inevitable rumours of sightings and stories of what might or might not have happened, there had been no concrete news of his well-being or whereabouts since then. The great Screedius and his magnificent sky ship had simply vanished into the heart of the Great Storm, never to be seen again.

And he was just the first of many knights academic to depart. Every time the dark anvil clouds boiled up and the air filled with sourmist particles, another one of them had been selected to sail forth. All of the original thirteen knights academic-in-waiting had now gone, with Screedius Tollinix the only one of them who had got even close. As for the others – Hophix, Dantius, Queritis, Phlax, Willandis, Xallix, and all the rest – their sky ships had turned turvey within minutes of launching into the air.

It was the flight-rocks. They just couldn't be controlled in this awful cold. And after poor old Xallix Flint's sky ship, the *Misthawk*, had shot straight up into Open Sky in front of the horrified crowds assembled on the Viaduct Steps, Ferule

223

had stopped going to the launches altogether. They could ring that bell on the Great Hall all they liked, but he for one had lost his appetite for the spectacle.

These days, it seemed, all it took was a whiff of sour-mist for that crazy hall master, Hax Vostillix, to order another stormchasing voyage. Why, those they were now sending were little more than squires, newly-knighted and still wet behind the ears. But then the Knights Academy was desperate – and it was a desper-ation shared by every single inhabitant of the great floating city, from the twin Most High Academes down to the lowliest minor-school servant.

And with lufwood logs at eight gold pieces a bundle, thought Ferule, rubbing a bony hand thoughtfully over his jutting jaw, who could blame them?

Just then, a thin tinkling sound broke the silence and Ferule's pale yellow eyes looked up at the small silver bell on the wall above him. It twitched as the bell-pull was yanked again and, with a weary sigh, Ferule climbed to his feet and made for the tower's spiral staircase.

'Who in Sky's name can *that* be?' he grumbled as he descended the stone stairs, made slippery by a layer of frost.

Ferule had no portrait sitters arranged for this late in the day, and he was certain there were no 'special' commissions due just at the moment. The bell tinkled a third time.

'Yes, yes, I'm coming,' he grumbled. 'Hold your prowlgrins!'

Reaching the front door, he pulled back the heavy bolts, top and bottom, and drew it open an inch, before pressing one yellow eye to the gap. A thin, sallow-faced youth dressed in the white cloak of a Knights Academy squire stood glaring back at him through a pair of tinted snow-goggles.

'Yes? Can I help you?' asked Ferule suspiciously. 'There's no fuel here, if that's what you're after.'

'Do I look like a timber scrounger?' said the youth, fixing the academic with a contemptuous look. 'I'm here on behalf of a good friend of mine. I believe you're amending his sword miniature . . .'

'You'd better come in,' said Ferule, opening the door a little further, and ushering the squire impatiently inside. 'Scrape that snow off your boots before you come up, there's a good squire,' he said. 'Oh, and you can keep your cloak on. The stove's not lit today.'

The squire did as he was told, stamping his feet, before following the painter up the stairs to the studio. As he emerged at the top, he took a sharp intake of breath. The room was crammed so full, there was scarcely room to turn round.

There were cupboards, cabinets and chests of drawers, and rows of shelves lining the walls, each one bowing in the middle under the weight of the countless objects crammed onto them.

Hundreds of jars, half-filled with heady solvents and viscous oils, and with brushes sticking out of the top, stood in rows. There were bottles and boxes, each one containing powders and pastes, and the vast array of ingredients in labelled jars that the painter used to create his range of pigments – as well as the stone mortars he mixed them in, and the heavy pestles to grind them.

Blood-beetles. Yellowbait. Emerald tics. Ambersap. The dried purple and magenta petals of swirewort and wintleweed, and the lesser spangleshrub's indigo roots. There were drawerfuls of crumbly rocks, excavated from marshy areas in the Deepwoods, that produced innumerable subtle shades of ochre and orange. And lullabee embers, that yielded the blackest of blacks.

Then there were the tools of his trade. The brushes and spatulas, the scrapers and scratchers, the sticks of charcoal and lumps of chalk. Pastels, crayons, inks and dyes; stacks of sketchbooks and heaps of canvas nailed to their frames. And, filling up the centre of the room, the props and backcloths the artist used to compose his portraits, as well as the tall rickety easels, with paintings in various states of completion balanced upon them.

'Now, this friend of yours,' said Ferule, as he picked his way across the cluttered room to his even more cluttered workbench, 'does he have a name?'

'Here,' said the squire, thrusting a scrap of barkscroll at him. Ferule took the scroll and scrutinized the clear, beautifully-formed handwriting on its smooth surface.

Quintinius Verginix, he read, as the sallow-faced squire continued to look round, *Lower Hall squire of the Knights Academy, requests the return of his sword miniature furnished to Professor Ferule Gleet of the School of Colour and Light Studies for amendment – namely the addition to the background of the tower of the Loftus Observatory, symbol of the squire's mentor, the twin Most High Academe, the Professor of Light, payment of three gold pieces having been supplied.*

'Ah, yes,' said Ferule at last, his pale yellow eyes looking the squire up and down. 'I remember the lad. Friend of yours, you say . . .'

'That's right,' said the youth, making no move to take off either the tinted snow-goggles or the thick scarf that covered half his face.

'And you are?' asked Ferule quietly, as he bent over to examine the minia-tures spread out on the workbench before him.

'Just a good friend,' replied the squire. 'Quintinius Verginix has been chosen to ascend to the Upper Halls of the Knights Academy,' he went on, 'and I'm sure you know what *that* means . . .'

Ferule gave a low chuckle, picked up a miniature from the workbench and examined it carefully.

'Indeed I do, young squire. Indeed I do. This noble-looking young friend of yours, so splendid in his shining armour, will one day become a knight academic . . .'

He held the miniature of Quint up to the light, between a thumb and a forefinger.

'First time I clapped eyes on him, I knew,' he said. 'It was something to do with the way he held himself – and the questing expression in those deep indigo eyes of his, as dark as the stormclouds rolling in from beyond the Edge themselves . . .'

The squire watched impatiently as Ferule's own pale eyes glazed over thoughtfully.

'I can just see him now, passing up from the Lower to the Upper Halls,' he said, the trace of a smile on his lips. 'Bowing to the hall masters at the foot of the staircase, saying goodbye to the other squires who have just become academics-at-arms – and are all trying to hide their disappointment . . . Then climbing the great Central Staircase to present his sword, hilt first, to the High Professors of the Upper Halls.' He paused. 'When *is* the Elevation Ceremony?'

'Soon,' said the squire smoothly. 'Very soon.' He held out a gloved hand, and Ferule carefully placed the miniature of Quint in it. The squire's fingers closed around it. '. . . Which brings me,' he continued, 'to the second, and rather more delicate, part of my errand.'

'Delicate?' said Ferule suspiciously.

The squire smiled as he placed the miniature in an

inside pocket of his cloak and drew out a small leather pouch.

'Quintinius Verginix is extremely busy preparing for his elevation, as I'm sure you'll understand . . .'

He untied the drawstring that fastened the pouch, and allowed its contents to fall open on the painter's workbench. A cluster of marsh-gems twinkled up at Ferule. There were jewels there for enough logs to keep his stove blazing for many, many months.

'Tell me more,' the painter said with a smile.

'He has a very close friend in Undertown who is desperate to hear from him,' the young squire went on, 'but he simply hasn't the time to write to her. Of course, *I* could write on his behalf, but just think how cold and impersonal that would seem to her . . .'

'Her?' said Ferule, counting the marsh-gems greedily with his yellow eyes.

'It would be a little deception, but I don't suppose, if I gave you a few scribbled words . . .' The squire pulled a second barkscroll from his cloak.

'. . . That *I* could supply that personal touch?' said Ferule with a smile.

The squire nodded. 'You read my mind,' he said, handing Ferule the scroll.

The painter looked from Quint's beautifully lettered barkscroll to the second barkscroll, which was covered in a thin, spidery scrawl – and then at the squire.

'Come back tomorrow night,' he said. 'I'll have it ready for you then.'

'It must be convincing,' the squire said, turning to go. 'She must believe it came from Quintinius . . .'

'Leave it with me,' smiled Ferule, scooping up the marsh-gems. 'When I'm finished, not even Quintinius himself will be able to swear that it's not his own hand-writing.'

The painter followed the squire down the stone stair-case and opened the door. The squire pulled his cloak around him and stepped into the numbing blizzard outside. Behind him, Ferule closed and bolted the door, before climbing the stairs once more. He had a long night's work ahead of him. After all, the young squire had paid for his very best work.

'How fortunate young Quintinius is,' he cackled sarcastically to himself, 'to have such a *very* good friend.'

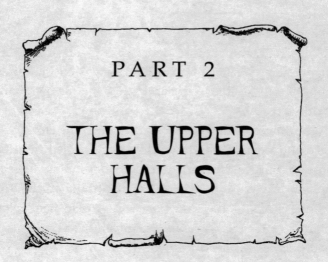

PART 2

THE UPPER
HALLS

·CHAPTER FIFTEEN·

THE SWORD MINIATURE

Quint took a deep breath and began to climb the great blackwood staircase. Beside him, he could hear Vilnix, his breath coming in short rasping gasps.

Beneath Quint's hand, the ornately carved banister felt smooth and cold to the touch. Even in the gloomy light, he could pick out extraordinary details in the bulbous black spindles and the carved treads and risers of the steps. Writhing hover worms bared their curling suckers, ornate quarms peered from behind carved clusters of delberries, while intricately coiling tarry-vines – their life-like tendrils seemingly searching for warm-blooded prey – snaked their way from tread to tread beneath his feet.

Quint desperately wanted to look back, but he knew he must fight the temptation. Squires who were elevated to the Upper Halls didn't look back. They kept their backs straight, their heads up and their eyes focused on the blackwood staircase winding its way up to the halls above.

Below him on the Central Landing, halfway between the Upper and Lower Halls, were all the other squires – Tonsor, Quiltis, and of course his best friend, Phin. A heavy lump rose in Quint's throat. After all the time they'd spent together in the Lower Halls, the laughs they'd had and adventures they'd shared, their parting had seemed so abrupt. Quint sighed. He could hear the sound of his friends' heavy boots retreating as they descended the staircase to begin their careers as academics-at-arms in the Academy Barracks below.

Two days earlier, it had all seemed so exciting when the cry went up that the graduation scroll had been posted. Immediately, all the squires had clustered round the newel post at the foot of the Central Staircase, good-naturedly jostling and shoving one another in their attempts to scrutinize the list.

'Look! Look!' Tonsor had shouted excitedly.

'I would do, if you'd just move your fat head for a moment,' Quiltis had laughed, pushing his friend out of the way to get a better look.

'The swivel catapults! Both of us! We've been assigned to the swivel catapults!' Tonsor had hugged his friend delightedly.

Phin had been peering to see over their heads. 'Yes!' he'd cried, when he saw his name. 'Belphinius Mendellix: Apprentice Swordmaster! And look, there's you, Quint,' he'd said, excitedly pulling Quint by the arm to the front of the jostling crowd of squires.

Quint's gaze had fallen on his own name, the words *Upper Halls – Knight's Squire* written beside it in neat, italic letters, and had felt his stomach lurch.

'What's wrong?' Phin had asked, when he saw his face. 'Isn't this what you always wanted?'

'It's not that,' Quint had replied quietly. 'It's just . . . Well, you'll be an academic-at-arms, and I'll be an Upper Hall squire . . .'

'We'll still see each other,' Phin had laughed, 'in the Eightways.' He slapped Quint on the shoulder. 'After all, even high-and-mighty Upper Hall squires have to eat!'

'Yes, but look . . .' Quint had pointed to the graduation scroll. Phin had narrowed his eyes and peered at the list.

'I don't believe it!' he'd gasped. 'Vilnix Pompolnius . . .'

'Upper Halls – Apprentice High Professor,' came a thin, sneering voice.

They had turned to see Vilnix standing behind them, with an unpleasant smirk on his face.

'Actually, Vilnix . . .' Quint had begun, pointing to the scroll, but a bony hand had shot out and seized him by the sleeve and he'd found himself being led away by the thin squire.

'We Upper Hall squires really ought to stick together, don't you think, Quint?' Vilnix had said in a wheedling voice, ignoring Phin completely. 'Now, I hear you have still to pick up your sword miniature from the School of Colour and Light Studies. Tut! Tut!' He'd shaken his head. 'Lucky for you, Quint, that you've got me looking out for you. After all, that's what friends are for.'

Vilnix, his friend! Who would have thought it? Quint snapped out of his daydream with a jolt. They were halfway up the staircase and the shadows were deepening. He cast a sideways look at the squire climbing the blackwood staircase beside him. Yet that was exactly what Vilnix seemed to think he was.

Quint didn't like to admit it, but there was something about Vilnix's sneering smile and wolfish grin that made his flesh crawl. That, and Vilnix's habit of sucking up to Hax Vostillix at every opportunity . . . After all, how else had he managed to be elevated to the Upper Halls? Vilnix was grinning now, Quint saw with a shudder, his face resembling that of the carved woodwolf they'd just passed on the stairs.

Strange, Quint thought as his mind began to wander again, that ever since that afternoon when Screedius Tollinix had set sail on the *Windcutter*, Vilnix's attitude to him had seemed to change. From that day on, the sour-faced squire always seemed to be hanging around, greeting him, chatting to him, offering to do him small favours.

At first, Quint had been suspicious, half-expecting Vilnix to trick him or get him into trouble with Hax. But as the months had gone by Quint had to admit that, despite his creepy ways and hostility towards the other squires, Vilnix actually did seem to want to be his friend – whether he liked it or not.

Take that incident just the other day with his sword miniature, for instance. Vilnix had absolutely insisted on picking it up for him, even though it had been blowing a blizzard outside. Quint shook his head. It wasn't as though there was any need; there had been plenty of time for him to pick it up himself before the Elevation Ceremony. But Vilnix simply wouldn't take 'no' for an answer, pestering Quint to write an explanatory note to the painter and then cooing delightedly over his beautiful handwriting when he'd done so.

Oh, yes, that Vilnix Pompolnius was a strange one, all right . . .

But what was that?

Quint snapped out of his reverie. Below them, there came the sound of raised voices from the Central Landing. Quint recognized the loudest voice – deep, guttural, with a slight lisp . . .

It belonged to the leader-elect of the academics-at-arms, Dengreeve Yellowtusk. He was a tall, rangy tufted goblin; a swordmaster with a tunic covered in the red 'duelling patches' that showed his prowess with the sword. Dengreeve was a hero-figure to Phin, and Quint had seen him many times in the Eightways.

'Has it come to this!' The swordmaster's voice sailed up to Quint and Vilnix as they continued up the staircase. 'Are the forges of the academy serving gatekeepers ahead of academics-at-arms now?'

'My gatekeepers need more weapons!' Daxiel Xaxis's voice rang out defiantly. 'To defend the academy!'

'Insolent fromp!' Dengreeve barked. 'The academics-at-arms defend *all* of Sanctaphrax, and what weapons the forges produce are ours, as of right!'

'As the only remaining hall master, *I* am the authority here!' Hax Vostillix's voice joined the argument.

Quint could see Vilnix's white-fanged smile out of the corner of his eye as they climbed on, but he kept his head up and his gaze forward.

'The Elevation Ceremony is no place for such arguments!' the hall master hissed. 'But the gatekeepers must have what they require . . .'

'This is outrageous!' Dengreeve bellowed – but Hax must have raised his staff to dismiss the swordmaster, because the next thing Quint heard was the sound of angry footsteps clattering down the staircase to the Lower Halls.

He and Vilnix were now approaching the top of the staircase, and in the deep shadows ahead of him Quint looked up to see a magnificent blackwood arch. It was formed from two mighty carved banderbears who were positioned on either side of the staircase, their great arms raised above their heads and joined at the top.

Every tusk, every claw, every tooth, every hair on their bodies, had been carved with such exquisite detail and accuracy that Quint had to look twice to convince himself that the great beasts weren't real.

This was it. With his heart in his mouth, Quint stepped through the archway and into the vast, echoey Common Hall of the Upper Halls.

The walls were lined with ornately patterned panels, from the wooden-tiled floor right up to the great vaulted beams that spanned the ceiling. The afternoon sun pierced the high shuttered windows, sending shafts of glittering light diagonally through the air. Ahead of them, sprouting from the floor like mighty lullabee trees in a Deepwoods

grove were the Common Hall pulpits.

Raffix had told Quint about them, but nothing he'd said had quite prepared Quint for the sight before him. Each pulpit had been carved with unique patterns; a cornucopia of circles and spirals, whorls, wheels, flutes and volutes. Thirty strides tall, they stood, with dais-like platforms at the top, accessible only by flimsy ladders, where forty or so squires and professors could gather at a time.

It was here that the great theories of sky-flight had been hammered out, breakthroughs in stormchasing discussed, and fantastic notions dreamt up and put to the test. The hairs on the back of Quint's neck stood on end. This was the heart of the Knights Academy and it was every bit as magnificent as he had hoped it would be.

Just then, he felt a sharp dig in the ribs. It was Vilnix. He nodded towards the huge pulpit in front of them, which was illuminated by a glittering shaft of light. The pulpits on either side of it were crowded with squires all peering down at them, while the one in front held the thirteen knights academic-in-waiting and the thirteen high professors.

Quint recognized several of the high professors from their visits to lecture in the Lower Halls. There was grim-faced Graydle Flax and the smiling Fluvius Hume. Others, he knew only by reputation. Fabius Dydex, for example, was unmistakable.

The most brilliant scholar of his generation, Fabius would have been a great knight academic, but for a leg crippled in a riding accident. He used a silverwood cane, rumoured to contain a sword and – unusually for a high professor – wore upper body armour and had several duelling patches on his robes.

Everywhere he went, Fabius Dydex was accompanied by his two tame quarms, Squeak and Howler, who, even as Quint looked on, chattered from the high professor's shoulders. Many believed that Fabius was a new 'Linius Pallitax' and would one day become Most High Academe of Sanctaphrax. Quint, although a little nervous, couldn't wait to meet him.

The knights academic, on the other hand, were unfamiliar. All the old faces had long gone, to be replaced by nervous-looking senior squires, hastily knighted. They looked uncomfortable in their newly-minted armour which, despite the forge masters' best endeavours, seemed too large for their bony frames. Their faces, too, Quint thought, looked pale and drawn from the strain of awaiting their ever more desperate stormchasing voyages.

From the pulpit, Graydle Flax motioned for Quint and Vilnix to approach.

'Welcome, squires, to the Upper Halls, where all are equal in their service to Sanctaphrax,' intoned the high professor in a soft yet sonorous voice as Quint and Vilnix reached the top of the ladder and stepped into the pulpit. 'Please present your miniatures.'

Their hands shaking with nerves and excitement, the two squires reached for the tilderleather pouches at their belts, and removed their tiny lufwood portraits. They held them out to the high professors and knights academic, who gathered round.

In the palm of his hand, Quint's portrait seemed

almost to glow as he looked down at it. How young he looked, despite the shiny armour; how optimistic and carefree, despite the dark intensity in his indigo eyes. Behind his head, the Loftus Observatory glinted against the snowy background.

Quint smiled. He had made it to the Upper Halls! And who knows, he thought, one day maybe he too could become a knight academic.

Next to him, Vilnix looked down at the portrait in his hand. The artist had captured the thin determined mouth with its hint of an upward curl. The eyes were dark and narrowed, as if against the light, and the lower jaw was thrust defiantly forward.

As he waited for the high professor to continue, Vilnix smirked. Now at last, he could really begin to show these haughty knights academic and high professors a thing or two. First as an apprentice high professor, then a high professor, and then . . .

'Now present your swords,' Graydle said in his calm, hushed voice.

Quint drew out the heavy, curved sky pirate sword that his father, Wind Jackal, had given him, and a wave of pride mixed with sadness washed over him. If only his father could be here to witness this, he thought.

Vilnix drew the thin rapier from the scabbard at his belt, the razor-sharp blade making hardly a sound as it slid out. An intense feeling of expectation mingled with delicious malice lit up his eyes.

He was hungry for power, and these fools were giving him the keys to the larder!

Two knights academic stepped forward carrying small glowing braziers suspended by silver chains in their gauntleted hands. Each contained a thimble of glowing ironwood sap, bubbling in the flames. Graydle took the lufwood miniatures and applied the ironwood sap to their unpainted sides, filling Quint's nostrils with the smell of toasting pine cones as he did so. Then, taking care to align them, the high professor pressed the portraits gently into place on the pommel of each sword.

'Welcome, Quintinius Verginix, knight's squire,' he smiled.

'Welcome,' the knights and high professors echoed his words.

'Welcome, Vilnix Pompolnius, knight's squire.' Graydle fixed the squire with a level, unblinking gaze.

Vilnix's smirk froze on his face.

Had he misheard? A knight's squire? But he was supposed to be an apprentice high professor ...

'Welcome,' the knights and high professors' voices sounded as one.

'Y ... you're mistaken ... surely ...' stuttered Vilnix, his face turning ashen grey. 'The Hall Master of High Cloud promised me a high professor apprenticeship ...'

'There will be no high professor apprenticeships until further notice,' said Graydle Flax gravely. 'Sanctaphrax is sorely in need of knights academic and their squires.'

Around him, the pale faces of the knights academic-in-waiting nodded solemnly.

'But Hax, he told me ...'

'The orders come from Hax Vostillix himself,' said Graydle, turning to leave. 'Here, we are all equal in our service to Sanctaphrax.'

A stunned Vilnix looked on as the knights and high professors left the pulpit one by one. His stomach knotted and a cold fury gripped him. What good was it becoming a knight's squire? That path led to a knighthood, stormchasing – and certain death. You just had to look at the faces of those stupid fools in their ill-fitting armour to see that.

Hax Vostillix had promised him a high professor apprenticeship for all the favours, all the information, all the little services he'd performed for him ... Why, Vilnix hadn't even bothered to read his name on the graduation list because it was a foregone conclusion ...

What a fool he'd been! He could see that now.

Next to him, that idiot Quint was grinning from ear to ear, actually pleased that they'd both received what amounted to a death sentence.

Well, if anyone was going to die, Vilnix thought, turning away from Quint, who was following the last of the knights down the pulpit ladder clutching that stupid ungainly sky pirate sword of his, it wasn't going to be Vilnix Pompolnius.

He narrowed his eyes as he stepped into the shaft of light that lit up the centre of the pulpit. A thin, wolfish smile spread across his face as a plan began to take shape in his mind . . . A brilliant plan. A plan worthy of that devious, lying old fraud Hax Vostillix himself!

·CHAPTER SIXTEEN·

THE CLOUDSLAYER

i
The Gantry Tower

Whumf! Whumf! Whumf! Whumf!

Quint looked up. High above him, the old sky ship strained at its tether as it circled the Gantry Tower. With each rotation, it bucked and lurched as the gusts of icy wind buffeted its ancient timbers.

Whumf! Whumf! Whumf!

The armoured figure of a knight academic-in-waiting stood on the bridge battling with the flight-levers as he struggled to control the vessel. As Quint watched, it suddenly listed to one side, and he could make out the chipped gold lettering on the old sky ship's prow: the *Cloudslayer*.

One day, thought Quint, that would be him up there training for a voyage. And, judging by the rate at which the academy was losing its knights, perhaps sooner than he imagined. Only yesterday, young Hemphix Root had been chosen as the next knight to depart, and was now waiting anxiously in his tower for Hax to confirm the arrival of the Great Storm by ringing the Great Hall bell.

Quint wondered which of the Upper Hall squires would take his place. It wouldn't be him, that much was certain, not if he couldn't even master a solo descent.

'Move, Sky curse you,' Quint grunted as he struggled with the frozen winch-lever. '*Move!*'

Beneath him, his prowlgrin – suspended in its harness from ropes which hung down from the gantry pole above – squirmed and kicked out. Tash was a fully-grown yearling now, set apart from the other Knights Academic mounts by its lustrous orange coat and magnificent chin-mane. When the gatekeepers had taken over the Hall of Grey Cloud, the Knights Academic had withdrawn their precious prowlgrins to the safety of temporary roosts in the wood stores beneath the Upper Halls. That oaf, Daxiel Xaxis, had protested but the knights and high professors had forced him to back down. Now Tash and his fellow prowlgrins were spared the punishing work on the great treadmills.

'Easy, boy,' Quint said, patting the creature reassuringly with his left hand as he continued to battle the stubborn lever with his right.

This wasn't the way it was meant to be, he thought bitterly. He'd listened intently to Fabius Dydex's lecture in the pulpit the evening before, not allowing himself to be distracted by the tame quarms that skittered and squeaked from the high professor's shoulders as he spoke.

A knight academic must harness and lower his prowlgrin and himself into the Twilight Woods, a skill mastered by long hours of practice in the Gantry Tower . . .

And so, bright and early the following morning, Quint had left his spacious study in the Upper Halls, collected Tash, and made his way to the top of the tall, wooden Gantry Tower, to do just that. He'd run through Dydex's instructions in his head, and then begun.

It had all gone well – at first.

To start with, while still on the gantry, he was to buckle his prowlgrin into the hanging-harness and attach it to a gantry pole – which he'd done. Next, he was to climb up into the saddle – which he'd done. Then, he was to spur his prowlgrin on, so that it leaped into the air from the gantry – which he'd also done. And now, hanging in the air from the projecting gantry pole, like an oozefish on the end of a fishing line, he was supposed to release the winch-lever and lower himself slowly and gracefully down the tower. But that he simply could not do.

Not that he had any intention of giving up . . . Quint twisted round and seized the lever.

'One, two, three,' he muttered grimly. 'Pull!'

He tugged at it with every ounce of strength. There was a grinding noise and a loud *crack* as the lever shot across, followed by a sudden jolt, and the rope began to feed out at last. Slowly – though since Tash was still kicking out, not very gracefully – prowlgrin and rider descended through the air.

'Easy, Tash. It's all right,' said Quint, leaning down to stroke the snorting, bucking creature round its sensitive nostrils as he continued to let the rope slip round the pulley-wheels. 'Easy there, boy.'

All at once, as the pair of them reached the halfway mark of the tall tower, the prowlgrin suddenly stopped struggling. Quint patted him warmly, realizing that his mount had been reacting neither to the dizzy height, nor to being suspended so precariously, but rather to his own agitation. Now that the winch was working and he had calmed down, Tash, too, was fine. And as he lowered himself still further, Quint could imagine the pair of them descending from his stormchasing sky ship, down into the Twilight Woods below . . .

Whumf! Whumf! Whumf!

Above him, the *Cloudslayer* juddered as it circled the Gantry Tower. Once it had been a proud sky pirate ship, soaring through the skies. But its days of plying a lucrative trade – anything from buoyant timber to illicit mire-pearls – between the Deepwoods and Undertown were long behind it. Now it was fit only to be a training vessel for young knights to perfect their skills while they awaited the delivery of their sleek new 'stormchasers' from the cradles of Undertown.

Below Quint, as the icy wind whistled through the ropes, the landing-platform at the bottom of the Gantry Tower came closer.

Now for the tricky part, thought Quint, going over the

high professor's words in his head. *Harness release must be smooth but quick, freeing the prowlgrin to land cleanly.* Quint tugged on the harness release, once, twice . . . *The worst fate that can befall a knight is to be caught in his harness, suspended above the forest floor.* Dydex had paused for a moment before continuing. *Suspended for all eternity!*

Quint shuddered and pulled desperately at the catch. It clicked open and the harness fell away, just as the rope snapped taut. With a whinny, Tash dropped to the platform on powerful legs.

'Good lad!' Quint exclaimed, quickly dismounting. 'Well done!'

He tickled the creature through its long, luxuriant mane. Tash gave a long, growling purr and rolled its eyes with pleasure.

'Why, you're just a big, soppy pup, aren't you, boy?' Quint laughed, and was about to lead the prowlgrin off the landing-platform when a high, metallic screech from above made him look up.

The *Cloudslayer* had flipped completely over and shot up directly above the Gantry Tower. The screech was coming from the chain which, now stretched almost to breaking-point, was only just managing to prevent it from disappearing into Open Sky.

As Quint anxiously watched, the knight academic tumbled down from the upturned helm, the black parawings strapped to his back billowing out like the wings of a giant ratbird. With his heavy armour accelerating the descent, it was all the knight could do to twist round and brace himself

before he crashed into the landing-platform in a flurry of snow and splintered wood.

Quint raced over to the stricken figure. He crouched down, clicked back the collar fastenings and pulled the heavy helmet from the knight's head. A familiar face smiled up at him.

'Raff?' Quint said.

The young knight sat up. 'Quint, old chap!' he exclaimed. 'Didn't see you there.' He nodded across at the prowlgrin. 'Getting in a bit of harness-practice, eh? Good show.'

'Yes, I was,' said Quint. 'But . . . but *you*, Raff. You're in full armour . . .'

Raffix grinned lop-sidedly and pushed his glasses up his nose. 'You noticed,' he said with a laugh. 'It's what all the best knights academic-in-waiting are wearing, I hear.'

'You? A knight?' Quint was taken by surprise.

'That's right, old chap,' said Raffix. 'Well, almost, that is . . .' He struggled to his feet and brushed the snow from his armour. 'When old Hemphix sets off, they've chosen yours truly to take his place as a knight academic-in-waiting.'

'But Raff—' Quint began. His friend held up a gauntleted hand to silence him.

'I know, I know,' he said, looking up at the Gantry Tower, where a group of hall servants had emerged from the upper gantry and were busy winching the upturned *Cloudslayer* back down. 'The prospects for stormchasing don't look too good, I'll concede . . .'

'Don't look too good?' Quint echoed him incredulously. 'It's madness trying to fly in this weather. You know it and I know it.' He snorted. 'The only person who doesn't seem to know it is Hax Vostillix!'

'Now, that's just where you're wrong,' said Raffix, a broad grin spreading over his face. He wiped some snow from his glasses. 'There is one other person who reckons that it's possible to control a flight-rock in this weather.'

'Who?' asked Quint.

Raffix chuckled. 'A very good friend of ours . . .'

*

ii
The Academy Barracks

The Academy Barracks were bustling. Beneath the lofty vaulted ceiling, with its clusters of hanging copperwood lamps, groups of academics-at-arms lounged in high-back armchairs of tilderleather, small buoyant tables tethered at their sides.

Some consulted cloud charts or ballistics lists, or joined in lively discussions on tactics with their colleagues in neighbouring armchairs. Some polished swords, some cleaned ornate crossbow mechanisms; some helped themselves to the contents of laden trays brought to them by the army of barracks servants, whilst others allowed their heads to nod over empty tankards of woodale.

In various parts of the great barracks hall, groups of academics-at-arms were engaged in weapon practice of all kinds, from swordplay and pikestaff drill, to knife-throwing and crossbow practice. In the centre of the hall, bathed in the light streaming in from the great circular window set into the north wall, Dengreeve Yellowtusk – swordmaster and leader elect of the academics-at-arms – threw up his hands in mock horror.

'No! No! No! Master Phin!' he exclaimed in his deep voice, with just that hint of a lisp. 'You're letting your guard down, opening yourself up to a parry from the left.'

He motioned for the young swordmaster apprentice to step aside and unsheathed his rapier. In front of him, a sumpwood dummy hovered in mid air. Dengreeve's blade swished this way and that in a blur of sudden movement, before the swordmaster stepped back and sheathed his sword.

Phin gasped. A spiral of sawdust hovered like a halo over the sumpwood dummy, which slowly listed over to one side.

'Practise, Master Phin,' laughed Dengreeve when he saw the look on the young academic's face, 'if you want a tunic full of duelling patches!'

Just then, the heavy leadwood doors at the far end of the hall burst open, and a detachment of academics-at-arms strode in, stamping the snow from their boots and unbuckling their armour and heavy cloaks. They were instantly surrounded by barracks servants, who took their snow-drenched clothes and gave them fresh robes warmed by the fire. Most settled into armchairs and called for mulled sapwine, but one of the academics-at-arms approached the swordmaster.

'It's about the catapults on the ramparts by the College of Rain,' he began.

Dengreeve dismissed Phin with a smile, and turned to greet the academic. 'I hadn't forgotten, Mardel, old friend,' he said. 'I raised the matter with the hall master just this morning.'

'Well, if those furnace masters in the forge don't overhaul the mechanisms on those catapults, and soon, then I can't ask our academics to go on operating them.' Mardel shook his head. 'It seems they can't do enough for the gatekeepers, whilst we academics-at-arms are last in line.'

Dengreeve nodded. 'Hax Vostillix can think only of these crazy stormchasing voyages,' he growled.

'Meanwhile, those gatekeepers do as they please,' added Mardel grimly. 'And talking of crazy stormchasing voyages . . .' He motioned towards the great oval window. 'There goes another one now.'

Dengreeve turned and looked up. Sure enough, rising up from the top of the viaduct, a stormchaser – the varnish on its timber still glistening wet from the ship cradles of Undertown – was setting sail.

Several academics-at-arms rose from their armchairs at the sight, but most carried on with what they were doing. Few in Sanctaphrax believed in stormchasing any longer, preferring instead to pray that the winter would end before it was too late.

From a vantage point halfway up the suspended stair-case to the study rooms, Phin peered through the glass of the oval window. On the top of the viaduct, he could just make out the ragged figure of Hax Vostillix. The hall master's arms were raised, and his robes and beard flapped in the snowflecked wind as he urged the sky ship on.

As the wind spun and the snow thickened, the sky ship faltered and shook. For one incongruous moment, it seemed almost to grind to a complete halt. An instant later, the sails slumped and the vessel flipped over, so that the mast was pointing back down to the earth. Then, as Phin looked on, the helpless sky ship – its flight-rock chilled to super buoyancy – shot up into Open Sky.

Back at the viaduct, a gaunt Hax Vostillix abruptly doubled over and clutched his head in his hands. The stocky figure of Daxiel Xaxis, Captain of the Gatekeepers, appeared at his side. He turned towards Hax, wrapped a comforting arm around his shoulder and led the broken-looking hall master away.

Phin turned away from the window. Who had it been this time? He'd heard Tonsor mention the name – that's right, Hemphix Root. Phin had seen him slumped unhappily over his hammelhorn steak in the Eightways a couple of nights earlier. Now he was gone, just like that.

Who would be next? he wondered. One day, he realized miserably, it would be his friend Quint. It was only a matter of time . . .

Phin continued up the stairs and, turning into the

corridor at the top, made his way towards his study alcove. Phin loved his alcove. Unlike the dormitory closets of the Lower Halls, where the squires slept in cupboards stacked from floor to ceiling, the academic-at-arms study alcoves were spacious and comfortable. Phin had his own floating lectern, a soft bed and more cupboard space than he knew what to do with. There was even a little lufwood stove in one corner to keep him nice and warm.

In fact, it was perfect in every respect but one. The study alcove was situated at the westward end of the Academy Barracks, where they adjoined the Hall of High Cloud – too close to Hax Vostillix for Phin's liking. But then you couldn't have everything, he told himself.

Reaching his study alcove, Phin was just about to draw back the heavy tilderwool curtain and enter, when he heard a thin, wailing cry.

'Help! Help!'

It was coming from the passage that led into the Hall of High Cloud. Phin hesitated for a moment.

'Help! Please help!'

There it was again – fragile-sounding and pathetic, but with an urgent note that Phin couldn't ignore. He turned from his alcove and headed down the unlit passage at the end of the corridor. He paused outside a small lufwood door that stood slightly ajar. The grander chambers of the High Cloud academics and that of Hax Vostillix himself were on the other side of the building, overlooking the Inner Courtyard. So far as Phin knew, the small rooms along this passage were mostly stockrooms or timber-stores . . .

'Help!'

Phin pushed open the door, and entered. In front of him, in a cluttered but freezing room, sat none other than Philius Embertine, the disgraced Hall Master of White Cloud.

He was slumped in a buoyant sumpwood chair and, instead of the familiar knight academic armour he usually wore, the old hall master was swathed in scarves, mufflers, quilted vests and padded leggings. At the foot of the sumpwood chair was a bundle of barkscrolls and an upturned tallow candle. Phin took a sharp breath. Crackling and spitting, the flames were consuming the tinder-dry barkscrolls and threatening to ignite the sumpwood chair hovering above.

'*Help!*' cried Embertine, waving the barkscroll he clutched in a mittened hand in Phin's direction.

Without another thought, Phin dashed into the room, pushed Philius's buoyant chair aside and began stamping on the blazing scrolls, extinguishing the flames.

'I was ... reading ... when ... when ...' gasped the old professor, looking up and blinking round the gloomy room as he struggled to make sense of what was going on.

'It's all right,' said Phin. 'You must have dropped your candle . . . Lucky I was passing and heard you. It could have been far worse . . .'

'Worse? Worse?' Embertine said, his brow creasing with concern. 'It'll get far, far worse soon enough!'

All at once, he leaned forwards and grabbed at the young apprentice's sleeve. He pulled him close, until Phin found himself staring deep into the old hall master's piercingly blue eyes.

'You're an academic-at-arms, aren't you?' he croaked. 'Can I *trust* you, lad? Can I?'

Phin nodded.

'You must take this scroll,' he said, thrusting the barkscroll he was clutching into Phin's hands, 'and go to my apartments in the Hall of Storm Cloud. In my bed-chamber there is a panel in the wall beside the carved quarm . . . Have you got that, lad?'

Again, Phin nodded.

'Slide the panel back,' the old knight gasped weakly. 'Behind it, you'll find a light-casket. Take it and the scroll to my good friend, Screedius Tollinix, knight academic-in-waiting. Tell him the time has come, "not to take from the sky, but to give back". *He'll* know what must be done . . .'

Phin nodded, a lump forming in his throat. Poor old Philius Embertine was as confused as ever. He didn't have the heart to tell the old hall master that Screedius Tollinix was gone, probably lost for ever out in Open Sky, like all those other knights academic who had followed after him.

'I . . . I'll see what I can do,' said Phin softly.

'Now go quickly,' Philius told him, his eyes gazing at him imploringly. 'Before they get back.' His eyes narrowed and his grip on Phin's arm tightened. 'They're in Hax's employ,' he hissed, 'and they're keeping me prisoner here.'

Phin rolled up the barkscroll and pushed it inside his robes. 'Is there anything else I can do?' he asked, pity and compassion bringing tears to his eyes.

'Just take the scroll and go to my apartments,' Philius whispered urgently. 'As quickly as you can. The future of Sanctaphrax depends on it!'

'I shall,' Phin replied as he pulled himself away and hurried from the room. Scrolls? he thought. Panels? The future of Sanctaphrax? The poor old knight academic had clearly lost his reason.

Phin had just made it to the end of the passage when he heard the sound of loud voices and heavy footsteps coming along the corridor behind him. Glancing round, he saw a couple of rough-looking gatekeepers turning into Philius's chamber.

'What in Sky's name have you been up to now, you senile old woodgoat?' one of them bellowed. 'There's ashes everywhere.'

'Can't leave you alone for a minute, can we?' roared the other. 'Do you want to be chained up?' he demanded. '*Do* you?'

Phin gulped. Maybe old Philius wasn't so confused after all, he mused.

*

iii
The Forge

The grey goblin forge-hand stared into the depths of the roaring furnace. He was wearing a heavy tilderleather apron, reinforced gloves and a tall conical forge hood, yet he could still feel the intense heat beginning to burn his skin.

'Just a little longer,' he whispered to himself, blinking away the sweat that was stinging his eyes.

In one hand he gripped a pair of long-handled tongs, in the other a thin metal taper. On the end of the taper, a ball of molten metal glowed in the furnace heat.

Taking great care, the forge-hand teased a glowing strand from the molten ball with the long-handled tongs and twisted it around and back on itself. Once, twice, three times, like a spinner teasing a strand of tilderwool into a ball, the forge-hand spun the strand of molten metal until it took on the form of an exquisite glowing cage.

This was where it usually went wrong. The intense furnace heat would become unbearable and force the forge-hand to retreat, only to see the molten cage collapse in on itself and fall to the floor to produce a useless puddle of liquid metal.

Not surprising really, if you thought about it, Stope realized. After all, the idea of spinning molten metal the way a woodspider spun a web was crazy, even *he* had to admit.

The idea had occurred to him when he'd been watching from the West Landing as the huge log burners warmed the Sanctaphrax rock. If only flight-rocks could be warmed in the same way, then perhaps those brave knights academic would stand a better chance of controlling their sky ships, Stope had thought.

He'd hurried back to the forge in the Hall of White Cloud to work on the problem. Instead of logs, which were far too cumbersome and fast burning, Stope had decided on sumpwood charcoal – light as a feather and with a slow, intense burn.

But how to encase it? That was the problem. He'd tried cage-like boxes, solid metal braziers and oval casings drilled with holes, but none of them worked properly. Either

263

they stifled the heat or they allowed the charcoal embers to fall through the bars. The answer, Stope realized, after long hours at the forge – usually late at night when the furnace masters had retired to bed – was a spherical metal cage, so fine that the heat could pass freely through, while its intricate mesh would contain the glowing sumpwood securely.

And so he'd started his metal spinning. His friend Raffix, the gangly Upper Hall squire, had encouraged him, often coming down to the forge late in the night and staying on until almost dawn, working the furnace bellows, and laughing and joking to keep his spirits up.

The heat of the furnace seared Stope's face as he forced himself to keep his eyes focused on its fiery heart. Six . . . seven . . . eight loops, he counted off. And now . . .

He leaped back from the furnace and swept the long-handled tongs round in a fiery arc, down into the quenching-trough. A loud hiss was followed by billowing clouds of acrid steam as Stope tore off his forge hood and stared down into the bubbling water. There, cooling from glowing white, to bright yellow, to intense coppery red, was an intricate cage of spun metal.

Stope held it up to the early dawn light that was now streaming in through the high, narrow windows of the forge. The metal cage glinted and glistened. A small opening secured by tiny silver hinges and a gold clasp, and it would be complete. Stope smiled delightedly. He couldn't wait to show Raffix.

He turned the cage round in the light. 'A fire float,' he whispered.

iv
The Loftus Observatory

'What was that?' the Professor of Light murmured distractedly to himself.

He looked up from the great telescope and peered round the shadowy observatory tower. He'd heard something, he was sure of it . . . But maybe it was just his imagination. That was what came of spending too long staring into Open Sky.

He'd been busy scouring the heavens for some sign of poor Hemphix Root, the latest knight academic to be dispatched to the Twilight Woods in search of stormphrax. He shook his head sadly. The sky ship had turned turvey almost at once, and been blown away into Open Sky before Hemphix had had a chance to abandon ship and parawing himself to safety.

Another brave young knight academic lost, and for what?

'To satisfy the crazed fantasies of Hax Vostillix,' the professor muttered to himself.

So far as he was concerned, there hadn't even been a hint of sourmist in the wind. But Hax wouldn't listen, and as head of the Knights Academy, it was *his* decision – not even the twin Most High Academes could overrule him.

'Madness, utter madness,' the professor grumbled as he climbed to his feet and made his way down the ladder to the Observatory Chamber below.

The moment he stepped down from the final rung,

he noticed that some-
thing was wrong. There
was a cold draught; a
banging noise ... He
turned to see that one of
the four glass-panelled
doors, each of which led
out onto individual
gantry platforms, was
flapping open.

'How did that hap-
pen?' he wondered out
loud, and tutted with irritation. 'Must be my other
half getting careless in his
old age again.'

He crossed to the door,
still muttering under his
breath about the
Professor of Darkness,
and pushed it to. There
was, he discovered,
something the matter
with the lock – as though it had been forced – and he had
to push the door firmly in order to lock it. As he did so,
his feet slipped on several metal bolts lying on the floor,
which skittered away into the shadows.

'What's the old fool up to, leaving his bits and pieces
lying about?' he said, turning away. 'I could have
slipped and broken my neck!'

Outside, the blizzard was closing in once more, with the wind blowing more ferociously that ever. The gantry platform creaked and shuddered. And, as the professor made his way slowly and carefully down the spiral flight of stairs, he grumbled to himself, unaware of the curious double echo his footsteps made, as if there were four, not two, feet on the stone steps.

·CHAPTER SEVENTEEN·

HAX

i

The Captain of the Gatekeepers

With a flourish of his thick cape – fur-trimmed and emblazoned with the red logworm insignia – Daxiel Xaxis shoved the tall arched doors of the Hall of Grey Cloud open and strutted inside. It was bitterly cold in the cavernous hall.

Since there was no timber to spare Daxiel had ordered that the braziers be left unlit. 'The prowlgrins are here to work, not to be pampered,' he'd snarled when the head stable-hand had objected. 'Take this rabble,' he'd added, pointing to the grooms, ostlers, stable-hands and byre-gillies, who were busy tending the roost pillars, 'and assign them to the treadmills!' Reluctantly, all the servants in the Hall of Grey Cloud had obeyed their new master.

It wasn't long before the warm, earthy, slightly musky smell of the stables had been replaced with a sour,

eye-watering stench – a mixture of rotten offal, rancid
fat, and old straw, putrid with prowlgrin droppings.
Daxiel Xaxis, Captain of the Gatekeepers of the Knights
Academy, never seemed to notice the smell, however. He
strode through the hall now, head up and eyes narrowed, inspecting the roost pillars above.

'What's that skewbald doing up there when there's
work to be done?' he demanded of a young stable-hand,
nodding towards a brown and white prowlgrin perched
on a low branch of a roost pillar.

'It's lame, sir,' came the reply. 'Damaged its left leg on
the treadmill last week, it did.'

Xaxis rounded angrily on the trembling stable-hand.
'Last week!' he stormed. 'How many times do I have to
tell you people? If they can't work, they're dead meat.
Understand?'

'Y . . . yes, sir,' the stable-hand replied,
on the verge of tears.

It had been so different
in the old
days, when
Hall Master
F e n v i e l
V e n d i x
had been
in charge.
Strict and
stern he
m i g h t
have been,

but it wasn't unknown for Fenviel to stay up for nights at a time tending a lame prowlgrin personally. When Daxiel Xaxis and his gatekeepers had taken over, Hax Vostillix had given them one order, and one order only. 'Keep the treadmills turning, day and night!'

Before long, the neverending labour at the East and West Landings had taken a terrible toll on the prowl-grins of the Hall of Grey Cloud, and the rigid order of the roost pillars had broken down completely. If it was to maintain a perch, every prowlgrin now had no option but to work hard, day in, day out – and the ever-grow-ing number of gatekeepers in the hall, with their logworm tunics and freshly forged weapons, made sure that they did so.

There were no more 'retirement' pillars for those crea-tures who had served Sanctaphrax, no matter how well. Any old or sick prowlgrins were simply slaughtered, becoming stew or glue, depending on their age. Neither were there sire-roosts or brood-roosts any longer. There was no time to raise and nurture pups, ensuring they grew strong and healthy, to replace the losses. Instead, to maintain numbers, prowlgrins were supplied by the leaguesmen in Undertown, who made a healthy profit from the flocks of sickly malnourished specimens they shipped up from their stinking hatching pens.

And as for the magnificent knights' pillar roost, since the original thirteen highly trained pedigree prowlgrins had departed on their ill-fated voyages, their places had been taken by increasingly young and skittish creatures, as ill at ease as their young masters.

Acknowledging the salutes of a cluster of newly-recruited gatekeepers, Xaxis left the great hall through a low arched doorway and marched briskly up the stairs on the other side. It had been a long and trying day. As if secretly building up his army of gatekeepers and getting the furnace masters to equip them with the weapons they needed wasn't enough, Daxiel had also had to run after Hax Vostillix from the moment he'd got up.

With each failed stormchasing launch, Hax felt less and less secure, and now insisted that his Captain of the Gatekeepers stayed at his side at all times. It was tiring, and a bore, Daxiel thought, especially when he had his own plans to attend to . . .

He hurried along the corridor, seized the gold handle of his blackwood door and burst into his chamber, only to be confronted by the looming figure of a leaguesman standing by the window with his back towards him. At the sound of the door slamming shut, the intruder spun round.

His face was red and sweaty, and he was wearing clothes which, though opulent, were clearly old and worn, as if the owner couldn't bring himself to replace them. The embroidered patterns on the quilted jacket were of the finest silver thread, carefully patched in numerous places, while the ruffs at his neck and cuffs were flamboyant, but frayed.

'What are *you* doing here, Heft?' Xaxis demanded, his hand moving automatically to the handle of his sword. 'I thought I told you not to come to the academy. It looks suspicious if you keep turning up . . .'

'I wouldn't have to,' said Heft Vespius, his whiny voice laced with a hint of menace, 'if you kept your side of the bargain. I've found you new gate-keepers – the meanest, toughest, fiercest tavern brawlers that Undertown has to offer. And it wasn't easy, I can tell you.' His eyes  narrowed. 'Now I want to be gangmaster of the East and West Landings, just like we agreed.'

'It's not that easy, Heft,' said Xaxis smoothly. 'You know that. This isn't Undertown, where the leagues can throw their weight around with impunity.'

He joined the fat leaguesman at the window and stared out at the snow-capped towers and spires outside.

'In Sanctaphrax, you need to watch and wait, flatter and deceive, calculate just the right moment, then . . .' He raised a gloved fist. 'Strike!'

273

Daxiel slammed the fist into Heft's flabby midriff.

'*Ooophh!*' Heft doubled up in pain and collapsed at Daxiel's feet.

'Perhaps you'll listen in future when I tell you not to come here – especially now of all times . . .'

'Why . . . now . . .?' gasped Heft, turning a red, fear-filled face up towards the Captain of the Gatekeepers.

'Because, my fat friend,' said Daxiel, with an evil sneer, 'the academics-at-arms are getting suspicious. That jumped-up little swordmaster is looking for any excuse to demand that Hax Vostillix disbands the gate-keepers, and if the Captain of the Gatekeepers is seen meeting leaguesmen in his chambers, it's just the excuse he needs.' Daxiel held out his hand and smiled grimly. 'But let's not quarrel,' he said.

Heft gingerly took the captain's outstretched hand and pulled himself sheepishly to his feet.

'If you could just see your way to having a word with Hax. Get him to make me the gangmaster,' he said in his whiny voice, 'like you promised . . .'

'Yes, yes,' said Daxiel wearily. 'Hax.'

It really was becoming irksome having to bow and scrape to the Hall Master of High Cloud, who could think only of cloudwatching and stormchasing, and who saw phantom earth-scholars hiding in every corner. He smiled humourlessly. If he was going to advance any further, there would have to be some radical changes in the Knights Academy.

'Don't worry, old friend,' Daxiel said. 'You leave Hax Vostillix to me . . .'

ii
The Swordmaster

Dengreeve Yellowtusk strode down the broad avenue past the sprawling clusters of minor academies, their spires, turrets, cupolas and balconies swathed in a thick blanket of snow. Behind him marched another twenty heavily-armed and armoured academics-at-arms.

Snow had fallen throughout the hours of daylight, with the clouds clearing and the temperature plummeting at dusk. Now, the billowing drifts had frozen solid, and resembled nothing so much as great marble quilts. The sound of the academics-at-arms' heavy boots, creaking and crunching in the hard snow, bounced back and forth from building

275

to building. A hundred strides on, the avenue opened up into a wide square, fringed with more schools – Sleet, Squall, Whirlwind, Dawn and Hailstones – and at the far end, an imposing stone emplacement built into the city wall.

Dengreeve Yellowtusk, swordmaster and leader elect of the academics-at-arms of the Knights Academy, crossed the snowy square and climbed the stairs to the top of the emplacement. There, like the bones of some giant creature, was a heap of splintered struts, supports and beams – all that remained of the two-seat swivel catapult which had once formed part of the great float-ing city's defences. Beside it, his gloved hands resting on the parapet wall as he stared down, was a solitary aca-demic-at-arms.

At the sound of the swordmaster's footsteps, the aca-demic started back and spun round. He was little more than a callow youth; gaunt, pale and hollow-eyed, dis-tress distorting his even features. A look of recognition flashed across his face.

'Swordmaster,' he said, his expression brightening up for a moment. 'Thank Sky you've come.'

'What happened, academic?' said Dengreeve.

'Happened?' he said blankly. 'It was so sudden . . .' He swallowed. 'The . . . the catapult . . . It just snapped . . . They didn't stand a chance, either of them . . .'

'It's all right, son,' Dengreeve said, his voice low and reassuringly calm. He'd seen shock like this before in academics-at-arms who had seen action; the blank expression, the stuttering words . . . He set the contin-gent of academics-at-arms he'd brought with him to the task of picking through the wreckage of the giant cata-pult. Then, stepping forwards, he gripped the young academic by the shoulders. 'Wendip, isn't it?' he said. 'Wendip Throx, if I'm not mistaken.'

Dengreeve Yellowtusk prided himself on knowing the names of all the academics-at-arms in the Academy Barracks. The youth nodded.

'Well, I want you to start at the beginning, Wendip,' said the great tufted goblin, 'and tell me everything that happened. In your own time . . .'

The young academic nodded bravely, and sniffed. 'It was approaching eight hours,' he said, 'and we were almost at the end of our watch.' He sniffed again. 'We'd had a pretty uneventful day all told, and were looking for-ward to getting warm and having a good meal in the . . .' He paused, his face crumpling up as tears threatened to overwhelm him. '. . . in the Eightways.'

'Carry on,' Dengreeve Yellowtusk told him firmly.

'I was on look-out,' the youth continued. 'The other two were seated at the catapult . . . We hadn't been able to do much all day, what with the blizzards and all. But when it stopped, we decided . . . well, we thought . . . Just for a laugh . . .'

'Yes?' said Dengreeve gravely.

'Well, sir, we thought we'd have a bit of firing practice. Just a few shots . . . To make sure the spring mechanism and angle-aligners were all working properly.'

'And what exactly were you intending to practise with?' said Dengreeve. 'Your supply of cliff rocks, maybe? Or the flaming leadwood balls over there?'

'No, sir,' said Wendip. 'Of course not! We wouldn't waste real ammunition . . .' He hung his head.

'So what was it then, Wendip?' Dengreeve asked.

'Snowballs,' the young apprentice replied quietly.

The swordmaster shook his head. It wouldn't be the first time since the bad weather had struck that the young academics-at-arms on guard-duty had been caught using the great swivel catapults to indulge in snowball fights, hurling the great balls of snow and ice out into the sky over the Edge.

'And then what happened?' he said.

'As I said, sir, something just snapped,' Wendip said. 'There was a loud crack. I turned round, and saw the catapult arm fly off its mounting, taking Tonsor and Quiltis with it . . .' He shook his head. 'They never stood a chance.'

Just then a cry went up from the heap of splintered wood and twisted metal. Dengreeve and Wendip looked round to see one of the academics-at-arms kneeling in the midst of it all, one arm raised, and a large metal bolt glinting in his fingers.

'I've found it, sir,' he announced. He climbed to his feet and took it to the swordmaster for him to inspect. 'It's one of the mounting-bolts,' he announced. 'It's old and worn. Should have been replaced – an accident waiting to happen . . .'

The colour drained from Dengreeve Yellowtusk's face. 'I asked those furnace masters in the Hall of White Cloud,' he growled. 'I pleaded with them. The catapults need a complete overhaul, I said; replacing, if need be . . . But no, they were too busy supplying the gatekeepers' every request!'

He slammed his fist down on the parapet, dislodging a flurry of snow. Tonsor Wexis and Quiltis Wistelweb? Dengreeve's blood began to boil as he recollected the two young academics-at-arms. They'd only just come from the Lower Halls. Inseparable they were, full of life and laughter; delighted they'd been assigned to serve on the swivel catapults together – and just look where it had got them.

The swordmaster's eyes blazed as they scanned the void beyond the Edge. The furnace masters had ignored the academics-at-arms in favour of the gatekeepers because that jumped-up gatekeeper captain had ordered them to – and everybody knew who Daxiel Xaxis's master was . . .

The academics-at-arms were all staring at the swordmaster now, the looks on their faces showing clearly that they shared his anger. Dengreeve gave way to his mounting fury.

'Hax Vostillix!' he shouted at the darkening sky. 'You will pay for this! Two brave academics-at-arms are dead! As Sky is my witness, you will pay!'

iii

The Former Hall Master of Grey Cloud

Fenviel lowered his dark goggles, pulled the hood of his cape up over his head and slipped out from the shadows of the archway. Keeping close to the wall, he made his way towards the huge wooden wheel at the end of the East Landing.

Despite the goggles, Fenviel Vendix, former Hall Master of Grey Cloud, raised his hand to shield his eyes as he drew closer. The sun had only just set, and the distant horizon curdled and swirled with bright, turbulent cloud. There would be more snow before the night was through, that much was certain. The prowlgrins and giant fromps would have to work hard that night, raising and lowering the mighty log burners to maintain the warmth of the great floating rock.

Ahead of him, they were working now. Eighty prowlgrins and two giant fromps, all in harness, marching ceaselessly, driving the great barrel-shaped wheel round and round. As it turned, so the boards creaked and groaned, and the axle bearings squealed. Each revolution of the great

wheel caused the log burner to descend thirty strides. It continued down until the rope had all been paid out when, at a cry from below, the hoist-lever at the side of the wheel was wrenched across, the mounting-reel flipped over, and the rope began to pull the burner up again.

Fenviel paused behind one of the basket-posts and eyed the prowlgrins sadly. The poor creatures were being worked to death. Already so many of his favourites from the roost pillars were gone, while their replacements from Undertown were faring no better. Their coats were dull, their ribs stuck out and there were scars and running sores across their backs from the constant whippings and beatings they were given. Undernourished and ill-treated, they were – why, he'd even heard that the stables they dragged themselves back to were now unheated.

'Mind your backs!' bellowed a voice from behind him. *'Get out of the way!'*

He turned to see a fresh contingent of prowlgrins being driven along the landing towards him by a group of stable-hands and grooms from the Hall of Grey Cloud. Watching them closely were the gatekeepers. It was they who were barking out the commands. Each of them had a whip in one hand and a riding crop in the other, which they weren't afraid to use – both on the creatures and on those looking after them.

'Get over there, Sky damn you!' shouted a tall, stocky gatekeeper with a flat, brutal face and lop-ears, and he slashed his crop at the scarred rear of a grey prowlgrin.

Fenviel winced as if he'd been struck himself. The creature let out a plaintive cry and scampered over towards the others.

The next moment, a loud klaxon sounded, the rasping noise cutting through the air like a rusty blade. The day shift was about to give way to the night shift. It was followed at once by the barks and howls of the prowlgrins in the treadmill who, recognizing the noise, knew that it signalled the end of their toil – at least for a while.

As they were unhitched from their harnesses and led back onto the landing, their places were taken by the prowlgrins that had just been brought up from the roost perches. The operation was carried out in a chaotic scramble of exhausted prowlgrins, stumbling and pushing against each other as they were beaten and bellowed at by the oafish gatekeepers.

Meanwhile above them, the two giant fromps – who were forced to do two shifts to each of the prowlgrin's one, and were only halfway through their day's work – looked round bleakly, and, raising their trunk-like snouts, hooted mournfully. Their feathery ears hung limply at the sides of their heads, while their once-sleek dappled coats were drab and mangy, and covered in patches of red-raw skin where the rough harnesses chafed.

'Keep going!' one of the gatekeepers roared, and struck the giant fromps viciously on their backs. 'Keep going!'

Fenviel Vendix looked on, impotent rage boiling up inside him. The huge creatures were famously mild-

mannered and biddable and, in the right hands, would need only the gentlest of coaxing to do as they were asked. Out in the Deepwoods, they were used in construction work high up in the ironwood glades and, handled by tree goblins, were also used to harvest lullabee grubs, the prized delicacies which, when roasted, yielded a purple juice that induced dream-filled sleep.

He knew, too, that sometimes the tree goblins used giant fromps in battle, where they proved themselves to be wily and fearless fighters. And as he watched, Fenviel wished with all his heart that these fromps would also fight – that they would rise up against their tormentors and tear them limb from limb . . . But it would never happen, Fenviel realized. The poor, miserable creatures before him were too cowed, their spirit crushed by the continual beatings.

'Yow-wah-aiii-aiii-aiii . . .'

All at once, a cry went up. One of the prowlgrins – tired and hungry and disorientated after so many hours of turning the wheel – had stumbled as it stepped off the treadmill, and collapsed. A gatekeeper stood over the fallen creature, cursing loudly and lashing out with his whip, causing it to yelp with pain.

All round it, the other prowlgrins skittered about nervously, their eyes rolling in their great heads as they reared up and pawed at the air. The stable-hands gripped their reins and tried their best to calm them down and lead them away.

'I'll show you, you lazy, stinking, good-for-nothing beast!' shouted the gatekeeper, raising his whip high above his head.

Fenviel strode up to the treadmill, his riding crop clutched in a white-knuckled fist. How dare these vicious, violent oafs treat *any* living creature in such a way. But especially his beloved prowlgrins! It was barbaric. Inexcusable. Intolerable . . .

'Stand back,' he barked.

The gatekeeper spun round to confront the insolent stable-hand who had had the nerve to challenge him. Fenviel Vendix slowly removed his goggles and fixed the red-faced gatekeeper with an unblinking stare.

'Stand back,' he repeated.

The gatekeeper lowered his whip and, with a shrug of his shoulders, turned away. 'Stupid prowlgrins is one thing,' he muttered as he joined his comrades, 'but crazy academics is another!'

Fenviel bent down and tenderly stroked the prowlgrin's head. But it was too late. The prowlgrin's breath was coming in short, shuddering gasps and, as the former hall master continued to stroke it, the eyes glazed over and it quietly died.

Fenviel closed his eyes and lowered his head. A moment later, he felt a hand on his shoulder and, looking up, saw Tuggel, the gnokgoblin groom from the Hall of Grey Cloud, looking down at him, his face full of concern.

'You should be careful, Hall Master,' Tuggel whispered urgently. 'If the gatekeepers report back to Hax Vostillix that you've been interfering . . .'

Fenviel rose to his feet and snapped his riding crop in two, as he barked a single word. 'Hax!'

iv
The Hall Master of High Cloud

The only remaining hall master of the Lower Halls stared at the bowl of tilder stew in front him. The spoon in his bony fingers shook so badly that its contents dripped down onto his robes.

'Sky blast it!' he grunted, dropping the spoon back into the bowl, seizing his napkin and dabbing at the brown stain.

A moment later, he frowned. His hand froze. He continued to stare down at his front.

'Marsh-gems,' he murmured. 'These purple robes were once decorated with marsh-gems . . .'

It seemed, for a moment, like the final straw. Someone – a hall servant or squire, probably – had painstakingly picked the precious marsh-gems from his robe; every last one of them! Did they really hate him so much? Hax Vostillix, Hall Master of High Cloud and sole head of the Knights Academy, thought gloomily.

He reached for his spoon again, but stayed his hand. He wasn't hungry. Abandoning all thought of eating the stew, he returned the full bowl to the silver tray and pushed the whole lot away. Like the day before, and the day before that, he simply had no appetite.

How could he eat at a time like this, anyway? he asked himself, when the sky yielded only snow and ice, and the sacred floating rock grew more buoyant with every blizzard.

He turned towards the window, his dark-ringed eyes searching the sky for a sign, however small, that the weather was changing. But, he noted with a sinking heart, the blizzard was still raging outside – and there wasn't even the faintest whiff of sourmist in the air. If there had been, he would have ordered a voyage at once – for all the good it would do. Yet he had no other choice.

He shook his head bleakly.

'Why is this happening to me, a faithful sky-scholar?' he groaned. 'Haven't I done enough? I've banished earth-scholarship. I've purified the Knights Academy.' He picked idly at the threads on his robes. 'I've taken the purge into the schools and academies of Sanctaphrax, rooting out earth-scholarship wherever it occurs ... Yet still the sky shows its displeasure ...'

Seeds of doubt, already sown, had begun to swell and grow. Could he have been wrong with the predictions about the imminent arrival of a Great Storm after all?

He clenched a fist and slammed it down on the table top, making the dishes jump and upsetting a goblet of sapwine.

No! he thought. I cannot think like that, not after sending all those brave knights academic off into the storm-racked skies. I must not! I am Hax Vostillix, the greatest sky-scholar there has ever been!

But he'd seen the way the two Most High Academes looked at him. *And* the others; the professors, the squires, the academics-at-arms . . . They'd all lost confidence in him.

He shook his head again as memories came flooding back.

It had all been so different that afternoon in the great Lecture Dome. They'd listened to him then as, with Daxiel Xaxis and the gatekeepers by his side, he'd purged the Lower Halls of those scoundrels and infidels posing as loyal sky-scholars. Why, even Screedius Tollinix had come round to his way of thinking in the end, and set off to serve Sanctaphrax . . .

What *had* happened to the brave young knight? he wondered.

No, things had certainly changed. Back then, they'd looked up to him. Now they despised him. Hated him. He looked down at his purple robes, picked clean of their marsh-gems. Yes, they hated him all right, he thought bitterly. If it wasn't for Daxiel Xaxis and his army of gatekeepers, the academics would surely have risen up and thrown him out of Sanctaphrax long before now. Yet he had to be careful, Hax told himself; make sure Daxiel Xaxis himself didn't get too big for his boots.

'After all, we don't want the servant becoming the master, do we?' he murmured.

He looked back down at his desk. It was strewn with sky charts, weather predictions, mist readings and . . .

He frowned. 'What's that?' he wondered.

There on his silver tray, nestling next to the jug of sap-wine, was a small gold bowl with sugared delberry bonbons in it.

Someone had taken the time to coat the little delberries in a fine dusting of exquisite icing and present them in a small gold bowl for his pleasure. Clearly, not everyone hated him, Hax thought, with a little smile.

He picked one up with a thumb and forefinger and turned it in the light. The sugar glittered. Hax licked his lips. A hall master eating bonbons! He really shouldn't – but one couldn't possibly hurt.

He popped it in his mouth and closed his eyes. The bonbon slowly melted on his tongue. It tasted so sweet . . .

·CHAPTER EIGHTEEN·

THE BARKSCROLLS

*D*ear Maris,
   I'm pleased you enjoyed my last letter. I'm afraid this one will be much shorter. I'm giving it to Vilnix Pompolnius to deliver to you because, despite my initial impressions, he has turned out to be a trustworthy comrade and a loyal companion. You know, I really misjudged him, and am only sorry to have passed on my silly misgivings to you.

   Which brings me to my big news! Both Vilnix and I are to be elevated to the Upper Halls! I shall be a knight's squire and Vilnix will be an apprentice high professor (which is no less than he deserves, considering all his hard work). Our Elevation Ceremony is in three days' time, and I need to collect my sword miniature, buy some new robes, get my sword polished and sharpened – a hundred and one things.

   Unfortunately, they all cost money, and I have already run through my father's allowance. What's more, my mentor, the Professor of Light, is turning out to be as mean as everybody here says he is. Vilnix is so lucky to have the Professor of Darkness as <u>his</u> mentor!

I don't suppose you could lend me a small sum – say fifty gold pieces? After all, your father must have left you plenty. You could put the money in the copperwood urn I've concealed this barkscroll in, and give it to Vilnix in the market-place tomorrow.

I know you won't let me down,

Your friend,

Quintinius Verginix

Upper Hall Squire

Dear Quint,

Since when do you sign yourself 'Quintinius Verginix' when you write to me? It sounds so formal and odd! I do hope your elevation to the Upper Halls isn't going to make you too high and mighty!

I'm only teasing . . .

I do understand about the money, and how expensive it must be getting all the things you need for your Elevation Ceremony, but you're quite wrong about my having plenty. Heft is such a terrible old miser, and Dacia is just as bad. You should see the clothes they wear. All full of patches and holes, and the very latest in fashion – about fifty years ago!

Heft has taken everything Father left me and locked it away with all his other gold. It is so unfair, but whenever I protest, he just waves the will that Father wrote making him my guardian, and says it's his to look after until I'm 'grown up and sensible'. I can't wait to be grown up, but I hope I'm never 'sensible' if sensible means acting like Heft and Dacia and their boring friends.

Oh, which reminds me! Something is definitely going on, because the other evening, that Daxiel Xaxis person showed up in his white cape with the horrible badge on it, and had a long meeting with Heft. I couldn't hear much from my room (my door was locked again, just like most other evenings!) – just some shouting. But Delby – she's the tearful mobgnome chambermaid I told you about – had to bring a log for the fire, so she filled me in later on the details of their big argument.

She said that Daxiel wanted Heft to find even more Undertowners to join those horrid gatekeepers of his, because soon he'd need every one of them he could get! Heft just kept whining (he's very good at whining, by the way – when he's not bullying) and saying that he'd already spent too much of his hard-earned gold finding recruits for Daxiel, and that now he wanted 'a return on his investment'. I suppose he means that stupid job controlling the log burners on the East and West Landings that he's always going on about.

Then, apparently, Daxiel said something <u>really</u> interesting. He said that Heft should be patient, find him some more recruits and wait for the moment when 'under shall rule above'. But Heft kept on pestering him, and they ended up shouting at each other. Daxiel warned Heft not to come to the Knights Academy until he was sent for, and then he stormed off.

Don't you think that's strange?

I think you should tell the twin Most High Academes about this, as I'm pretty sure that Hax Vostillix is behind the whole thing. Is he as mad as they all say he is? I heard that they're planning to send another knight academic stormchasing again, even though hardly anyone believes that these blizzards we keep having are Great Storms, or anything close.

Oh, do be careful up there, Quint, won't you? Although it's not much, I have been saving the allowance Dacia gives me once a week – it's five gold pieces all together, and it took me ages to save it! Heft keeps all <u>his</u> gold in a great big lufwood chest at the foot of his bed – or so Delby says. And he opens it up and counts it every night before he goes to bed. He is such a miser!

Sorry I can't send more. You know I would if I could. I'll give it to Vilnix with this letter like you said – and good luck with the Elevation Ceremony.

Your friend,

Madame Maris Pallitax-Vespius

(only joking!)

P.S. The funniest thing, Quint. Your letter – the barkscroll parchment you wrote it on – it is exactly the same sort that Father wrote his will on. Smooth texture, with small grey flecks on it. I remember thinking it was odd at the time because Father always used sumpwood barkscrolls (more grainy and lighter). But it was definitely his writing. And now, here you are, using the same sort!

Dear Maris,

I'm sorry you found it formal and odd that I signed myself
Quintinius Verginix in my last letter, but you must understand that I have moved on to the Upper Halls and left
childish things behind. You might only be teasing, but these
things matter. And as daughter of a Most High Academe, I
would expect you to understand this.

I am very disappointed that you only sent me five gold
pieces, and can only count myself fortunate that my loyal
friend, Vilnix Pompolnius, came to my aid at the Elevation
Ceremony. He sharpened the blade of my sword beautifully
and ran all sorts of useful errands for me, including picking
up your letter — and the measly gold coins you decided to let
me have.

If you were as true and loyal a friend to me as Vilnix,
you would find a way to take the gold your guardian
has taken from you, and send it to me. I'm sure it's
what your poor dear father would have wanted — especially
as my new mentor, the Professor of Light, has turned
out to be so tight-fisted. As my true friend, you would
take as much of the gold as you could and give it to Vilnix
in this copperwood urn. He will pass by your window each
week on market day until you wave a red kerchief to show
you have been successful. Do not expect any further
barkscrolls from me until you have proved your friendship
by doing this.

I shall pass on your concerns to the Professors of Light. I
certainly wouldn't be at all surprised if Hax Vostillix _was_
up to something — he is not only mad, but also devious, as
poor Vilnix has found out to his cost. After doing him many

kindnesses and small acts of service, Vilnix was promised a position in the Upper Halls as an apprentice high professor. But Hax Vostillix cruelly betrayed him, sending him to the Upper Halls and making him a knight academic squire instead, even though he has no interest in or intention of going stormchasing.

I was so angry when Vilnix told me this that I felt like murdering Hax Vostillix with my own two hands. It is no more than he deserves! That is what true friends do for each other.

Do not let me down again.

Yours,

Quintinius Verginix

Upper Hall Squire

Dear Quintinius,

I was very hurt by the tone of your last letter. In fact, I cried for a whole week, if you must know. I do want to be a good friend to you, you know I do. I don't think murdering anybody – even Hax Vostillix – with your bare hands is proof of friendship, and even though you seem to think so highly of Vilnix, I'm afraid he still gives me the creeps.

For three weeks he's been appearing outside my window on Market Day, with that horrid little twisted smile on his face. It's almost as if he's happy that you're angry with me and that I'm miserable. Indeed, I've been so miserable that I have actually gone and done what you asked me to. It was against my better judgement, because stealing is wrong, and both of us know that.

I managed to sneak into Heft and Dacia's bedchamber last night, and watched while the loathsome fat barkslug quaffed sapwine and rocked back and forth while he counted out that gold of his. Dacia was as drunk as he was, and they kept singing 'under shall rule above', and laughing. It was horrible!

But eventually they both fell asleep and I managed to tiptoe from behind the hanging drapes and take about a hundred gold pieces out of the lufwood trunk, literally from under Heft's big fat snoring nose!

I say 'about' because I'm sure you'll understand I couldn't stop to count it out. There, so I've done it! You'll find them in the copperwood urn with this letter. I'll give it to Vilnix when he turns up tomorrow (which I'm sure he will). Perhaps it'll wipe that horrid little smirk off his face!

When Heft finds out, I'll be in big trouble, I know, but you asked me to prove my friendship, and I have, so there! And I say 'when' not 'if' because he knows exactly how much he's got – or rather, how much he had. I'm not proud of what I've done, and I intend to slip away as soon as I can. I'll go to the twin Most High Academes and throw myself on their mercy. I've decided to tell them everything, Quint – I'm sure it'll be for the best.

Your <u>true</u> friend,
Maris

Dear Maris,

We must see each other. Don't, I beg of you, do anything stupid!

You must escape and get to the Loftus Observatory. Wait for me on the north gantry platform of the Observatory Chamber at eight hours tomorrow morning and I will explain everything . . .

Please excuse my poor handwriting, but I injured my hand at Gantry Tower practice.

Thank you for the money. You are a true friend.

Your friend,

Quint

Maris slipped a coin into the calloused palm of the old gnokgoblin basket-puller and stepped onto the West Landing. She shivered and lowered her head. With the howling wind tugging at her cape, it seemed, if anything, even colder up here on the great floating rock than back in Undertown.

From behind her there came the creaking noise of the great wooden treadmill as it raised and lowered the log burners – the huge glowing cage-like structures she'd watched so often from the window of her bedchamber. Up close, she could now hear the barks and whinnies of the hardworking prowlgrins that turned it, as well as the curious mournful hooting of the giant fromps.

So many changes since I was last here, she thought.

She scurried along the jutting platform, keeping to the long, early-morning shadows as best she could. There were gatekeepers everywhere, she noticed with a shudder, in their white tunics with the horrible red insignia. But they were too busy shouting and bullying the stable-hands to pay her any attention. How different from the days when her father had been Most High Academe. He would never have allowed Hax Vostillix to build up his own personal army . . .

Still, she thought, as she reached the end of the landing and stepped down onto the broad, snow-covered avenue that led, in a majestic sweep, from the Great Library to the Loftus Observatory, the twin Most High Academes would put a stop to it, she was sure. Especially as she was going to tell them all about the Captain of the Gatekeeper's suspicious meetings with her guardian, Heft. But first she had to get to the Loftus Observatory before eight hours, to meet Quint.

Her heart gave a leap. Quint! It was going to be so good to see him again after all this time.

There was so much she wanted to say to him, and so many questions she couldn't wait to ask. What was it *really* like being an Upper Hall squire? To ride a prowlgrin, and learn to sail a stormchaser? And his friends; she wanted to know all about them – Stope, Raffix, Phin and . . . even Vilnix.

What *did* he see in that thin, shifty-eyed apprentice whose twisted smile made her flesh creep?

These sorts of things couldn't be explained in barkscroll letters, but Maris was sure Quint would explain everything to her now that, at last, they were going to meet face to face. She quickened her pace.

Cutting through an alleyway at the back of the School of Mist, she emerged on the main avenue, the tall towers of the College of Cloud ahead of her. There were mob-gnomes and cloddertrogs out clearing the snow as best they could, and the air was filled with the sound of scraping shovels. Above her, though, the early morning sunlight was already being blocked out by an approaching bank of black cloud. She turned right. The Loftus Observatory loomed ahead of her.

Not far now, she told herself, and she'd see Quint again and could tell him everything. About the long, lonely, cold nights locked up in her room, about the petty unkindnesses and meanness of her guardians and the deep ache in the middle of her chest whenever she allowed herself to think about her former life in the great floating city.

And then there was the hurt. The angry hurt that his letter had caused her, with its haughty tone and accusation that she wasn't 'a real friend'. It had stung her so deeply that Maris had seized the first opportunity to prove him wrong. She hadn't had to wait long . . .

A gatekeeper had arrived with a message for Heft which had transformed her moaning bully of a guardian into a laughing, giggling fool. He'd pranced delightedly round the palace, ordering the servants to bring the sap-wine, and shouting for Dacia to come and celebrate with him. Before long, the pair of them were roaring drunk and staggering off to their bedchamber, singing, 'Under shall rule above!' – and forgetting to lock Maris's door on their way.

Heart in her mouth, Maris had slipped out of her room and tiptoed down the corridor and into her guardians' bedchamber. There, she'd nipped behind the heavy window drapes at the far end of the huge room. With her heart hammering in her chest, she'd peeked through a gap in the drapes. Dacia had collapsed on the enormous carved lufwood bed and was snoring like a woodhog, while Heft was kneeling in front of an open chest at the foot of the bed.

As Maris watched, his eyes grew heavy and closed and his head lolled forward. Soon, he too was snoring thunderously, crouched over the treasure chest as if worshipping its contents.

Maris had waited a while, just to be sure they weren't about to stir. Then, with a deep breath, she emerged from behind the curtains and tiptoed over to the open chest.

How full it had been! she remembered indignantly. It contained more gold coins than she had ever seen before – all glinting and gleaming in the yellow light of the two-groat tallow candle that flickered on the lampstand. Without a second thought, she hitched up her skirt and scooped several handfuls of coins – a fraction, she was sure, of what her father had left her – into the folds of material. Then, scarcely daring to breathe, she hurried away from the bedchamber.

Back in her own room, she'd wrapped the coins up with her letter in a small cloth and stuffed the whole lot inside the copperwood urn. Then – unable to sleep, her head spinning with the thought of what she'd just done – she sat up the whole night, waiting for morning. By daybreak, the market stalls had already been set up and there, lurking in the shadows once more, was Vilnix Pompolnius. For the first time ever, she was pleased to see him. Instead of ignoring him, as she'd done on all the other occasions, she pulled the red kerchief from her sleeve and waved.

Then she'd pushed the urn through the bars at her window and lowered it on a length of knotted sheet into Vilnix's waiting arms. He'd grabbed it, pushed it inside his jacket and dashed away without even the slightest acknowledgement.

Well, she'd thought, with a bitter feeling of triumph. At least Quint would realize that she was a 'true friend' now. But she would pay a high price for proving her friendship when Heft counted his gold again. And she didn't have much time – a day or so at most . . .

An hour later, dressed in her warmest clothes, with her belongings wrapped up in a small bundle under her arm, Maris had set off to confess everything to the twin Most High Academes. Up in their bedchamber, Heft and Dacia were still sleeping off the effects of the sapwine as she slipped out of their apartments.

She hadn't gone more than half a dozen paces when she felt a tug on her sleeve. With a terrified gasp, she'd spun round – to be confronted once more with the leering face of Vilnix Pompolnius.

'I'm glad I caught you,' he said, his nasal voice breathy and urgent. He reached inside his jacket and pulled out a barkscroll, which he'd thrust into her hands. 'I've just come back down from Sanctaphrax – Quint told me to give you this. It's very important, so read it now!'

Then he'd dashed away before she could stop him.

What a strange barkscroll it had been, summoning her here to the Loftus Observatory with no explanation. And the handwriting! A thin, spidery scrawl so unlike Quint's usual beautiful penmanship.

Something was wrong, Maris was certain, and now she was going to get to the bottom of it. Pushing open the door to the observatory, she began to climb the stairs, two at a time. By the time she'd reached the circular Observatory Chamber, Maris was panting with exertion. Outside, high up at the top of the Great Hall, the bell chimed a quarter off eight hours.

'Quint?' she called, rushing to the door to the north gantry platform and stepping through it. 'Quint? Are you there?'

Quint strode towards the Loftus Observatory through the thick snow. In the distance, the Great Hall bell was chiming a quarter off eight hours. His heavy black cape billowed out behind him as he quickened his pace, the glowing lamp-staff in his gauntleted fist throwing a glinting light onto the battered old suit of armour he wore.

How inconvenient of his mentor, the Professor of Light, to summon him to the Loftus Observatory on this morning of all mornings, Quint thought.

Until about a couple of hours ago, the plan that Quint, Phin, Stope and Raffix had been working on for weeks now had been going perfectly. Stope's work in the forge was completed, Raffix had prepared the *Galerider* and

Phin had retrieved the light-casket from Philius Embertine's bedchamber. All that had been left was for Quint to equip himself. He'd sneaked down to the lecture theatre in the Hall of White Cloud and carefully unhooked the old knight academic armour from its stand. It was surprisingly light, and Quint had experienced a guilty thrill as, piece by piece, he'd buckled the armour on.

So this is what it felt like to be a knight academic in full armour, he'd thought, and smiled to himself.

The suit was clearly too big for him, and was battered and worn, but Quint felt magnificent as he quietly left the hall and made his way up the Central Staircase, taking care to conceal it beneath his heavy black robe. He'd just got to the Central Landing when who should come sneaking up behind him but

Vilnix, his thin face red from running, and his voice an urgent, panting whisper.

'Thank Sky I've found you, Quint! I've been looking for you everywhere. Why aren't you in your study?' Vilnix had gasped.

'I couldn't sleep,' Quint had lied. The last thing they needed was the sneaky squire discovering their plan. Fortunately, Vilnix seemed to have other things on his mind, for he didn't give Quint's heavy cloak or armoured boots a second glance.

'That's just as well,' said Vilnix, 'because the Professor of Light wants to see you urgently on the north gantry platform of the Loftus Observatory at eight hours. And don't be late,' he'd said, and smiled wolfishly at Quint. 'Your very future depends on it!'

Vilnix had gone off, chuckling to himself and rubbing his hands together. Try as he might, Quint couldn't work him out. But then, he thought, as he hurried up to meet Raffix in the Central Hall of the Upper Halls, he had more important things than the workings of Vilnix Pompolnius's mind to worry about.

He reached the entrance to the Loftus Observatory and rushed inside. He hoped this meeting with his mentor wouldn't take too long. Raffix and the others were waiting for him back at the Knights Academy. Quint arrived at the Observatory Chamber, gasping for breath. The armour had felt light at first, but now, after climbing all those stairs, it seemed to weigh more than stormphrax itself.

The north gantry door was ajar. Quint walked

over to it and pulled it open.

'Maris!' he exclaimed. 'What are *you* doing here?'

Maris turned from the balustrade, a look of joy on her face. 'Quint!' she gasped. 'At last.'

Quint stepped onto the gantry. As he did so, there was a loud *crack,* and the look of joy on Maris's face turned to horror as the platform beneath her feet suddenly gave way.

With lightning reflexes, Quint shot out a gauntleted hand and grasped Maris by the wrist, hanging onto the handle of the creaking gantry door with the other. Below them, the platform clattered and clanged against the sides of the tower as it crashed to the ground. Above him, Quint felt the door hinges shudder as they began to give way. Four metal bolts buckling under the strain was all that stood between them and certain death.

Maris turned a tear-streaked face up towards his, and Quint tightened his grip on her wrist. His arms felt as if they were being wrenched from their sockets, and sharp stabs of pain shot through his shoulders. The gantry door began to buckle and, below him, Maris seemed to sense this . . .

As she dangled precariously over the edge, she screamed, 'Save yourself, Quint!'

·CHAPTER NINETEEN·

BLOOD IN THE SNOW

The skies over sleeping Sanctaphrax were pitch black, with dark turbulent clouds delaying the onset of dawn. Inside the Hall of White Cloud, although the furnaces had burned down low and needed stoking, the glowing embers cast a soft crimson light throughout the forge.

In the far corner, behind a clump of twisting flue-pipes, a wiry young grey goblin emerged from a nest of rags, rubbed the sleep from his eyes and gathered together the small bundle he'd prepared the previous evening. He slung it over his shoulder and, checking that there was no-one else up and about at such an early hour, he crept softly out of the forge and headed for the Central Staircase.

At the other end of the Knights Academy, in a study alcove of the Academy Barracks, a sleepy-headed academic-at-arms yawned, stretched and scratched his head before climbing gingerly out of bed. He stood for a moment, shivering. The little lufwood stove had gone out in the night, and despite the heavy tilderwool blanket that hung at the entrance, his study alcove was bitterly cold. Still shivering, he grabbed his clothes and hurriedly dressed. Then, having buckled the breast-plate and upper armour of an apprentice swordmaster into place, he hurried off down the corridor towards the Central Staircase.

In the Central Hall of the Upper Halls, a gangly young knight academic-in-waiting with oval spectacles paced the floor. His brow was furrowed. Pausing for a moment beneath one of the tall, ornately decorated pulpits, he reached out and, with his forefinger, traced the twists and curves of a carved tarry-vine with his forefinger. This was the pulpit where the Fellowship of the First Scholars held their debates.

He walked on, looking up at the towering pulpits all round him. In the one to his left, the Knights of the Great Storm held their secretive meetings; and in that one over by the back wall, he knew that the Friends of Mist and Fog would meet to talk endlessly of the weather . . .

So much discussion and debate, he thought with a wry smile, and pushed his spectacles back up his nose. The Pulpit Societies of the Upper Halls generated enough hot air to warm the Sanctaphrax rock to its core. Yet for all their talk, not one of the squires, knights or high professors who gathered there could explain this endless winter – nor decide what to do about it.

Just then, he heard the sound of footsteps and turned to see two figures approaching. One was a slightly built forge-hand, the other an apprentice swordmaster.

'Where's Quint?' the apprentice swordmaster whispered, his face drawn and anxious-looking.

'He's been called to meet his mentor at the Loftus Observatory at eight hours,' said the young knight. 'He only heard a few moments ago . . .'

'So what do we do now?' asked the forge-hand, urgently. 'We can't call it off. We might not get another chance . . .'

'Well, we can't leave Quint behind,' said the knight, as calmly as he could manage. 'I think we should go ahead as planned, get everything prepared. Quint will join us as soon as he can. Now,' he said, with a smile, 'Instead of standing round here debating like some Pulpit Society, let's get a move on.'

They were about to slip away when the sound of more footsteps echoed round the vast, empty hall. The group turned to see a thin, hunched Upper Hall squire crossing the floor, rubbing his hands together gleefully as he did so. Catching sight of the three figures over by the pulpit, the squire paused for a moment. He seemed as surprised as they were to find anyone else up at this hour. He approached them, the smirk on his face changing to a sneer.

'Who have we here, then?' he asked. 'Raffix, Phin! And . . . let me see . . . Ah yes, Stope the forge-hand, I remember you . . .'

'Vilnix Pompolnius,' said Raffix. 'What are you doing creeping about this early in the morning?'

'I could ask you the same question,' said Vilnix, his eyes narrowing suspiciously.

'Us?' said Raffix nonchalantly. 'Oh, um . . . We've just formed a Pulpit Society . . . Though only a small one, you understand . . .'

'How interesting,' Vilnix sneered. 'And what's this Pulpit Society of yours called?'

'Called?' said Raffix, his face reddening.

Vilnix chuckled. 'You mean to say you've dragged an academic-at-arms and a grubby little forge-hand up from the Lower Halls to form a Pulpit Society, and you haven't even thought up a name?'

'It's . . .' Raffix began.

'Perhaps *I* can help,' Vilnix interrupted. 'The Apprentice Windbags! Or the Ranting Ratbirds . . . Or no, I've got it – the Boring Barkslugs!' He sniggered at his own joke.

Raffix bridled, colour flushing his cheeks. 'If you must know,' he said stiffly, struggling to come up with a plausible name that would wipe the smile off the squire's smug features, 'we are called . . . the Winter Knights.'

*

The bedchamber of the Hall Master of High Cloud was dark and cold. A moaning sound, low and eerie, was coming from the large sumpwood bed, chained to the centre of the floor. The bed swayed and lurched as its occupant thrashed about and clawed at the bedclothes.

Hax Vostillix was having a bad dream.

He was on board a stormchaser, gripping the balustrades grimly as the fragile vessel rolled and swayed, pitched and plunged. One moment he was unbearably hot, as though his body were in flames; the next, as the fragile sky ship was swallowed up by the freezing ice-blizzards, he became so cold that his teeth chattered and his body shook uncontrollably.

All at once, a loud screeching sound filled his ears, and he looked down to see thousands of ratbirds streaming from the hull of the ship, twisting round in the air, before speeding off towards the far horizon. The sky ship was out of control and, in a fast and furious spiral, spinning down towards the white mud of the Mire . . .

Hax Vostillix's eyes snapped open. He was bathed in sweat, his skin dripping and his nightgown soaked right through. But he was cold. Bitterly cold. His fingers and toes were so frozen he could barely feel them, and yet inside, his belly was on fire, churning and convulsing. And then there was the pain . . .

Hax had never known pain like it. It wrenched and racked his stomach, like a thousand red-hot needles that stabbed and slashed, twisting his guts into knots.

'*Wooorgh!*' he groaned. '*Aaoouurgh . . .*'

Spasm after spasm of intense pain drove though him, folding him up double as it cramped and branded. Grunting with utter misery, Hax rolled over and crawled from the swaying sumpwood bed. He stumbled across to his desk – its surface strewn with cloud charts, weather predictions, ballistics lists and mist readings – and slumped down into the chair.

The pain grew more intense than ever, and the words and figures on the barkscrolls swam before his eyes, seeming to taunt him and goad him. He pushed them aside, and as he did so, his hands knocked against the silver tray with its untouched plate of food, the jug of sapwine, the small gold bowl . . .

All at once, he doubled up violently again, his chin on his knees, as a fiery convulsion erupted inside him. The pain was so bad, it felt as if his belly was about to explode.

'Must be something . . . I . . . ate . . .' he moaned.

His gaze fell on the gold bowl . . .

Of course! The delberry bonbons. And he had taken them as proof that not everyone hated him. How could he have been so stupid? So careless?

The searing pain inside him grew more and more intense. Hax's vision clouded over. The fire surged up from his belly, into his throat . . .

'*Aaaargh!*' he screamed, twisting out of the chair and crumpling, open-mouthed, to the marble floor like a gutted oozefish on a slab.

It took several moments before the convulsions ceased, the limbs stopped thrashing and the Hall

Master of High Cloud fell still. As a bright streak of blood trickled from the corner of Hax's mouth onto his white beard, a low buzzing sound came up from his throat.

The next moment, a single dark striped insect appeared. It rested on Hax's swollen, protruding tongue for a few seconds, its feelers quivering as it tasted the air. Then the tiny creature spread its glistening wings and, with a rasping buzz, took flight.

Another insect appeared in its place . . .

And another, and another – until there was a thick stream of them, spewing out from the hall master's gaping mouth. Soon, the bedchamber was filled with the sound of angry buzzing as the swarm of newly-hatched woodwasps swirled round the room, while Hax's lifeless eyes stared sightlessly at the ceiling.

'Murder! Murder!'

Daxiel Xaxis stormed into the Hall of Grey Cloud, his face disfigured by a mass of weeping purple blisters. He seized the nearest gatekeeper and thrust his swollen, pustular features into the startled guard's.

'Rouse all the gatekeepers!' he wheezed through blistered lips. 'There is no time to lose! Hax Vostillix, our beloved leader, has been murdered!'

'Murder!'

'Murder!'

'Murder!'

The news flew round, and before long the Hall of Grey Cloud was resounding with the indignant cries of the gatekeepers as they scrambled from their hammocks and benches, clambered into their white robes and grabbed whatever weapon was closest to hand. They clustered round the Captain of the Gatekeepers, who angrily pushed away the byre-gillie fussily attempting to apply a hyleberry poultice to the wasp stings. He raised his hand for silence.

'When I took the Hall Master of High Cloud his supper last night, he was in good spirits,' Daxiel began, wincing with pain. 'Yet this morning, at seven hours, when I opened the doors to his chamber, I found the hall master dead and the place infested with woodwasps!'

All round him, there was a sharp intake of breath, and the gatekeepers exchanged dark looks.

'Yes, yes, I know what you're thinking,' said Daxiel. 'Woodwasp eggs – an earth-scholar trick! But that's just what they want you to believe!'

'They?' asked a heavily-tattooed flat-head goblin with a puzzled frown.

'The academics-at-arms, of course!' snarled Daxiel. 'They, and their friends in the Upper Halls. Sanctaphrax born and bred, the lot of them, and they hated Hax

Vostillix because he wouldn't stand for their stuck-up ways! That's why he took on Undertowners like us to be his gatekeepers.'

Daxiel surveyed the heavily-armed ranks that filled the hall, their numbers swollen with recruits from the very worst parts of Undertown. Heft Vespius had chosen well.

'That Dengreeve Yellowtusk was always trying to get him to disband the gatekeepers,' he went on. 'And when he wouldn't, he got one of his sneaky Sanctaphrax academics-at-arms to murder our beloved leader! Well, we're not going to let them get away with it! The gatekeepers will teach all them in the Academy Barracks a lesson they'll never forget . . .'

The hall was filled with nodding heads and grunts of approval.

'And we won't stop when we've done that neither,' he shouted. 'We'll go on and show the whole of Sanctaphrax that they can't push us Undertowners around any more. I, your captain, have made powerful friends in the leagues. Together, we're going to change this floating city for ever!'

The gatekeepers roared their approval. Daxiel drew his sword and raised it high above his head.

'Under shall rule above!' he roared.

All round the hall, the gatekeepers took up the cry, 'Under shall rule above! Under shall rule above! . . .'

'The time to act has come!' Daxiel told them. 'We shall lock every gate, bolt every door and seal every entrance in the Knights Academy. Anyone found wandering about in the communal areas is to be killed. By the time those idle, in-bred academics-at-arms stir, they'll find the entrance doors to their Academy Barracks secured and bolted from outside.' He smiled. 'Penned up like hammelhorns on market day, they'll be,' he said. 'Penned up and awaiting slaughter!'

A bloodcurdling cry went up, so loud that the rafters high up in the vaulted ceilings trembled and the sound of the Great Hall bell chiming eight hours was all but drowned out.

Soon there were gatekeepers running everywhere. Up stairs and down corridors, and out across the Inner Courtyard, blocking off entrances, barricading doors and bolting gates shut. There was no time to lose if they were to take control of the Knights Academy, and certainly the gatekeepers were far too preoccupied to notice the rickety stormchaser high up at the top of the Gantry Tower as it loosed its mooring tether and swooped off into the snow-flecked sky . . .

'Locked?' queried Dengreeve Yellowtusk. 'What do you mean, locked?'

'Exactly that, swordmaster,' the young academic-at-arms replied, fear and excitement in his eyes. 'The main doors have been locked . . . from the outside.'

'The pair of us were just off to relieve the night-watch,' his comrade added, his eyes flashing brightly. 'At the eastern slingshots . . .'

'And we couldn't get out . . .'

'What's more,' the first one said, 'all the side entrances

and the corridors have also been blocked – by the gate-keepers.'

Dengreeve's eyes narrowed as he sat back in the high-backed chair. 'So, Hax Vostillix has made his move at last,' he murmured.

Just then, a group of academics-at-arms strode through the barracks hall, two of them carrying a grey-faced mobgnome stable-hand, his tunic stained with blood.

'Swordmaster.' The heavily armoured academic saluted Dengreeve. 'I think you should hear this.' He gestured for the stable-hand to speak.

'Sir, Hax Vostillix is dead ... Murdered!' the mob-gnome gasped once he'd been placed in a chair. There was a crossbow bolt embedded in his side, and he was clearly struggling for breath.

'Wessel, here, is a stable-hand in the Hall of Grey Cloud,' the academic-at-arms said, bending down and speaking in a low voice in Dengreeve's ear. 'He escaped across the rooftops of the dormitory closets and climbed over the battlements of the barracks ...'

'The gatekeepers have locked every entrance in the academy ...' gasped Wessel, his face greyer than ever. 'They got me just as I reached the barracks wall ... But I kept going ...' He fell back, exhausted.

'Well, Quelf?' Dengreeve demanded. 'Who committed this outrage? Eh? Who murdered Hax Vostillix?'

The academic's face reddened, and he leaned closer to Dengreeve's ear. 'The gatekeepers think that *you* did, Captain.'

*

Outside, as a cold yellow-grey sun rose up above the glistening West Wall and a bitter wind howled round the towers of the Knights Academy, a flock of raucous white ravens circled high in the sky. The neverending winter had culled their numbers, for though many creatures had perished in the icy conditions, their bodies were instantly lost, entombed in impenetrable snow. Now the vicious, half-starved scavengers cawed and screeched with excitement, tumbling over one another as they wheeled around, as if sensing that the ground below would soon furnish them with a great feast.

Already, the crisp white snow of the Inner Courtyard was criss-crossed with footprints where the gatekeepers had taken up their positions. Daxiel Xaxis, his face swathed in bandages, stared across the carpet of snow towards the great leadwood doors of the Academy Barracks. Around him, his personal guard of massive cloddertrogs from the boom-docks – hand-picked by Heft Vespius himself – grasped their heavy spiked cudgels. In front of them, a vast unruly mass of gatekeepers armed with a bewildering array of weaponry jostled each other and stared at the Academy Barracks ahead.

'Easy, lads,' growled Daxiel, from behind his mask of bandages. 'Let them come to us – and then we shall feed them to the ravens . . .'

Boom!

High above, the white ravens squawked with alarm as something heavy thudded noisily into the leadwood doors from inside.

CRASH!!!

The doors slammed to the ground, torn from their hinges by the solid ironwood pillar that now skidded across the snow and crashed into the Knights' Tower on the corner of the West Wall. Behind it lumbered a fully-armoured party of academics-at-arms, dragging a heavy lufwood slingshot behind them.

They came to a halt by the steps of the Hall of High Cloud as gatekeepers appeared on the roof and sent a volley of crossbow bolts raining down on them.

Several academics screamed and fell, the lethal bolts finding the weak spots in their hard armour and embedding themselves in the soft flesh beneath. Some fell still at once; some writhed and twisted in the snow, blood spurting from their helmet visors and beneath their arms, evidence of where they'd been hit.

The others hastily loaded the slingshot with another missile – a heavy refectory table – and, as the crossbow bolts glanced off their armour, they cranked back the sling.

'FIRE!'

The command rang out, and the sling snapped back, sending the great plank of wood hurtling at the mass of gatekeepers that Daxiel had sent racing across the snowy courtyard towards the academics-at-arms. It slammed into the midst of them with a splintering crash of wood and bone, and a sickening gush of blood.

At that moment, with a bloodcurdling cry, Dengreeve and his swordmasters raced out of the barracks. They charged past the slingshot crew, bellowing loudly, and fell heavily upon the gatekeepers.

Eyes glinting from behind his bandage mask, Daxiel signalled for his cloddertrogs to advance. As they lumbered forward, he turned and strode back across the courtyard towards the Hall of Grey Cloud.

Behind him, the swordmasters – though heavily out-numbered – were making short work of their gatekeeper adversaries. Leaping high in the air, their swords whirring about their heads, they left great spirals of red splattered across the white snow in their path as the heavy blades slashed and stabbed and plunged.

No Undertown tavern brawl could have prepared the gatekeepers for this controlled ferocity. With cries of terror they fled back across the courtyard, pushing past the massive cloddertrogs in their desperation to escape the flashing blades.

Meanwhile, a detachment

of catapults up on the battlements of the barracks had managed to clear the adjoining hall roof of gatekeeper crossbows – though at a heavy price to the great dome of the Lecture Hall in shattered panes of glass. Down below, the cloddertrogs gave huge throaty roars and charged at Dengreeve and his swordmasters.

'Come on, then,' Dengreeve muttered coldly.

He ducked down below his opponent's guard as an attacking cloddertrog got close, skewered him through the heart with a single thrust – and spun neatly to one side. The cloddertrog crashed to the ground like a stricken ironwood pine, followed by twenty of his companions, as each of the other swordmasters struck home.

Now, out from the Academy Barracks ran the rest of the academics-at-arms – young missile-loaders, catapult and slingshot look-outs, cage-masters and rock-guardians, clutching axes, bludgeons, pikestaffs and any other weapons they could find. And, as the sword-masters looked on contemptuously, the remaining cloddertrogs turned on their heels and lumbered away towards the Hall of Grey Cloud.

Just then, to the sound of breaking glass and splinter-ing wood, the entrance to the dormitory closets burst open, and a high professor from the Upper Halls stepped out into the snow. His robes were torn and spat-tered with blood, and on his shoulders was a pair of quarms, skittering and squeaking. Behind him trooped the rest of the Upper Hall academics, their swords red with gatekeeper blood.

Dengreeve looked across and smiled broadly, his

yellow tusks glinting. 'Why, if it isn't my good friend, High Professor Fabius Dydex – and Squeak and Howler!' He bowed low.

The high professor crossed the courtyard, his boots leaving bloody footprints in the snow. He looked about him.

'The ravens will feed well tonight,' he said with a grim smile. 'And we've left a whole lot more of the traitorous wretches decorating the Central Staircase ...' Fabius wiped his swordstick on his tattered robes. 'Though it was a hot fight, Dengreeve, I can tell you. There was more than one moment when I thought our time was up.' He shook his head. 'What *was* old Hax up to, allowing Xaxis to build up such an army here in the academy?'

Dengreeve walked over to the high professor and tickled one of the quarms affectionately under the chin.

'Sky knows, Fabius,' he growled. 'But this is where it ends!'

Dengreeve motioned to the academics-at-arms to follow him and strode, grim-faced, across the snowy courtyard towards the high-arched door of the Hall of Grey Cloud. Fabius and the Upper Hall academics followed; white-faced squires grimly clutching their swords, shocked-looking high professors in blood-stained robes and young knights academic-in-waiting, their armour dented and stained.

Halting outside the hall, Dengreeve slammed his fist against the doors and roared, 'Come out, Xaxis, and face the wrath of the Knights Academy!'

For a moment, there was complete silence, broken only by the squawks of the circling ravens overhead, and the faint coughs and barks of prowlgrins in the stables inside. Then without any warning the high-arched doors abruptly sprang open, unleashing a terrible, fetid stench that forced the academics-at-arms to step back and raise their hands to their faces.

And then it hit them . . .

A charge of crazed, whip-scarred, semi-starved prowlgrins, ridden by Daxiel Xaxis and his most fanatical lieutenants. And behind them, vast ranks of white-tunicked gatekeepers who'd been waiting silently in the Hall of Grey Cloud for the academics-at-arms to come out into the open.

Dengreeve was sent sprawling as the prowl-grins leaped over the academics-at-arms.

'The tilt trees!' shouted Fabius Dydex desperately. 'Take cover in the tilt trees!'

He grasped Dengreeve, hauled him to his feet

and set off across the courtyard at a run.

From all round them came screams and despairing cries as academics-at-arms, Upper Hall squires and professors alike fell beneath the surging onslaught of the mounted gatekeepers. While overhead, Daxiel and his prowlgrin riders picked off the swordmasters and knights academic with deadly bolts, taking care as they did so to keep well clear of their enemies' flashing sword thrusts.

As they reached the comparative safety of the tilt trees, Fabius and Dengreeve threw themselves into the forest of poles and struts as crossbow bolts whistled about their ears. Gasping for breath, Dengreeve quickly assessed their situation.

It wasn't good.

Certainly the trees deflected the flights of the incoming bolts – but they also made it all but impossible for the academics to swing their swords. What was more, since the tilt trees had been designed especially for the prowlgrins to practise their battle-technique, it was surely only a matter of time before the mounted gatekeepers penetrated the forest from above.

As he looked round, Dengreeve realized that barely a hundred individuals from the Academy Barracks and Upper Halls had made it into the tilt trees – and most of them nimble young squires and fresh-faced academics-at-arms. Out in the courtyard, the bodies of their fallen comrades were staining the white snow red, while on the far side, the stream of gatekeepers pouring out of the Hall of High Cloud and encircling the tilt trees seemed endless. At their head, on a wild-eyed prowlgrin, Daxiel Xaxis punched the air in triumph, the leering grin all but hidden beneath his bandages.

'The wrath of the Knights Academy, eh, Dengreeve?' he taunted. 'Now it is *your* turn to come and face the wrath of the gatekeepers!'

'Sky blast the impudent wretch!' growled Dengreeve, gripping his sword. 'If he wants us so badly, he'll have to come in and get us, Fabius . . .' He frowned. 'Fabius?'

Dengreeve was startled by the look on his colleague's face. The high professor was staring out at the white and red expanse of courtyard between the tilt trees and the ranks of the gatekeepers – an expression of shock mixed with an unblinking intensity. On his shoulder, one of the quarms gave odd, bleating little cries. Dengreeve followed Fabius's gaze.

There, halfway between the gatekeepers and themselves, was the high professor's other quarm, a crossbow bolt through its tiny chest. As Dengreeve watched, it raised its small furry head and let out a cry of pain.

'Squeak!' Fabius Dydex breathed, so quietly that Dengreeve could barely hear him. 'Don't worry, boy . . .'

'Fabius, no!' Dengreeve Yellowtusk said gruffly. 'Don't be a fool!'

But the high professor did not hear him. With a guttural cry of rage, he sprang from the cover of the tilt trees and sped across the snow towards the dying quarm as fast as his bad leg would allow . . . only to fall heavily a moment later, twenty ironwood crossbow bolts peppering his body.

With a trembling hand, Fabius stretched out and touched the lifeless body of his tiny companion. Then, with a sigh, his head slumped forward into the snow, now red with his own blood.

Dengreeve Yellowtusk groaned and buried his head in his hands. It was all over. The Knights Academy – the finest school in all Sanctaphrax, and sole protector for everyone on the great floating rock – had fallen into the hands of Daxiel Xaxis!

All at once, from close by, there came a piercing scream. Dengreeve looked up. It had come from the Gates of Humility in the West Wall, just beside the tilt trees. The gate creaked open and a stooped figure shuffled out into the courtyard and rose slowly from its knees. In one mighty, tattooed fist was a terrified gatekeeper, held by the scruff of the neck; in the other was the great curved sword of a flat-head goblin warrior.

Sigbord, Captain of the Treasury Guard, surveyed the massed ranks of the gatekeepers from beneath the massive ridge of his brows. The scars on his face showed evidence of his recent torture.

'Throw down your weapons and surrender!' he roared. 'By order of the twin Most High Academes!'

'The Most High Academes have no authority over the Knights Academy!' Daxiel shouted back, his eyes burning with rage. 'Only the hall masters can give such an order!'

'Then, surrender!' came a barked command. Another figure, tall and gaunt and clutching a prowlgrin crop bound together with woodtwine, emerged from the Gates of Humility.

'You!' Daxiel Xaxis pulled viciously on the reins of his prowlgrin, which was rearing up and pawing the ground.

Fenviel Vendix, Hall Master of Grey Cloud, eyed his usurper coolly. 'Surrender!' he barked again.

Sigbord raised his sword and the top of the West Wall suddenly bristled with the fearsome goblins of the treasury guard.

Behind him, Daxiel heard the clatter of metal as the more faint-hearted of the gatekeepers dropped their weapons.

'Never!' he screamed, digging his jagged spurs into the sides of the prowlgrin and charging at the hall master full tilt.

Fenviel raised two fingers to his lips and gave a sharp, high-pitched whistle. In answer, a deep hooting cry sounded from the other side of the West Wall and the ranks of the treasury guard parted as two giant tree fromps clambered over the ramparts and down into the courtyard.

Daxiel gave a scream as one giant tree fromp swept him from the saddle in mid-charge with a huge clawed paw, and slammed him to the ground at Sigbord's feet. The other fromp gave another impassioned hoot and strode towards its former tormentors on the treadmills. At the creature's approach, the ranks of the gatekeepers broke up in panic, and again the clatter of falling weaponry filled the air as the last of them abandoned the fight.

With a short whistle, Fenviel called the huge creature off.

Overhead, the sky was full of squawking white ravens circling ever lower over the tempting feast spread out across the Inner Courtyard.

Daxiel Xaxis stared up at the Captain of the Treasury Guard, his eyes wide with fear between the swathes of bandages. Sigbord ran a finger down the angry-looking scars on his face where, to make him sign the false confession, he had been branded with searing metal. He'd dreamed of this day for a long time. A smile plucked at the corners of his mouth.

'You and I have a little unfinished business,' he said, and with that, he thrust the blade of his sword through the Captain of the Gatekeeper's heart and turned away.

'Let the ravens feast!' he growled triumphantly.

Just then, and with no warning, the ground gave a violent lurch, sending the treasury guard, gatekeepers and academics alike reeling. Emerging from the tilt trees, Dengreeve Yellowtusk brushed the snow from his blood-stained tunic, the quarm on his shoulders squeaking mournfully.

'Let them feast indeed, Captain Sigbord,' he said grimly. 'Yet if this winter doesn't end soon, we shall all end up as raven meat.'

·CHAPTER TWENTY·

THE WINTER KNIGHTS

An Ancient Barkscroll from the
Great Library of Sanctaphrax

I, *Quode Quanx-Querix, first Knight-Scholar of Sanctaphrax, must set this down in blackroot ink on barkscroll parchment, and lodge it for all time in the Great Library, newly built this short while since, that the scholars who come after might heed my warning, if, as I fervently hope, our young city survives.*

I, who built the Great Pulpit Hall, the first building on the sacred rock of Sanctaphrax, and founded the Order of Knight-Scholars, have seen much in my long life. I have seen the First Scholars conjure marvels from the air, spread the light of knowledge from the shining beacon of Sanctaphrax into the farthest reaches of the dark Deepwoods, from whence all manner of diverse tribes and creatures have been drawn to encamp below our floating rock. I, too, have seen the darkness that has been sucked from the sky and made manifest in the Great Laboratory of the First Scholars; an abomination that, even now, makes my blood run cold.

I, and my fellow Knight-Scholars, did battle the monstrous creation the First Scholars unleashed into the stonecomb, and many brave souls had the life sucked from their bodies. But we prevailed, and entombed the abomination in a chamber deep within the rock from whence there is no escape. Loud were the lamentations when the Great Laboratory was likewise sealed for all time, its terrible history recorded in the blackwood carvings in the Palace of Lights, but even the most fervent of the First Scholars conceded the wisdom of this act.

If only I could record that here the sorry history of the First Scholars' sky-meddling came to an end, but I fear I cannot, for it is not so. Their experiments with the very matter of the sky have had consequences too terrible to have been foretold. The sky has sickened over Sanctaphrax, the balmy breezes and fragrant zephyrs have curdled into blizzards of snow and ice that have no end. There can be but one answer to this wintry plague that even the sealing of the Great Laboratory has not assuaged.

The sky must be purified, and there is only one substance in all the Edgelands that has the power this task demands. I speak of sacred stormphrax, most precious distillation of the Great Storm, the shards of which I, Quode Quanx-Querix, founding Knight-Scholar of Sanctaphrax, was the first to bring back from the Woods of Twilight.

Now I shall set forth on my final voyage into Open Sky beyond the Edge to restore the stricken sky, by seeding it with stormphrax. This, my final testament, shall be read by scholars hence, only if my desperate enterprise meets with success.

Farewell.

'Are you sure, Phin, old chap?'

'Take a look for yourself!' Phin turned and thrust the brass telescope into Raffix's hand as he joined him on the foredeck of the old sky ship.

A strong north-easterly wind was buffeting the starboard side of the *Cloudslayer*, making the rickety vessel creak and groan as it bobbed about on the end of its tether. Below them, on the ship's flight-rock platform, Stope the grey goblin forge-hand fought to keep his balance as he attached the last of the fire floats to the flight-rock, and released them.

Dancing on the end of thin, silver chains, the intricate metal floats fanned out around the rock like a swarm of luminescent fireflies. Another gust of icy wind hit the flight-rock, and the floats clustered here and there over its surface as the glowing sumpwood charcoal inside was drawn to the coldest spots. The *Cloudslayer* stopped bucking and swaying and Stope climbed to his feet, smiling broadly.

'They work!' he exclaimed. 'The fire floats work! I always knew they would – in theory. But now . . .'

Just then, in the distance, the bell at the top of the Great Hall tolled eight hours. From far below the Gantry Tower, there came the sounds of raised voices, and the thuds and clangs of doors and gates being slammed and barred.

'Quick, Phin!' shouted Raffix, snapping the telescope shut and racing over to the helm. 'Release the tether!'

Phin didn't need telling twice. He tore over to the ship's prow and sliced through the tolley-rope with a single blow of his sword.

'Tether released!' he bellowed back.

Silhouetted against the low milky sun, the great sky ship rose up from the Gantry Tower, creaking and groaning louder than ever as it did so. At the helm, Raffix's hands darted feverishly over the flight-levers, raising and lowering the weights and sails, as the *Cloudslayer* was caught by a gust of icy wind.

'Hold on tight!' he shouted to the others as the old sky ship sped high over the rooftops of the Knights Academy.

Round the Great Library it wheeled, the hanging-weights grazing the building's pointed wooden roofs as they passed overhead; then on low between two tall swaying towers which tinkled and chimed in the wind. They skirted the tall latticed tower of the College of Cloud. They darted between a cluster of Minor Academy domed minarets . . .

'Mind that archway!' Phin bellowed.

Raffix tugged hard on the flight-levers. Stope shut his eyes tight and clasped the main mast as, all round his head, the fire floats whirred in a sparkling cloud. The sky ship skimmed the top of the arched walkway – causing two academics to duck down, and then wave their fists angrily after the runaway vessel as it soared back into the air.

'Loftus Observatory ahead!' Phin yelled from the prow. 'Quick, Raff! *Quick!*'

On the rock-platform, Stope opened his eyes and gasped. Suddenly he understood why the other two had set sail so urgently. 'Quint!' he cried out. 'Hold on! We're coming!'

Far up the observatory tower, just below the top, one of the gantry platforms had collapsed. And there, hanging precariously from an open door, was Quint. Dressed in an old suit of stormchasing armour, he clutched the handle of the door with one gauntleted hand, while in the other, he clung to the wrist of a girl who dangled below. Only moments before, they had been standing on the gantry platform staring open-mouthed with surprise at each other. Then, with an awful metallic *clang!* the platform had given way.

'Save yourself, Quint!' Maris screamed. 'Save yourself!'

Quint's shoulders felt as if they were on fire. His eyes were blinded with sweat and he could feel the door beginning to give way as, one by one, the screws holding the hinges popped out and clinked against his armour as they fell.

'Won't . . . let go . . .' he grunted, as the door gave a sickening jolt. 'Won't . . . *Won't!*'

'*Aaaargh!*' screamed Maris.

All at once the door hinges gave way with a splintering creak. For a moment, it came almost as a relief to Quint that the intense pain had suddenly lifted and that he was falling. His hand still clutched Maris's wrist as the heavy gantry door whistled past them . . .

Ummph!

All the air was knocked out of his lungs as, suddenly, his fall was cut short and the roaring sound in his ears was replaced with the sound of creaking wood and strange whirring hums.

'I've got him!' a familiar voice rang out somewhere above him.

Quint squinted up into the pale yellow sunlight. And there, overhead, was the gnarled and pitted hull of the *Cloudslayer* coming closer by the second as he was winched up by the scruff of his heavy black cloak. The pain had returned, tearing at the muscles of his right shoulder, but Quint no longer minded.

'Phin? Is that you?' he croaked, his throat dry and sore.

'Hold on, Quint,' his friend shouted down. 'Just a moment longer . . .'

His armour clanked against the rickety balustrade as Phin, helped by Stope, hauled Quint aboard, followed by the limp body of Maris, her wrist still clamped in Quint's gauntleted hand.

They all collapsed in a heap on the foredeck. And as the old sky ship swooped off over the ice-bound city, they lay there for a moment, panting and struggling for breath. Phin was the first to climb to his feet. He detached the grappling hook from Quint's cloak and smiled down at him.

'Thought we'd lost you for a moment there,' he said. 'And who's this?'

He nodded towards Maris, who had come to, and was looking up at him with startled eyes. She turned her gaze away and inspected her wrist.

'You can let go now, Quint,' she said softly.

'Why, this is Mistress Maris, Master Quint's friend,' said Stope. 'Good old gauntlet locks!' he muttered as he clambered to his knees and bent down over Quint, who was still gasping for air.

The grey goblin flicked the catch on Quint's cuff, and the gauntleted fingers clicked back.

Quint sat up with a groan of pain, and turned to Maris. 'I thought . . . I feared . . .' He shook his head. 'Oh, Maris, what were you *doing* up there?' he said, his voice hoarse and racked with emotion.

'Me? What do you mean?' she said, her own voice beginning to crack and quaver. 'You *told* me to meet you there . . .'

Quint's brow furrowed. '*I* told you?'

'Yes, you. In your last letter,' said Maris. Her cheeks were turning pink and blotchy. 'Oh, those horrible letters, Quint. All that unpleasantness about the money . . .'

Quint tore off his gauntlets and took her hands in his own. 'Maris,' he said softly. 'Maris, I don't know what you're talking about . . .'

'And how in Sky's name could you say I wasn't a true friend?' She was sobbing now. 'A true friend! Why, I've done everything you asked me to in those letters of yours,' she wailed. 'I'm as true a friend to you as Vilnix Pompolnius!'

'Vilnix?' Quint said, startled. 'What's *he* got to do with this?'

Maris paused and wiped her eyes. 'He brought

me your letters . . .' she began.

'No, miss, I brought you Master Quint's barkscrolls,' Stope interrupted. 'All wrapped in a lullabee burner I made myself,' he added. 'Remember?'

'Not *that* letter,' said Maris, smiling at the grey goblin. 'That was a lovely one . . .' She turned back to Quint. 'I mean the other letters you sent. The ones you gave Vilnix to give to me . . .'

Quint frowned. 'I didn't give *any* letters to Vilnix Pompolnius,' he said, cold anger growing in his voice.

'But they were in your handwriting, Quint, I swear . . .' Maris began.

'Why, the crafty little barkslug!' exclaimed Phin, shaking his head, 'forging your handwriting, while all the time sucking up to you. The nerve of that Vilnix Pompolnius! Did he really think he could get away with it?'

Quint lowered his head. 'He almost did,' he said, with a shudder. He squeezed Maris's hand softly. 'Leave Vilnix to me. The important thing is that you're safe now. Or at least, you will be when we drop you off in Undertown . . .'

'Drop me off!' Maris exclaimed, getting to her feet. 'Nobody's going to drop me off! Now I've got back to Sanctaphrax, I'm staying – and I don't care what anybody says!'

'But Maris,' said Quint. 'We're leaving Sanctaphrax . . .'

Maris's jaw dropped. 'You *are*?' she said, startled. It was true. The sky ship had already sailed beyond the West Landing – where there seemed to be some commotion going on at the treadmills – and was high above Undertown. 'But where are you going?'

Quint strode over to the prow and pointed into the dark clouds billowing beyond the Stone Gardens.

'Open Sky,' he said.

Maris looked up from the ancient barkscroll with its beautiful writing – slanting and angular, and decorated with great ornate loops. The blackroot ink had scarcely faded since the day Quanx-Querix's sharpened snow-bird quill had first dipped into the ink-pot.

'And Philius Embertine found this in the Great Library?' she asked.

Phin nodded. They were all clustered round the helm, where Raffix was busily adjusting the flight-levers as the *Cloudslayer* sailed on, its sides buffeted by snow-flecked winds.

'But he's shut up in the Hall of High Cloud now,' Phin said. 'Hax is keeping him a virtual prisoner there.'

'A prisoner?' said Maris with a shake of her head. 'How terrible.' She glanced round at Quint. 'I mean I knew he was ill, but this . . .'

'The thing is,' Phin went on, 'Philius realized how important the barkscroll was. That's why he went to so much trouble to get hold of stormphrax. He wanted Screedius Tollinix to cancel his stormchasing voyage and sail into Open Sky instead – "not to take from the sky, but to give back". Those were his words. I didn't under-stand them until later when I read the barkscroll . . .'

'But his friend Screedius left before he could tell him of his discovery,' said Stope.

'Which is why Phin, Stope, Quint and I realized it was

up to us to carry out the old hall master's wishes,' said Raffix, realigning the neben-weights.

'By flying into Open Sky and purifying it with this,' said Quint, holding up the light-casket.

Maris's eyes widened. 'Stormphrax,' she breathed. 'But how?'

'Don't you see,' said Quint, urgently. 'By giving *back* to the sky, not taking *from* it.'

'And we do it, the Winter Knights!' added Raffix, proudly.

Maris held out a hand and touched the small hatch on top of the illuminated box.

'Careful!' warned Quint. 'It's only stable in twilight, remember! When the time comes, one of us will release it into Open Sky . . .'

'Which one of you?' asked Maris, scarcely able to believe what she was being told.

'We haven't decided yet,' said Phin. 'Raffix is most senior, but Quint thinks it should be him – says he feels responsible for everything that has happened . . .'

Quint's face reddened.

'But *why*, Quint?' Maris began. She stopped and put a hand to her mouth. '. . . It's because you served as my father's apprentice, isn't it?' she said. 'He opened up the Great Laboratory, and you helped him . . .'

Quint stared back into her eyes and, without saying a word, nodded grimly.

'Oh, Quint,' Maris sighed.

'It still isn't too late for us to drop you off somewhere safe,' said Quint. 'If that's what you'd prefer.'

But Maris shook her head. 'I thought you knew me better than that, Quint,' she said sharply. 'When I make up my mind about something, I don't change it . . .' Her voice dropped to a low whisper. 'By using the Great Laboratory, my father not only summoned up a gloam-glozer, but because of his experiments . . .' She looked down at the barkscroll and traced a line with her finger. *The sky has sickened over Sanctaphrax,* she read, *the balmy breezes and fragrant zephyrs have curdled into blizzards of snow and ice that have no end.*

Quint nodded. 'And it's up to me to put that right,' he said, his voice low, yet determined.

'It's up to all of us, old chap,' said Raffix. 'Now look lively, everyone. We're passing over the Stone Gardens!'

Quint and Maris crossed the deck and, hands resting on the balustrade of the port bow, looked below them. The great stone stacks were buried in snow, pitted here and there with holes made by rocks freezing and breaking free. Quint turned to Maris and, seeing her eyes full of tears, remembered the last time the pair of them had been in the Stone Gardens.

'You're thinking of your father, aren't you?' he said, putting his hand on hers and squeezing it warmly.

She nodded. 'I used to think he was so clever, so brave . . . Yet he died because of that monster he created. And now this . . .' She swept her arm in a wide arc that encompassed the snow-covered scene below them. 'If he truly *was* responsible for this endless winter, then instead of uniting Sanctaphrax by bringing earth- and sky-scholars together, he succeeded only in' – her voice

faltered – 'destroying everything he cared for most . . .'

She stopped, unable to go any further.

Quint put his arm around her shoulder. 'Not every-thing,' he said. '*You're* still here . . .'

'We're approaching the Edge!' Phin's agitated voice rang out above the sound of the gathering wind that whistled through the hull-rigging and set the mainsail slapping against the mast.

Quint looked down. Sure enough, far below them, was the Edge itself. Snow had started falling once again – a swirl of huge, feathery white snowflakes that clung to the hull-rigging and coated the decks. The fire floats whirred and hummed round the rapidly cooling flight-

rock like angry wood-wasps and a shudder passed through the beams of the old sky ship. Quint's heart missed a beat.

Mark well, the three rules of sky sailing, Quint, his father's voice echoed in his head. *Never set sail before you've plotted a course. Never fly higher than your longest grappling rope. And on no account venture into the uncharted areas of Open Sky.* Yet that, Quint realized, was precisely what he and the other Winter Knights were about to do.

Below them now, at the very tip of the jutting rock, was the Edgewater River, frozen solid in its cascade. Like the drippings of some mighty candle, the frozen river had formed a vast colonnade that stretched from the lip of the rock down into the void below. For a moment it stood out, sparkling and clear, before swirling mists and thickening blizzards closed in around the *Cloudslayer* and, like a dream, the vast pillar of ice faded from view.

Quint gripped the balustrade as the *Cloudslayer* began to buck and sway. Despite the best efforts of Stope's fire floats, it was clear that the old sky ship couldn't withstand the icy onslaught much longer. The snow on her decks thickened as the howl and wail of the snow-laden winds rose, until all other sounds – even the shouts of the *Cloudslayer*'s crew and the splintering creaks of its protesting timbers – were drowned out.

A bank of freezing mist shot by and the heavy clouds abruptly parted. It was at that moment that Quint looked up and saw a sight that only Quode Quanx-Querix, founding Knight-Scholar of Sanctaphrax, had ever seen before . . .

·CHAPTER TWENTY-ONE·

CLOUDEATER

The massive eye – as big as the great oval window in the barracks hall of the Knights Academy – swivelled in an ice-pitted socket, the light glistening on its gelatinous surface. A thick filmy mucus swam across it, and gathered in a claggy mass in one corner.

A moment later, with the sound of splintering icicles, a huge snow-encrusted eyelid peeled back to reveal a second eye, then a third and a fourth – until there were a dozen bulging eyeballs clustered like glistening wood-grapes around the first. At the centre of each sphere was a pulsating indigo circle, which contracted, then dilated – spreading out like an ink blot on yellowing parchment – as it focused on the tiny sky ship hurtling towards it.

'Raff! Watch out!' screamed Quint. He tore himself away from the balustrade and dashed towards the helm, where the young knight academic was standing trans-fixed by the monstrous, staring eyes in the sky ahead.

Pushing Raffix aside, Quint yanked the flight-levers back, and spun the heavy lufwood wheel hard to the right. Suddenly the massive eyes blurred as the *Cloudslayer* lurched violently, keeled over to one side and swerved upwards in a squeal of creaking timbers and flapping sails.

'Hold on!' Quint shouted, his breath billowing in the freezing air, as the old sky ship went into a near vertical climb, the wind whistling through its rigging, and jagged shards of ice and swirls of snow buffeting its pitted hull.

He battled against the wheel in his hands, which bucked and juddered and fought to break free – but Quint maintained his grip.

He knew that if he let go, the *Cloudslayer* would turn turvey. And if that happened, the ascent would become uncontrollable and the whole sky ship would tear itself apart . . .

Slowly, straining to hold the wheel steady with one hand, Quint reached out with the other towards the flight-levers. One by one, he pushed them forward, gingerly adjusting the sails and realigning the flight-weights, a fraction of an inch at a time. As he did so, the sound of the wind roaring past his ears gradually began to subside, as did the sound of the protesting timbers. And, by degrees, the *Cloudslayer*'s wild, hurtling ascent began to slow.

Soon, Quint was able to make out the resonant hum of the glowing fire floats as they swarmed busily around the flight-rock; that, and the excited shouts of the Winter Knights.

'Phin, are you all right?'

'I'm fine, Mistress Maris. Where's Stope?'

'Here, Master Phin! With Master Raffix – he's hit his head.'

'It's nothing, dear chap,' Raffix's voice sounded from the quarterdeck, below the helm. 'Thank goodness for armour . . .' There was a clanking sound as he scrambled back to his feet. 'I say, sorry about that, Quint. Taken by surprise just then . . .'

Looking up from the bone-handled flight-levers, Quint saw Raffix's rueful head appear at the foot of the stairs. His spectacles were lopsided and there was a red bump on his forehead, but otherwise he looked none the worse for his fall.

'Never mind that, Raff,' he said, turning the wheel to starboard. The *Cloudslayer* levelled off, a stiff breeze setting its patched and tattered sails fluttering. He brought it gently round until the prow was dipping down. 'Look at that!'

The other Winter Knights scrambled up to the helm, clustered round Quint at the wheel and peered down.

'What in Sky's name . . . ?' breathed Raffix.

Far beneath them, hovering in the sky, was some kind of monstrous creature. It was lumpy, ill-shapen and encased in a glistening carapace of ice and snow – its surface scarred and pitted with what looked like weeping sores and oozing boils. The creature was massive. Its bulbous head alone was twice the size of the Sanctaphrax rock, while its coiling, sinuous body, which trailed back across the sky towards the Edge, could have circled Undertown three times over. The creature's immense, frozen body tapered into gigantic fraying strands which ended in wispy tendrils, stretched taut in the sky, as if held by some invisible force.

Beyond these tendrils, in the distance, as the clouds thinned, the great gleaming column of ice hanging from the Edge cliff shone out for a moment. And beyond that, the hazy outline of the Stone Gardens and the floating rock could just be glimpsed.

With a sigh – a dry, rasping sound like the wind blowing through ironwood pines – the immense creature curved round in the sky, its numerous eyes glittering hungrily. Approaching it was a mountainous bank of silver-edged clouds, billowing in from Open Sky towards the Edge on a balmy breeze as warm gusts enveloped the *Cloudslayer*, so different from the freezing winds Quint had become used to in the ice-bound floating city. The words of the ancient barkscroll came back to him once more: *The balmy breezes and fragrant zephyrs have curdled into blizzards of snow and ice . . .*

Just then, with a deep and sonorous cry – like a muffled clap of thunder – the creature swung round, drifting across the sky, until its great head was hovering just ahead of the approaching cloudbank. Its jaws opened wide and, with a thick, gurgling sound, the creature began to swallow the cloudbank.

It gulped greedily, huge lumps of compacted snow and shards of ice falling away from its body as it swelled and contracted, like a wood-python swallowing a fromp. As the Winter Knights watched, the creature sucked the very last strands of cloud into its great gaping mouth, leaving nothing but empty sky in its place. The mouth closed and, for a moment, the creature seemed to pause.

Then its eyes swivelled and its long, coiled body writhed and swayed. From deep inside it, there came a low rumbling sound, as it began to ripple, to convulse . . .

All at once, a particularly violent spasm passed from its bulbous head, all the way down towards the fraying strands at the end of its tail. The wispy tendrils trembled and strained, but remained stretched taut in the sky, as if trapped in an invisible vice. However violently the creature twisted its immense body, the tail seemed to tether it in the sky.

The rumbling grew louder and louder, and was joined by a long moaning hiss. Maris gasped. Quint held his breath . . .

The next moment, exploding from the ducts along its great ice-encrusted body, came huge billowing jets of freezing air which stabbed the sky like great glistening spikes, before dissolving at their ends into white clouds. As they did so, the very sky itself seemed to curdle, and the creature ululated with a low, wailing howl.

From their vantage point, high up above, the Winter Knights watched as the clouds which had been expelled by the creature sped across the sky towards the Edge in great swirling blizzards of snow and ice. Soon the Edge cliff, the Stone Gardens and the floating rock itself were lost from view, swallowed up by the ice and snow being expelled from the creature's writhing body.

Even at this distance from the creature, those on board the sky ship were not spared. With a sudden rushing sound, the Cloudslayer was abruptly engulfed in a wave of ice-cold air that set the vessel pitching precariously to and fro. Several of the fire floats were extinguished in the blast, and the flight-rock juddered violently, threatening at any moment to turn super-buoyant and pitch them into the farthest reaches of Open Sky, a place from which there would be no return.

'So this . . . this . . . *thing*,' said Phin with a shudder as he gripped the balustrade, 'is what's causing the endless winter?'

'It certainly looks like it,' said Raffix grimly. 'Gobbling up cloud and spewing out ice and snow like that . . . Quanx-Querix must have discovered something just like it, and slain it with stormphrax.' His lip curled. 'Hideous, loathsome, evil creature . . .'

'No,' said Maris softly. 'Not evil . . .'

Quint stared at its frost-encrusted body, the outer carapace pitted and cracked. Thick, pale liquids oozed from the fissures – liquids which froze and melted, melted and froze, as the wheezing creature breathed painfully in and out. Its eyes were dim and misted. They swivelled round, some pale blue, others milky white and dripping with filmy mucus. Its jaws shuddered, its mouth opened a crack, and a thick glutinous stream of half-frozen fluid drooled from the corners.

'No, not evil,' he echoed Maris. 'But sick.' He continued to gaze at the creature. There was something about it that seemed horribly familiar. It reminded him of the formless monster which had roamed the stonecomb – the blood-red glister which had been created by the ancient scholars in their Great Laboratory from the curious, ethereal glisters that inhabited the depths of the Sanctaphrax rock. They were creatures of the air, sucked into the glass tubes of the laboratory, and horribly deformed there. The writhing, shifting body, the clusters of glistening eyes, the long tendrils that swayed and swung in the sky like ragged ribbons blowing in the wind . . .

'Whatever it is, it's a creature of the air,' he said, shaking his head. 'When your father re-opened the Great Laboratory and attempted to create life, it must have been drawn here from Open Sky. And now,' he sighed, 'it is trapped, look . . .'

Quint pointed to the long fraying tail. The Winter Knights followed his gaze. As the creature writhed and twisted, the taut strands of its tail looked, more than ever, like strands of rope from which it was struggling to break free.

'It's as if it's frozen from the tail up,' said Stope, 'and every time it gulps down the warm clouds and tries to blast itself free, it just freezes up a little more . . .'

'And freezes Sanctaphrax and Undertown along with it,' interrupted Raffix. 'We'll have to kill it . . .'

'The poor thing can't help it. It's only trying to break free,' said Maris. 'We can't just kill it . . .'

Quint motioned to Raffix to take the wheel, and walked away. When he returned a few moments later, he was wearing a pair of parawings and holding the glowing light-casket in his gauntleted hands.

'If we don't kill it, then Sanctaphrax is doomed,' he said grimly. 'But I was your father's apprentice, Maris. I am responsible. I can't ask the rest of you to risk your lives.'

He turned to Raffix. 'Do you think you can get close enough for me to jump?'

Raffix smiled. 'Oh, I reckon I can get us close enough all right, old chap,' he said. 'But we're the Winter Knights, remember. We stick together. There's going to be no jumping.'

Phin and Stope both nodded, and Maris grabbed Quint's hand. 'The Winter Knights stick together, Quint,' she said. 'You mustn't do anything stupid. Promise me you won't.'

'I promise,' said Quint.

Far below them, the creature swayed back and forth in the sky, icy blasts of snow-filled air bursting from the ducts along its body as it swallowed another bank of incoming cloud.

'Everybody rope themselves down!' Raffix called out. 'I'm taking us in!'

With its ragged, patched sails billowing and hull-weights swinging, the old sky ship swooped down in a wide arc, gathering speed as it did so. The sound of protesting timbers filled the air as the topmast cracked, the rudder creaked and the fore-decking buckled and groaned. Ice particles and snow flurries flew towards them, clinging to the hull-weights, settling in the folds of the now frozen sails and, despite the fire floats, beginning to clog up the porous flight-rock.

Tied to the helm, Raffix clenched his jaw as his hands raced over the flight-levers. On the rock-platform, Stope and Phin – their faces pale, their bodies trembling – had lashed themselves to the mast. Behind them, the fire floats on the ends of their silver chains – twists of dark, aromatic smoke coiling from the orange sumpwood charcoal as it hissed and glowed – spread out from the flight-rock like the wings of a giant snowbird.

Up at the battered prow, Quint stood like a carved figurehead in full knight academic armour with the shining light-casket clutched to his breast-plate in both hands while Maris crouched behind him, the rope around her waist tied to the foredeck balustrade. She was staring up at her friend, her face drawn and white with fear.

They sailed out further into Open Sky, then turned and raced back towards the Edge, through the gathering clouds. Up ahead of them, the cloudeater loomed. And as they drew closer, the glistening eyes focused once more on the tiny sky ship.

With a shudder, Quint saw that the eyeballs were tinged a jaundiced yellow colour and that the surface of every one was covered in a latticework of broken capillaries. The filmy discharge had thickened, becoming as viscous and opaque as prowlgrin glue. It hung down beneath the lower eyelids in pleated ribbons of frozen mucus.

From behind him, Quint heard Maris gasp. And from the helm, Raffix's voice rang out.

'I'll follow this cloudbank in as far as I can, Quint, old chap. Then, I'll pull up sharp. But we're only going to get one go at it, so be ready to release the stormphrax on my command!'

Ahead of him, through the thinning clouds, Quint saw the lips of the great creature slowly part to reveal a huge, cavernous mouth. Out of it came a long, silent roar.

For a moment, warm, sickly air enveloped the sky ship, melting the snow and ice and causing the flight-rock to sink in the sky ... But only for a moment. The next, the creature took in a huge, gulping breath, and the *Cloudslayer* hurtled towards the creature's great, gaping maw.

Quint gritted his teeth and raised the glowing light-casket.

'Now, Quint!' bellowed Raffix. 'Now!'

Quint looked up into the cavernous mouth of the monster, which filled the sky ahead, its glowing red edges disappearing into the inky blackness of the gullet at the centre. All he had to do was flick the catch at the top of the light-casket, and the precious shard of storm-phrax would be released. His fingers tensed inside the metal gauntlets.

Click!

The gauntlets jammed! He flexed and strained, but they wouldn't open. They wouldn't move! His hands were locked tightly into place around the glowing lamp . . .

'*Now, Quint!*' bellowed Raffix.

Desperately, Quint struggled to break free from the rope that tethered him to the ship. If he couldn't release the stormphrax crystal then he'd throw himself into the gaping mouth instead – light-casket, stormphrax and all!

With a grunt of effort, he wrenched himself free – only for Maris to grab him by the arm.

'Don't, Quint!' she shouted. 'You promised!'

With nimble fingers, she reached forward and flicked the catch on the light-casket. The door sprang open. There was a low hiss and the pungent scent of toasted almonds filled the air as the tiny crystal flew out of the box, as if shot from a crossbow. Sparking and flashing, it blazed a trail through the sky as it shot into the vast dark maw of the creature.

The next instant, as Raffix slammed the flight-levers back, Quint was knocked from his feet. The *Cloudslayer* pulled up hard, juddering to a halt in mid air, preventing it, too, from being swallowed up by the gargantuan creature.

A dazzling flash lit up the sky as the crystal exploded deep down inside the cloudeater's body. Every cell, every tendril, every scale of its icy carapace glowed as the fragment of stormphrax, made solid in the Twilight Woods, returned to its original form in Open Sky – pure energy, blindingly bright and blazing hot.

Suddenly the *Cloudslayer* was speeding across the sky back the way it had come, tossed and twisted on the bucking eddies as the shockwaves from the massive explosion rippled out through the air. For a moment, it seemed as if the sky ship's timbers had finally had enough and would shatter into fragments beneath the feet of the Winter Knights. The topmast splintered, the rudder shattered and much of the fore-decking was ripped to pieces – but somehow, the *Cloudslayer* stayed intact.

When it finally righted itself, and Raffix had brought it under control, Quint struggled to his feet and gazed out into Open Sky.

'Did we kill it?' he asked.

A warm wind was blowing in from Open Sky, and ahead the carapace of snow and ice that had enveloped the cloudeater was falling away. Icicles dripped, snapped off and plunged down through the air like dis-carded lances. Great disintegrating chunks cracked and slipped from the creature's back, breaking up in mid air, and turning to showers of ice fragments which seemed

almost to effervesce. And as they melted in the turbulent air, so the sky was filled with shimmering curtains of rainbow-coloured light – red and yellow, purple and green – that criss-crossed and collided with each other in shifting arcs of exquisite colour.

The Winter Knights watched, transfixed, as the last of the ice-cold carapace melted into thin air. From inside the grey and lumpy shell of ice, an extraordinary creature had emerged.

It was diaphanous, and translucent, as if moulded from the crystal air itself. Long, twisting tentacles fanned out from its glassy body, catching the sunbeams like a tasselled fringe of light. Its eyes were clear now, and sparkled like marsh-gems. And as the light passed through its body, it was rendered visible only by the ripples of its movement. Its mouth opened like a tremor on the surface of a crystal lake, and the cloudeater's great glassy body seemed to swell and surge forward.

All at once, with a rippling flick of its barely visible tail, the transparent fronds at the tip finally broke free from the warming sky with the sound of a thousand panes of glass shattering at the same instant. Then, with a second flick, like a fountain of crystal clear water, the mysterious cloudeater sped off into Open Sky in one long, languorous ripple of movement.

Maris turned to Quint, her eyes shining. 'We didn't kill it, Quint,' she said. 'We cured it!'

·CHAPTER TWENTY-TWO·

THE RATBIRD

With a high-pitched screech and a flap of its leathery wings, the tiny ratbird flew up from Quint's outstretched hands and darted through the open window at the north end of the Upper Halls. For a moment, it hovered in the sky, the warm sun beating down on its small, sleek body. It looked down at the Knights Academy below; at the thirteen towers, the Lower Halls, the wide expanse of the Inner Courtyard, then up at the great yellow clouds billowing over the towers and turrets of Sanctaphrax.

'Sky protect you, Nibblick, little friend,' breathed Quint as the little ratbird disappeared from view. 'I only hope my father has the answer to the question you carry.'

Then, as if making up its mind, it let out a second screech and, with a twitch of its whiskers and a flick of its tail, soared off into the sky towards the distant Deepwoods.

*

Three days earlier, a battered sky ship – its sails in shreds and its hull timbers creaking – had approached the Edge cliff through a warm sunlit sky. Far below, the Edgewater River swirled and writhed like a mighty logworm as a vast torrent of snowmelt brought its frozen waters back to life.

At the very tip of the cliff, the great frozen pillar of water groaned and shuddered as the newly-awakened river flowed over and around it, loosening its grip. As the lone sky ship passed high overhead, there came a resounding *crack!* and the mighty pillar of ice – three times the size of the Sanctaphrax rock – finally broke free, splintering and shattering into countless million brittle shards as it tumbled down into the void below.

The sky ship continued on its lonely way, high above the frothing turmoil of the swollen river now pouring freely once more over the edge. Ahead of the battered vessel lay the Stone Gardens.

Dropping down low over the once mighty stone stacks, which stood like islands amidst the swirling snowmelt, the crew of the sky ship gathered excitedly at its balustrades and gazed down. The rocks seemed to have retained their caps of snow, yet as they drew nearer, the crew could see that this covering of white was in fact alive. Thousands of white ravens had settled – cawing and screeching on the topmost stones – and were now flapping and jostling for position.

A command from the helm sent the crew scuttling back to their stations.

With Raffix at the helm, Stope and Phin at the

flight-rock and Quint and Maris at the prow, the *Cloudslayer* came down lower still as it approached the jumbled roofs and turrets of Undertown. Beneath them, the streets were alive with activity, as if some giant had just kicked over a woodant nest.

There were lugtrolls shovelling the dwindling drifts of snow away, gnokgoblins and cloddertrogs sweeping the pouring water down the drains. From the edge of every roof, icicles dripped, before shattering and breaking off as great chunks of compacted snow above them suddenly shifted, slid down the sloping tiles and tumbled noisily to the ground below. After so many months of snow and ice there was, at last, no need to remain barricaded in against the cold, and it seemed as though every door and every window in the great sprawling city had been flung wide open.

There was water everywhere, gushing down pipes and pouring along gutters, sluicing the dirt and dregs of winter away in a great frenzy of spring cleaning. And if Undertown was a changed place now that the stranglehold of ice and snow had finally released its grip, then Sanctaphrax was all but unrecognizable.

'Look,' gasped Maris, clutching at Quint's arm.

Melted water was pouring down from every rooftop, every gable, every ledge; every banked-lintel and flying-buttress; every archway, avenue, bridge and hanging-walkway. From the moment the thaw began, the water had been steadily seeping down into the porous floating rock and collecting in the stonecomb.

Now, all at once, the pressure which had been

building suddenly became too much. With a loud hiss and a high-pitched whine, the trapped water burst out of the rock from all sides. Countless jets showered out from every crack and crevice in the vast spherical rock, filling the air with a halo of spray that, in the sunlight, turned to a magnificent rainbow which bathed the floating city in dazzling coloured light. And, as the ice continued to melt, the jets grew thicker and stronger, cascading down onto Undertown below as the great floating rock glided across the sky on the end of its anchoring chain.

With a leisurely shift of a flight-lever, Raffix brought the old sky ship round in the sky and set a course for the floating city. Ahead, the Gantry

Tower stood tall above the rooftops at the eastern end of the Knights Academy. As the *Cloudslayer* approached, the smiles of its crew turned to frowns and they exchanged anxious looks. The snow might be melting, but it was clear that something was still terribly wrong in the Knights Academy below.

Take the Inner Courtyard, for example. It looked like a battlefield . . .

There were bodies everywhere. Some still lay where they had fallen, their bodies horribly twisted into grotesque shapes, blood staining the ground around them. Others had been moved and lay in rows, the thick white shrouds which covered them making it look, for a moment, as though the snow hadn't melted after all. At the far end of the courtyard, the great ironwood doors to the Academy Barracks hung shattered from their hinges, whilst in the distance the tilt trees were lying scattered in a mass of splinters and broken branches.

As Raffix brought the *Cloudslayer* carefully down in the sky, Phin jumped onto the landing jetty and tethered the tolley-rope to the mooring-ring of the Gantry Tower. One after the other, the Winter Knights climbed from the ship, their legs suddenly wobbly as they set foot on firm ground. The joy and elation they had all felt as they approached the academy had disappeared, to be replaced with shock and bewilderment.

Keeping close together, they trooped down the gantry steps, and in through the narrow side entrance that led to the Central Hall of the Upper Halls. As they stepped through the doorway, they were struck by the atmosphere of the place – the loud conversations, the stifling heat, the smell of blood . . . It was so different from the hushed, deserted hall they had left earlier that day.

The pulpits were now crowded, loud animated discussions taking place at their tops, while below them the hall resembled a vast sick-room, with low sumpwood cots laid out in rows and thick blankets draped over their occupants. High professors and Lower Hall squires alike passed among them, ministering to the wounds of the injured and closing the eyes of the dead.

At the end of one of the rows, Raffix noticed a tiny quarm crouched down at the foot of a floating cot. It was whimpering softly as it rocked slowly, back and forwards, back and forwards. The body of a second quarm lay nestled in the arms of the cot's occupant.

'Fabius Dydex,' Raffix whispered, shocked at the sight of the professor's waxen, lifeless face. He approached the cot and kneeled down, tenderly stroking the quivering head of the little quarm. 'There, there, Howler,' Raffix whispered. 'Your master's gone.'

As if in answer to his words, the quarm turned and scurried up onto Raffix's shoulders and buried its head in the folds of his cape.

'Looks like you've made a friend there,' said an Upper Hall squire, approaching the little group now gathered around the professor's cot.

Raffix looked up. 'Lubis?' he said, clearly shocked by the squire's appearance. 'Lubis, is that you?'

The Upper Hall squire attempted to smile. He was sallow and drained-looking, with hollow cheeks and sunken eyes. When he spoke, his voice was choked and raw, and the words seemed to tumble out in a torrent, like melting snow water.

'Daxiel Xaxis and the gatekeepers locked all the doors at dawn, and we woke to the sounds of battle down in the Inner Courtyard . . .' the squire began, fixing Raffix with a haunted stare. 'We couldn't just stay locked up there. The honour of the Upper Halls was at stake. Fabius Dydex rallied us, and we fought our way down the Central Staircase, paying in blood for every step we took – but making the gatekeepers pay as well!'

Raffix nodded, his heartbeat quickening.

'Flayle and Beltix fell on the Upper Landing,' Lubis continued. 'And Memdius . . . dear old Memdius. He died in my arms as we fought our way through the dormitory closets. But we made it out into the Inner Courtyard with Fabius Dydex at our head, and . . . and . . .'

The Upper Hall squire's face crumpled up, and he covered it with shaking, blood-stained hands.

'That's . . . where . . . he met his death . . .'

The little quarm on Raffix's shoulder shivered and let out a small, mournful howl.

'Where *were* you, Raffix,' the squire sobbed, 'when the Upper Halls needed you?'

The Winter Knights looked at each other. Suddenly it didn't seem right to boast of their great

triumph out in Open Sky – not here in this place of death and suffering.

The blood had drained from Raffix's face and his eyes sparkled from behind his spectacles.

'I was in the Gantry Tower, aboard the *Cloudslayer* . . .' he began, but the Upper Hall squire wasn't listening.

Slumped at the foot of the floating cot, he was sobbing and rocking back and forth, just as the little quarm had done.

Quint laid an arm on his friend's shoulder and led him away. 'Leave him, Raff,' he said gently. 'He won't understand right now, but there *is* someone who will.'

'Philius Embertine!' said Phin. 'Come on, we must tell him that everything the barkscroll said was true, and more!'

The five of them set off, hurrying from the Upper Halls, down the stairs and along the dark, narrow corridors towards the Hall of High Cloud, and the small, forgotten room where Philius Embertine was being held prisoner. Every step of the way was punctuated with the aftermath of the great battle they had missed – smashed doors, broken bits of weaponry and the discarded robes of the gatekeepers, their logworm insignias now torn and blood-spattered.

They arrived outside Embertine's room to find the corridor deserted except for the slumped body of a gatekeeper, a crossbow bolt embedded in his chest.

'It's one of the guards,' said Phin, stepping over the dead cloddertrog and pushing the door slowly open. He peered through the narrow crack into the shadowy room, a single candle beside the bed, low and sputtering. The soft, yellow light fell on the pinched and drawn face of the old hall master, who lay propped up against grubby pillows, his breath coming in snatched, wheezing gasps.

'Hall Master Embertine,' Phin whispered, striding into the room. 'It's me . . .'

All at once, there was a noise from behind the door and a brawny individual leaped out, grabbed Phin by the shirt and shoved him back against the wall, the blade of a long thin knife held to his neck.

'Who are you?' he growled. 'Speak up, before I slit your scurvy throat from ear to ear.'

Stepping silently into the room, Quint drew his own knife and pressed the point into the back of Phin's assailant.

'Drop the knife,' he hissed. 'Now.' There was a clatter as the knife fell to the floor. 'Now turn round and tell us who you are,' Quint demanded.

As the young guard turned, it was clear from his uniform that he was an academic-at-arms – a rock-guardian, judging from his half-armour and the twin crossbows strapped to his belt.

'I . . . I'm sorry,' he said. 'I thought . . . I thought . . .' He motioned towards the door. 'I thought you were gatekeepers,' he said. 'Like that evil guard out there.'

Quint nodded.

'They starved and beat the hall master, you know,' the young academic-at-arms said. He shook his head. 'And on Hax Vostillix's orders. Sky curse his soul!'

Raffix's eyebrows shot upwards. 'Hax Vostillix is dead?'

'Ay,' came the reply. 'Murdered in his chamber by earth-scholars – at least that's what some reckon. Poisoned by woodwasp larvae. Ate him, inside out. That's why the gatekeepers attacked us – it was the excuse they were looking for . . .'

Just then, from the bed, a faint voice could be heard. 'Someone . . . someone's there,' it said. 'Let me see your face.'

Quint turned and crossed the room to the bed. He placed his hands on Philius's shoulder, and was shocked to feel how thin and bony it had become. The old hall master stretched out a gnarled hand and clasped Quint's forearm, his fingers closing round the metal armour.

'Screedius?' the old professor wheezed. 'Screedius, is that you?'

Beside him, Phin reached into his jacket, pulled out the ancient barkscroll and handed it to Quint.

'We . . . we voyaged to Open Sky,'

Quint said gently. 'Just as Quanx-Querix did,' he added, waving the yellowed parchment in front of the old professor's face. 'And we took the stormphrax with us.'

'Oh, Screedius, Screedius.' Philius's weary eyes suddenly sparkled with life. He leaned forward and gripped Quint by his hand. 'Screedius, you gave the sacred stormphrax back to the sky, just as Quanx-Querix did before you? And did it work?' His frail voice rattled querulously. 'Did you heal the sky?'

'Yes, sir,' Quint assured him. 'Just as Quanx-Querix once did, we healed the sky and winter has passed . . .'

'Winter has passed,' the old professor repeated serenely, his face suddenly suffused with a beatific smile. 'Thank Sky for that. My old friend, Linius Pallitax, would be so happy to know that the sky has been healed. So happy to know that the evil he caused by opening the Great Laboratory has been undone . . . But you must promise me one thing, Screedius, for the sake of Linius Pallitax!'

The hall master's grip on Quint's arm tightened as he pulled Quint closer towards his own unseeing eyes.

'For the sake of the greatest, most honourable, the truest Most High Academe there ever was . . .'

Behind him, Quint heard Maris stifle a sob.

'Anything,' he whispered to Philius. 'Just name it.'

'You must never speak of your voyage again,' came the reply, 'to anyone. The Ancient Laboratory is locked, the stonecomb sealed. If Sanctaphrax ever learned that Linius was responsible for the terrible winter, his reputation would be ruined and his statue would be pulled from the viaduct and smashed to a thousand pieces ... Hax's thugs beat me and starved me, but I refused to tell them about the scroll and the stormphrax. And you, Screedius, have rewarded me ... Now promise never to speak of it again!'

'I promise,' said Quint softly.

Philius Embertine smiled and let go of Quint's arm. 'Thank you, Screedius Tollinix, Knight Academic,' he breathed. 'Now I can begin *my* voyage to Open Sky ...'

And with that, his eyelids flickered heavily and closed. Then, the same serene smile on his face, he breathed out – long and rasping – and fell still.

Quint reached forwards and pulled the old professor's sheet slowly up over his face.

'He's at peace now,' the academic-at-arms said softly. 'They can't hurt him any more ...'

He turned and looked at the two knights academic, one in armour as bright and shiny as if it had just been forged; the other's, battered and ancient-looking. And their three companions – a little grey goblin, a serious-faced girl with tears streaming down her cheeks, and an academic-at-arms who he seemed to vaguely recognize from the barracks; a swordmaster apprentice.

'What was he babbling about at the end?' he asked. 'Voyages and ancient laboratories ... and Open Sky?'

The small group exchanged looks, and then the knight in battered armour spoke.

'Nothing,' he said. A trace of a smile crossed his lips as he glanced at the girl. 'Nothing at all.'

*

Over the next few days life returned to normal in the Knights Academy. Little by little, bit by bit, the stains and scars of both the terrible winter and the bloody battle were removed.

The dead were dealt with as tradition decreed. Gnokgoblins, woodtrolls and mobgnomes were burned on floating funeral-pyres that their spirits might be released and ascend to Open Sky. Cloddertrogs were buried in the Mire outside Undertown, and the few waifs from amongst the hall servants who had died in the Battle of the Central Staircase were sent floating down the Edgewater on small coracles decorated with flowers.

Philius Embertine and Fabius Dydex were accorded different rituals, as their status demanded. Carried down to the Stone Gardens on raised biers, their bodies were laid out amongst the growing stacks and devoured by the flocks of white ravens. It was the first such ceremony since the funeral of Linius Pallitax himself.

As for the living, they too ensured that life would return to the way it had been before the momentous upheavals. The great ironwood wheels and the log burners they had shifted up and down the stricken rock were dismantled, and the giant fromps were returned to the Deepwoods and, on Fenviel Vendix's instructions, set free. The Hall of Grey Cloud had been stocked with prowlgrins once more. And the Knights Academic mounts, Tash included, were back on their perches on the central roost. The academics-at-arms – though diminished in number – assumed many of the roles of the erstwhile gatekeepers, the hated red-logworm insignias giving way to simple black tunics with numerous duelling patches.

The Winter Knights returned to their duties as if nothing had happened; Stope to the Forge, Phin to the Academy Barracks, and Quint and Raffix to the Upper Halls. Quint gave up his study dormitory to Maris and moved in with Raffix, just while the high professors set about re-organizing the ravaged Upper Halls – but they both knew that this arrangement couldn't last.

'You must go and see the twin Most High Academes as soon as the Grand Inquiry has finished,' Quint told her three days after their voyage to Open Sky. 'And I'll send Nibblick with word to my father. I'll ask him what he thinks you should do.'

'And what about Vilnix Pompolnius?' Maris asked.

'You leave him to me,' Quint said. 'He's hiding out somewhere in the academy, but he can't hide for ever. In the meantime, I've got an inquiry of my own to finish . . .'

He patted the miniature painting set into the handle of his sword – but when Maris pressed him, he wouldn't say any more.

The following day, the Professors of Light and Darkness convened a Grand Inquiry to report on the death of Hax Vostillix. As the sun rose high in the sky, academics from all parts of Sanctaphrax began streaming into the glistening Lecture Dome of the Hall of High Cloud, the windows that had been broken in the aborted uprising now mended.

The two professors – dressed respectively in their new white and black robes – had already taken their places on the ornate buoyant lectern before the first arrivals appeared at the doors. And, as the professors and under-professors, apprentices and acolytes took their places in the bench-tiers and balconies, the twin Most High Academes viewed them sternly, their two bearded faces revealing not a trace of emotion. Only when everyone was seated did the Professor of Darkness climb to his feet.

For a moment, the whispering grew louder, echoing round the great domed chamber like a mass of hissing hover worms. The Professor of Light raised his staff, and the hall fell still.

'As twin Most High Academes of Sanctaphrax,' he began, in his thin reedy voice, 'it is our sad duty to report on the untimely death of Hax Vostillix, Hall Master of High Cloud.'

'We have examined the circumstances and nature of this unfortunate occurrence,' continued the Professor of Darkness, his voice deep and rumbling, 'and have come to an inevitable conclusion . . .'

'Hax Vostillix was murdered!' the Professor of Light announced in ringing tones.

The Lecture Dome was absolutely silent. Everyone knew that Hax Vostillix had been murdered, and everyone had their own theory as to who had murdered him. After all, from the gossip-rich Viaduct Steps to the rumour-filled benches of the Great Refectory, talk was of little else. But, as tradition demanded, the Most High Academes were to have the final word.

'Many had good reason to hate the late Hall Master of High Cloud,' rumbled the Professor of Darkness. 'The other hall masters, unjustly thrown out of the academy.'

'Fenviel Vendix, Arboretum Sicklebough and the late Philius Embertine . . .' intoned the Professor of Light, reedily.

'We find them innocent of all charges!' announced the Professor of Darkness.

'On the evening of the murder, a young Upper Hall squire was taking a tray of food to Hax Vostillix's chamber when he was stopped by the Captain of the Gatekeepers, Daxiel Xaxis,' said the Professor of Light.

'This squire states that Daxiel Xaxis took the tray from

him and placed a bowl of bonbons upon it, before entering the hall master's chamber alone,' rumbled the Professor of Darkness.

· 'The eggs of the woodwasp dipped in honey and rolled in hyleberry sugar would resemble the sweetest of bonbons,' the Professor of Light trilled, 'until . . .'

'They hatch in the belly of one who consumes them and begin to sting their way out!' boomed the Professor of Darkness.

His voice was drowned by the rising tide of anger and revulsion that echoed round the hall as the gathered academics made their feelings known. The Professor of Light raised his staff for silence.

'It is the finding of this Grand Inquiry that Daxiel Xaxis, Captain of the Gatekeepers, believing that his master's increasingly erratic behaviour threatened his position, did murder Hax Vostillix, Hall Master of High Cloud, by woodwasp poison!'

The Professors of Light and Darkness's voices mingled as they announced their verdict in unison.

'Order has been restored to the Knights Academy, and the terrible winter has come to an end, Sky be praised!'

Cries of 'Sky be praised!' echoed round the gantries and balconies of the great Lecture Dome.

'Now let us put this matter behind us,' said the Professor of Light.

'And return to our studies,' said the Professor of Darkness.

At a signal from the Professor of Light, the buoyant lectern was hauled back down to the jetty, and the twin

Most High Academes made their way to the entrance, where a thin-faced Upper Hall squire with shifty-looking eyes was waiting. His eyes darted nervously back and forth over the crowd, as if he was afraid of being spotted at any moment.

'If that'll be all,' said the squire in a wheedling tone as the twin academes approached, 'I really must be getting back to *my* studies, too.'

'And what studies might they be?' said the Professor of Light scornfully. 'Hiding in the Gantry Tower? Or skulking in the wood-store of the Hall of Storm Cloud?'

The squire shot the professor a murderous look and turned imploringly to the Professor of Darkness.

'I've told you all I know,' he pleaded. 'Can't I go now?'

'Not just yet,' rumbled the Professor of Darkness, placing a hand on the squire's shoulder and leading him out of the Lecture Dome. The professor smiled kindly. 'There *is* just one other little matter you can help us with.'

Nothing unnerved Vilnix Pompolnius as a rule, and yet as he followed the Professors of Light and Darkness through Sanctaphrax to the School of Light and

Darkness, the former knife-grinder felt decidedly ill at ease. He passed through the imposing doorway, with its heavy studded leadwood doors; he climbed the sweeping marble staircase; he passed along the ornately decorated corridors – his heart racing a little faster with each step he took.

Suddenly, he was standing before the twin doors – one black and one white – of the professors' studies. The last time he'd been there was that early evening, all those months ago, when the Professor of Darkness had first confirmed that he was to sponsor him through the Knights Academy. How long ago that now seemed . . .

Then, of course, it hadn't just been him waiting to see the eminent professors. No, that snivelling son of a sky pirate, Quintinius Verginix, had also been present.

Vilnix felt a cold fury rising up and catching in his throat.

What had gone wrong with his plan? How had Quint and that stupid, spoilt girl not fallen to their deaths from the Loftus Observatory? It was a mystery. True, the two of them did seem to be keeping their mouths shut – but how long would that last? And meanwhile, Vilnix was getting weary of sleeping in the woodstore and hiding in the Gantry Tower. No, it couldn't go on. He'd have to fix them for good next time . . .

'Come in, Vilnix,' the Professor of Darkness said to him, as he pushed the black door open and entered the huge study on the other side.

It took a moment for Vilnix's eyes to grow accustomed to the light – or rather the lack of it – inside the great chamber. For, just as the Professor of Light's study was blindingly bright, ablaze with lanterns, lamps and blazing torches which were reflected back on themselves a thousand times in the mirrors which lined the walls, so the Professor of Darkness's study was the opposite. It was dark and sombre, with heavy blackout curtains at the windows and only the luminescent moonstone-chandelier throwing out any light.

Vilnix had never actually set foot in the study before, even when he'd returned the telescope over a year earlier. Now, he wasn't sure he was happy with this honour. Peering round uncertainly, his pupils slowly dilating, he was slowly able to take in his surroundings. He saw the shelves lining the walls, stacked with books. He saw cabinets filled with flasks and bottles, brass implements and glass instruments, and complicated multi-armed contraptions set with scales, dials, lenses and incandescent bulbs. And, over by a tall statue of an ancient scholar, a long padded sofa upon which Quint and Maris were sitting, their eyes fixed firmly on Vilnix.

'You can't prove a thing!' Vilnix blurted out, backing towards the door – only to find his way blocked by the Professor of Light. 'I was just a messenger for those barkscrolls. A masked squire – with goggles and scarf – he gave them to me and told me to deliver them to her . . .' he babbled, his voice rising to a guilty squeak. 'How was *I* to know they were forged? Probably one of those snooty Sanctaphrax-born and bred friends of his playing a trick on both of us . . .'

He turned to the Professor of Darkness imploringly –

aware, all the while, of Quint and Maris's eyes boring into him.

'You've got to believe me! I'm innocent! That gantry on the Loftus Observatory is a death trap – could have collapsed at any moment. Frost damage ... Yes, that's what it probably was. Frost damage.'

He ground to a halt, his cheeks blazing red and sweat running down his back.

The Professor of Darkness fixed him with an unblinking gaze, his face betraying no emotion. He shook his head.

'Oh, Vilnix, Vilnix,' he said softly.

Meanwhile the Professor of Light had crossed the room towards the window. 'Come out, Gleet,' he said.

There was the sound of shuffling from behind the heavy blackout curtain, which was abruptly pulled to one side to reveal a bony individual with a hooked nose and pale yellow eyes.

Vilnix stared at the forger from the viaduct School of Colour and Light Studies. 'I've never seen this academic in my life!' he protested desperately.

'But he has seen *you*, my dear Vilnix,' said the Professor of Darkness gently.

The painter smiled and nodded.

'We can't prove that you intercepted the barkscroll correspondence between Maris and Quint here,' said the Professor of Light, nodding towards the two of them sitting silently watching from the sofa. 'We can't prove that you tricked Quint into giving you a sample of his handwriting, which you took to Ferule Gleet here, for the purposes of forging barkscrolls to Maris.'

Vilnix stared at the Professor of Light, his face contorted into a mask of leering hatred.

'We can't prove that you used these forged barkscrolls to obtain gold coins from Maris. Nor that, when certain to be unmasked, you tampered with the gantry in order to send both Maris and Quint hurtling to their deaths, thus covering up your crimes . . .'

'Then what *can* you prove?' spat Vilnix, glancing wildly at the faces around the room.

'You've been a great help, my dear Vilnix,' continued the Professor of Light. 'Without your involvement, which we can't prove, of course, Quint would never have discovered that Ferule Gleet also forged the document granting the leaguesman Heft Vespius and his wife, Dacia, guardianship of Maris – a crime for which Heft has been made to pay with all the gold he possesses by my treasury guard.' The Professor of Light permitted himself a little smile.

'Why should I care?' snarled Vilnix, trying not to look at Quint or Maris.

'Why, indeed?' said the professor sarcastically. 'Why, indeed? But you *will* care, I think, that Quint also discovered that Ferule Gleet had some other interesting information.'

The professor motioned for the painter to speak. Ferule looked at Vilnix with his pale yellow eyes.

'I've seen you before, young master, indeed I have,' he rasped. 'Not wrapped up in scarf and snow-goggles and disguising your voice in my studio. Oh no. But bold as brass, on another occasion entirely, coming out of the viaduct School of Potions and Poisons just opposite, and glancing up at the stuffed vulpoon sign with an evil little sneer on your face as you pocketed a vial of woodwasp eggs.'

Vilnix's jaw dropped open, but no sound came out. For a moment, there was complete silence, before the Professor of Light spoke.

'Of course,' he said, 'we can't prove that those were the same woodwasp eggs that ended up in our poor, late Hall Master of High Cloud's stomach.'

A smile slowly crept across Vilnix's face. So that was it? That was the best they could do? He had got away with it after all. Of course, he always knew he would. He was just too clever; too clever for the lot of them.

'Well, if you'll excuse me,' he said, grinning, 'I'll just be running along back to the Knights Academy.'

'I'm afraid not,' said the Professor of Darkness, taking Vilnix by the arm and escorting him towards the door. 'You showed such great promise, Vilnix, when I first met you – and yet you have let me and yourself down. I'm afraid, as twin Most High Academes, we have no choice but to expel you from the academy.'

'On what grounds?' squeaked Vilnix, his voice shrill and high-pitched. 'The Professor of Light says you can't prove a thing . . .'

'You were identified coming out of the School of Potions and Poisons.'

'So?' protested Vilnix.

The professor leaned over the young squire and spoke softly and clearly, as if to a small child.

'It is forbidden for any but the senior academics to set foot in that school, for obvious reasons. Everyone in Sanctaphrax knows that.'

'Sanctaphrax born and bred, that is,' the Professor of Light added lightly.

'For a junior academic – a squire, no less – to do so is rank insubordination of the most serious kind.'

'I . . . I . . .' stammered Vilnix.

'It's true, I'm afraid,' said the Professor Darkness, opening the door for Vilnix. 'Gather your things and leave the Knights Academy tonight. I've arranged a place in the College of Rain, in the Faculty of Raintasters – a lowly, menial existence after what you've been used to here, but better than knife-grinding.

Goodbye, Vilnix. I'm so very sorry.'

The Professor of Darkness shook his head sadly as he propelled Vilnix through the door, and closed it behind him.

Outside, the youth straightened up, the expression of bewilderment and shock on his face turning to dark loathing.

'Insubordination,' he hissed. 'I'll get even with you, Quintinius Verginix – and you, you two pathetic buffoons – if it's the last thing I do.'

Quint and Maris emerged from the School of Light and Darkness and gazed up at the evening sky.

'The Professor of Darkness was right!' Quint said, turning to Maris excitedly. 'It *is* the *Galerider*!'

'He's a sky-scholar,' Maris laughed. 'He doesn't miss much with that telescope of his. It's what's right under his nose, like scheming knife-grinders, that he can't spot.'

Above them, the sky pirate ship cast a huge shadow on the ground below, all but blotting out the last remnants of the day as it approached one of the great mooring-rings set into the upper walls of the school. Moments later, Wind Jackal appeared at the portside balustrade.

'Quint, lad!' he shouted down. A long rope-ladder descended, uncurling as it dropped, and dangled in front of them. 'I got your message, I was on my way back to fetch you when the ratbird found me. Climb aboard, we haven't a moment to lose!'

'But Father, what about the Knights Academy? My studies? And Maris?' Quint called up in confusion as he gripped the coiling rope-ladder and set foot on the first rung.

'I'll tell you everything when you get on board,' said Wind Jackal.

'Not without Maris,' Quint persisted, as she grabbed him by the arm.

'The daughter of my oldest friend?' Wind Jackal called back. 'I wouldn't dream of leaving her behind. Now hurry!'

They climbed the swaying rope-ladder and, almost the moment their feet touched the deck, the *Galerider* leaped into the air and sped off across the darkening sky. Beside him, Quint felt Maris grab his arm and tighten her grip.

'I'm staying with you. I won't be left behind. Not this time,' she said fiercely. 'Not ever!'

EPILOGUE

Far out in the Mire, as the last rays of the setting sun fanned out across the bleached mud-flats, the broken body of a sky ship – a stormchaser – cast long, dark shadows back over the boggy ground. The vessel had clearly crash-landed, and badly. Its mast was broken, the hull smashed in on one side, while the flight-rock had broken in two. One half was still in the shattered cradle at the centre of the decks, the other some way off, half-buried in the sucking mud.

Beside it, sitting upon an upturned barrel, a raw, half-eaten oozefish clutched in his hands, was a knight academic. His armour was dirty, the pipes and dials clogged up with the same white mud. To his left, his heavy helmet lay discarded.

He was staring ahead, unblinking, at the Twilight Woods as he rocked slowly back and forwards, back and forwards. There – as the sun set and the sky about him darkened – the perpetual orange glow of twilight lit the flocks of fluffy clouds which gather above it.

'Lost,' he murmured, his voice cracked and gruff from lack of use. 'All is lost.'

And as he stared, so four figures emerged, their scrawny frames silhouetted against the glowing light.

He scrambled to his feet and stumbled across the Mire towards them. As he drew closer, he saw that they were a small family of gnokgoblins, stragglers who had braved the perils of the Twilight Woods in their attempt to travel from their Deepwoods home to a new beginning in Undertown.

Seeing the tall, noble-looking knight heading towards them, the party of goblins beckoned to him.

'Please, sir,' said the eldest – a wizened old'un – as they approached. 'We need help.'

'Help,' the knight murmured.

'We need shelter for the night,' the gnokgoblin matron explained. 'And a guide to help us across this wasteland . . .'

'Shelter,' the knight repeated. 'Guide.'

It was almost as though he hadn't noticed the gnokgoblin, for he wasn't looking at her as he spoke. Instead, he seemed transfixed by the tiny glittering particles which sparkled amongst the mud trapped both in the coarse tufts of hair between her toes and under her nails.

As his eyes stared down at the gnokgoblin's feet, a strange expression crossed his troubled face – as if he was struggling with a problem and slowly making up his mind.

'All is not lost,' he said at last, a hand lightly touching the handle of the knife at his side. 'Follow me.'

Turn the page to read an exclusive extract
from *Clash of the Sky Galleons*, the ninth
book in the Edge Chronicles.

Available in stores from September 2006.

· CHAPTER ONE ·

EDGE WRAITHS

'Not even here in this place of ghosts and demons and half-formed things . . .' bellowed the wild-eyed sky pirate captain, his voice cracking as he struggled to make himself heard above the screaming wind, 'not even here will you be safe from my vengeance!'

The sky ship bucked and swayed as it fought against the violent air currents which kept all but the most reckless or foolhardy from venturing over the lip of the Edge and down into the abyss below. For here, where the warm Mire mud cascaded down over the cliff face in huge oozing mudflows and met the icy air currents of the void below, gales and hurricanes and turbulent fog were whipped up into a frenzy.

'No matter how far down into these infernal depths you descend,' Wind Jackal raged, shaking his fist at the eternal gloom below, 'I shall hunt you down . . .'

'Father, please,' the young sky pirate by the

captain's side protested, and laid a hand on his shoulder. 'The crew . . .'

Wind Jackal turned from the balustrade at the helm of the *Galerider*, the look of glazed fury on his face giving way to a frown as he found the eyes of his crew upon him. There was Spillins, the ancient oakelf, high up in the caternest. Ratbit, the swivel-eyed mobgnome, his heavy jacket laden with charms. Steg Jambles, the harpooneer, with young Tem Barkwater, as ever, by his side. Sagbutt, the fierce flathead goblin, his neck-rings gleaming. And Maris Pallitax, still in her Sanctaphrax robes, staring up from the foredeck. They all shared the same expression – one of barely contained panic – as they stared wide-eyed at their captain, looking to him for reassurance.

Only the newest member of the crew seemed immune to the terror of this fearful place he had brought them to. The Stone Pilot. Concealed inside the tall conical hood that she never removed, and silent as the day she was rescued from the Deepwoods slave market, she tended the flight rock, seemingly oblivious to all around her. The sight of the Stone Pilot applying the cooling rods and adjusting the blazing sumpwood burners which surrounded the flight rock seemed to calm the captain, for he took the wheel from his son with a grim smile.

'Forgive me, Quint,' he said, running his hands over the flight levers. 'It's just that, after all these years, he seems so close . . . '

A blast of wind hit the *Galerider*, making the sky ship shudder from stem to stern, and forcing Wind Jackal to feverishly adjust the hull weights. His hands raced expertly over the bone-handled flight levers on either side of the great wheel, raising this one a tad, lowering that one.

'Sky curse this infernal wind!' he snarled, scanning the mud-clogged cliff edge. 'I can't hold her much longer. We must find somewhere to tether.'

Suddenly, the strident voice of Spillins, the *Galerider*'s lookout, cried out from the caternest. 'Jutting rock at fifty strides!'

'Thank Sky,' Wind Jackal murmured, removing his right hand from the hull-weight levers for a split second; just long enough to put the carved tilder-horn amulet gratefully to his lips. 'Hold her steady as you can, Stone Pilot. We're depending on you. Tem! Ratbit!' he bellowed. 'Man the winch! Steg, prepare to descend.'

A chorus of voices and a flurry of movement erupted all round the sky ship as the crew hurried to do their captain's bidding, taking up their positions and getting to grips with the ship's heavy equipment. Ratbit barked commands at Tem Barkwater as the pair of them swung the winding-winch round until the great ironwood wheel was jutting out over the port side of the sky ship. Steg Jambles secured a leather harness round his midriff, seized the rope that dangled from the winch-wheel and attached one to the other.

'Jutting rock directly beneath us!' Spillins shouted down.

Quint and Maris scurried across the deck – skirting round Filbus Queep, the tin-faced quartermaster, who had appeared from his quarters above the aft-hold – and peered over the side. Sure enough, there was the single jutting crag that Spillins had spotted, a small island of stillness and stability amidst the constantly shifting Mire. It stood proud of the oozing white mud, which swirled slowly round it, then poured over the edge in great globules that glistened for a moment, before disappearing into the eternal gloom below.

Quint turned and looked up at the flight-rock platform. The Stone Pilot was standing to the left of the great rock, her back towards him. Since the moment they'd first met, the mysterious figure had uttered not a single word. Yet the hunched urgency with which she worked now feverishly pumping the rock-bellows and riddling the ashes from the roaring furnace, spoke louder than any words.

Every moment the *Galerider* hovered hare, untethered over the void, it risked being swept away and lost for ever in Open Sky. But the Stone Pilot was a natural, whose skills seemed to grow with every passing day. Under her care, the heated flight rock was gradually becoming less buoyant and the *Galerider* was descending towards the jutting rock.

'Now, Steg! *Now!*' bellowed the captain, his hands leaping from lever to bone-handled lever as he fought to keep the sky ship hovering motionless in place.

Steg Jambles didn't need telling twice. He tested the rope with a quick tug – just to be on the safe side – before stepping off the side of the ship. Tem and Ratbit took the strain and, when Steg had gathered himself, began turning the pulley-lever. Slowly, carefully, they lowered the thick-set foredecker down through the air towards the jutting rock.

At the balustrade, Maris gripped Quint's arm and turned to look up at him, her dark eyes glistening with a mixture of awe and excitement.

'The great void,' she gasped. 'The realm of ghosts and demons and . . . What was it your father said?'

'Half-formed things,' said Quint, staring down at the foredecker dangling below.

'*Stop!*' Steg's bellowed command was just audible above the turbulent air.

Tem and Ratbit stopped turning the winch at once, and slid the locking bolt across. Far below, Steg gripped hold of a rough chunk of the jutting rock with one white-knuckled hand, while with the other, he unhooked the glinting rock-spike from his sky pirate coat.

'When you're ready, Master Steg!' Wind Jackal called out from the helm as he battled to hold the ship steady, as the howling wind battered and buffeted it, seemingly from all sides at once.

Steg thrust the pointed end of the spur into a

narrow crack in the rock then, with a great round-bowled hammer that he'd unhooked from his belt, he pounded the spike into place with a flurry of colossal blows. As the sound of Steg's hammer blows rose up from below, Wind Jackal smiled grimly.

'Be ready with that tolley-rope, Master Tem, ' he bellowed down at Steg's mate.

'Ay-ay, Captain,' Tem called back.

'Spike secured!' Steg's voice floated up from below. He had driven the metal spike deep into the crack in the rock.

'Tolley-rope, Master Tem!' Wind Jackal's command rang out.

Quint looked down to see Tem Barkwater lean out over the balustrade and hurl the length of thick rope down to Steg Jambles. It uncoiled as it dropped. One end was secured to a tolley-post at the prow, the other dropped into Steg's outstretched hands. With a deft turn, twist and threading through of the rope, he fashioned a perfect tilder-knot – so called because it was the type of knot used by slaughterer hunters to snare and bind any migrating tilder that happened past their hides – and slipped it over the head of the spike. He gave it a sharp tug. The rope closed round the shaft of metal.

'Tolley-rope secured!' he shouted. 'Pull me up!'

Tem and Ratbit jumped to the winch-handle and began turning. A moment later, Steg Jambles' tousled head appeared above the balustrade. He grinned.

'The old *Galerider* is tethered, Captain,' he said as he jumped down onto the deck.' Should hold for a little while yet.'

'Let's hope so, Master Steg,' said Wind Jackal, descending the stairs from the helm. He turned towards Quint, his eyes blazing with a frightening intensity. 'I've waited many a long year for this moment,' he said. 'For your mother's sake, Sky rest her soul, and your dear lost brothers ... Will you come with me and watch my back, Quint?'

'You know I will,' said Quint, clasping his father's arm and following him to the prow.

Maris gazed after them, the blood draining from her face. 'Sky protect you, Quint,' she said hoarsely, her voice little more than a whisper.

As Wind Jackal and Quint arrived on the foredeck, Tem and Ratbit realigned the winding-winch and swung a second winch round into position next to it. Quint eyed the dangling harnesses warily, his courage beginning to drain away.

'Don't just stand there, lad,' Wind Jackal was saying, looking up as he secured the harness straps around his legs and waist. 'Get yourself buckled in. I need you, lad ... If anything were to happen, I need to know that you'd finish the job off.'

Quint nodded. 'You can count on me, Father,' he said, climbing into his harness. 'After all, I was there, too, remember.'

The pair of them climbed up onto the balustrade.

Tem was manning Wind Jackal's winding winch; Steg Jambles, Quint's. At a word from Wind Jackal, both he and his son stepped off the *Galerider* and into mid-air.

Quint's stomach lurched. The harness tightened around the top of his legs as the winding-winch creaked into motion, and the rope began to descend. He'd seen how the wind had turned and twisted the suspended Steg, but nothing could have prepared him for the sheer violence of the turbulent air. It hit him like a blow to the ribs and sent him spinning round and round.

'Stick your legs out, son,' he heard Wind Jackal calling across to him and, when he looked round, he saw his father bent double, his legs jutting forwards at right-angles to his body.

Quint did the same. The spinning stopped and, as the rope continued to be let out, he found himself drawing level with the jutting rock the *Galerider* had been anchored to. A moment later, and the sheer rockface of the Edge itself was directly in front of him. He planted his legs squarely against the great wall of rock and, as the rope was released from above, began making his way down the vertical rockface in leaps.

The wind howled louder than ever down here in the perpetual shadow of the void beneath the Edge, and it was cold – so cold that, even though there was sweat running down his back, Quint's teeth chattered and his breath came in foggy puffs of air. Every so often, there would be a soft ploff-ploff sound from above him and a huge column of steaming Mire mud would whistle past him, breaking up as it did so and showering him and his father with a viscous, fetid-smelling spray.

Wind Jackal swung over towards his son and signalled for him to remain silent, before pointing down into the gloom below. Quint glanced down. There, huddled in the shadowy darkness some fifty or so strides below him, were a series of vivid scars cut into the cliff face. Jagged ledges, one above another, covered with the remains of lufwood roofing, splintered and wrecked by the howling winds.

These must be the abandoned ledges of the ancient cliff quarry from the time of the First Scholars, Quint realized with a shudder. It looked as strange and ghostly as the priceless rock that was quarried there.

Quint ran his hand over the rock before him. Dark and grainy, rough to the touch and stained with the white Mire mud, it did not look anything special. He knew, however, that when it was polished, the rock was transformed into a shimmering, shining material that glowed from within, as though countless glisters had been sealed within it, like insects inside fossilized pinesap.

At Wind Jackal's signal, Quint followed him down the cliff face towards the quarry ledges, fifty or so strides below. When they landed on the first narrow ledge carved into the cliff face, Quint noticed that his father had unsheathed his sward. Grim-faced, he motioned for Quint to do the same, then began inching his way along the narrow cutting, which was no wider than a window ledge. Here and there, overhead, the remains of a jutting awning – erected to protect the ancient quarry-workers from the howling wind and falling Mire mud – stuck out from the rock.

Not that it offered much protection now, for the jutting struts had snapped off, and the lufwood planks were splintered and warped. Those that remained creaked and groaned and seemed to give the howling wind a new and sinister voice, as if the spirits of the long-dead stone masons were calling out a ghostly warning. Quint tried to shut out the awful noise as he crept along the ledge after his father, but in vain . . .

'Don't allow our harness rope to get snagged,' Wind Jackal hissed over his shoulder,' or they'll never be able to winch us out of here.'

Following his father's example, Quint checked that the rope above his head was clear of the struts of the wrecked awning as he continued. At the end of the cutting, Wind Jackal paused for a moment, before swinging out across the cliff face and descending to the ledge below. Quint followed close behind, and again, they inched along the narrow cutting, their backs pressed against the smooth, quarried surface of the cliff face. Down they went, from ledge to ledge, until the gloom thickened and the ghostly howling made speech impossible.

Quint gripped his sword tightly and felt the

reassuring tautness of the harness rope tug at his shoulder. It was good knowing that up there, in the light, Steg Jambles was holding on to the other end. Three short tugs and the harpooner would winch him out of this waking nightmare.

Ghosts and demons and half-formed things . . . Quint swallowed hard as his father's words sounded in his head. How desperate was the one they hunted that he sought refuge in such a terrible place?

Still deep in thought, Quint felt his father's hand on his shoulder. They had come to the lowest of the quarry ledges. Below them, the cliff face sloped sharply away into an inky blackness, and in front of them, the narrow ledge ended beside a narrow crack in the rock face, like a gap in some huge stone curtain – deep, dark and only inches wide.

Wind Jackal raised the hilt of his great sky pirate sabre to his lips and kissed it, then, checking his harness rope, he stepped inside.

At the prow of the *Galerider* Tem Barkwater turned the winch-wheel, feeding out the rope as steadily as he could manage. Beside him, Steg Jambles was doing the same.

'How do you think they're getting on down there?' Tem murmured, his bony face wide-eyed with anxiety.

'Don't go concerning yourself with that, lad,' said Steg. 'The captain and his son have unfinished business to sort out down there. *Personal* business!' He fixed the gaunt youth with an unblinking stare. 'It's up to you and me to keep feeding this here rope out nice and steady until they're ready to come up.'

Tem nodded.

'And when they give three tugs on this rope, then—'

'We winch them up,' Tem blurted out eagerly.

Steg smiled. 'Like your life depends on it, Tem, lad. Like your life depends on it!'

The moment Wind Jackal and Quint stepped inside the narrow fissure in the cliff face, the howling of the wind was instantly shut out – only to be replaced with a dank and eerie stillness. Some way in the distance, a pale light was flickering. Quint's mouth was dry and gritty with Mire mud, and he could feel the blood thumping in his temples.

Just ahead of him his father crept along the narrow tunnel between the two huge walls of rock, his sword held out in front of him, the rope from his harness trailing out behind. Carefully, silently, scarcely daring to breathe, Quint followed. He must watch his father's back, he told himself, be prepared to step in if he was needed; if something should go wrong . . .

The light grew brighter and Wind Jackal hesitated, and motioned for Quint to join him. Just ahead of them, some sort of chamber had been carved out of the tunnel wall.

At its entrance, stacked against the wall, lay a heap of ancient chisels, rock hammers and quarrying tools, while above them was a row of hooks, from which hung decaying cloaks, frayed gloves and long, pointed hoods that looked for all the world like long-dead, desiccated woodmoths. Inside the chamber, a hunched figure was squatting beneath a huge, ancient lamp – its light pale and feeble as the last of its tilder oil burned itself out.

Quint glanced at his father and was shocked to see a look of pure hated contorting his features. With a hideous cry, like that of a wounded beast, Wind Jackal launched himself into the chamber and brought his heavy sabre down on the squatting figure in a savage, vicious sweep. There was an explosion of blood and guts as the bloated, lifeless sack disintegrated with the blow and Quint and Wind Jackal found themselves covered in stinking tilder entrails.

Wind Jackal stared for a moment at his son, his face blood-spluttered and shocked, before the lamp spluttered out and pitched them into absolute darkness.

'Nothing but a tilder leather sack, filled with blood . . . Sky curse my blind thirst for vengeance!' Quint's father groaned. 'I've led us into a trap'

'Father, I . . . Did you feel that?' Quint's harness rope twitched and bucked.

In the darkness, Quint heard the weary sky pirate captain sigh unhappily. Then the harness rope twitched again, more violently this time, and from the direction of the tunnel came an ominous rustling, scratching sound . . .

'Three tugs!' said Tem. 'I felt them'

'Me too,' agreed Steg Jambles. 'Well, what are you waiting for?' He frowned at the young deckhand. 'Winch, lad! Winch!'

Tem leapt at the winch-wheel and began winding it furiously. 'I know, I know, you don't have to tell me,' he shouted over his shoulder to the harpooneer. 'As if my life depends on it!'

'*Whoooah*!' Quint cried out, as he found himself being dragged back towards the tunnel entrance – and closer to the scratching, snuffling sounds.

Behind him, Wind Jackal stumbled on the end of his own harness rope. 'Whatever you do,' he shouted to Quint, 'don't cut the rope, or we'll never get out of here.'

'What's out there?' Quint whispered, as he slid and slithered through the pitch-black darkness of the tunnel, like an oozefish on the end of a line

'Only one way to find out,' answered his father, and Quint found something hard and shiny being pressed into his hand.

It was a type of sky crystal, Quint could tell from its smooth, round shape. He slammed it against the tunnel wall and it glowed in his hand with a warm, yellow light. Behind him, Wind Jackal did the same and together they held their glowing fists up above their heads as they approached the tunnel entrance, half running as the harness ropes dragged them ever faster.

There, blocking the narrow fissure, was a huge, white creature, its thin papery wings folded tightly behind it as it squeezed into the entrance. It had massive watery eyes that seemed far too big for its shrunken skull-like head, and long, spidery hindlegs that stretched out towards them, glinting with long, needle-like talons. Thin spittle-like drool dripped from its jaws which, as Quint watched, seemed to dislocate as they opened to become impossibly huge.

'*Khhhaaah!*'

The sound it let out was long, harsh and rasping, a blast of air that came from the very depths of its angular body and was expelled with great force from its gaping maw. Its head darted from side to side, the tiny nasal flaps at the top of its beak-like mouth flickering furiously. It was the smell of fetid tilder blood that had drawn it into the tunnel, like a woodmoth to a candle.

'The neck!' Wind Jackal shouted. 'Aim for the neck!'

Quint gripped his sword and raised his forearm to fend off the lunging attack that instantly came. He felt the vice-like jaws crunch into his arm with the pain of a thousand hot needles, before swinging his sword in an upward arc.

A high-pitched shriek choked off in mid-screech, followed by crunching bone and the crumpling of

413

papery wings filled Quint's ears – before he found himself bursting from the tunnel's entrance at the end of the harness rope and swinging free in the dark, freezing air.

Below him, the hideous creature tumbled away into the murky blackness, its glassy-eyed head separated from its body.

Some way behind him, Wind Jackal also swung clear of the tunnel, before rising up alongside Quint on the end of his own harness rope.

'Winch, you sky curs!' roared his father. 'Winch us out of here!'

In front of Quint, the quarry ledges and the rockface sped past in a blur, as the violent wind howled once more in his ears.

From below there came more hideous screeches, as three more creatures swooped up out of the infernal darkness. Their papery wingspans were the size of sky ships, and their gaping jaws wide enough to swallow a full-grown hammelhorn whole. Yet for all that, their white bodies were skeletally thin, and looked as delicate as a spindlebug's. Round they circled, calling to each other and coming ever closer to this tempting, dangling bait – so much tastier and more substantial than the dried out morsels of carrion that the Mire mud filtered down to them in the depths below.

In their harnesses, Quint and Wind Jackal flailed desperately with their swords as the creatures swooped, dived and snapped at them with their razor-sharp teeth. Each time a creature glided past, Quint caught sight of its huge, swivelling eyes, irises enlarging and contracting as if calculating exactly when and where to strike.

His arm was throbbing painfully now, and he was nearing exhaustion. How long could he keep these hideous creatures from the phantasmal depths at bay?

Quint glanced across at his father, dripping, like himself, with rancid tilder blood, and swinging his heavy sabre in a figure of eight in front of him. Above, the hull of the *Galerider* had come into view.

'Not far now,' he murmured to himself. 'Not far now . . .'

'*Waaaarch*!'

A creature – the pupils of its huge eyes fully dilated – managed to avoid the flashing blade, and glanced past Quint, tearing his sky-pirate coat at the shoulder with trailing talons as it did so.

'Winch! Sky take your souls!' Wind Jackal roared up at the sky ship as another of the creatures swooped and snarled above his head.

It glided round, its eyes wide and staring, and closed in for the kill. Then suddenly, as Quint was beginning to fear the worst, a bright arc of light shot through the air and straight through the papery wings of the vast flapping creatures. For a moment, they seemed to hover in mid air, before bursting – like great paper lanterns – into brilliant flame and hurtling down into the blackness. With a screech of alarm, the third creature broke off its attack and fled back to the safety of the void.

Moments later. Steg and Tem were hauling Quint and his father on board, looks of shock on their faces as they saw the blood-spattered state of their faces and clothes.

'Edge wraiths,' said Filbus Queep the quartermaster, shaking his head. 'Foul creatures of the void . . .'

'But what happened to them?' Quint asked, clambering out of his harness with the help of Tem.

'Harpoon dipped in flaming sumpwood tar,' said Steg proudly.

Quint looked up to see Maris smiling down at him, trying hard to conceal the look of fear and concern on her face.

'It was Mistress Maris's idea, and it worked a treat,' Steg continued. 'Now, with your permission, Captain, perhaps we can get out of this accursed place.'

But Wind Jackal wasn't listening. He was standing at the balustrade, gazing down into the bottomless void, his eyes glittering from beneath a mask of dried tilder blood.

'This isn't over,' he muttered through clenched teeth. 'In fact, this is just the beginning!'

Read *Clash of the Sky Galleons* to discover more about Wind Jackal and Quint's quest.